W9-AEU-412

Lusts

Books by Clark Blaise

LUSTS

LUNAR ATTRACTIONS

DAYS AND NIGHTS IN CALCUTTA *with Bharati Mukherjee*

TRIBAL JUSTICE

A NORTH AMERICAN EDUCATION

LUSTS

Clark Blaise

DOUBLEDAY & COMPANY, INC.
GARDEN CITY, NEW YORK
1983

*All of the characters in this book are fictitious
and any resemblance to persons, living or dead,
is purely coincidental.*

The author gratefully acknowledges the support
of the National Endowment for the Arts during the writing of this book.

DESIGNED BY LAURENCE ALEXANDER

Canadian Cataloguing in Publication Data

Blaise, Clark, 1940–
Lusts

ISBN 0-385-15474-7
I. Title.
PS8553.L34L87   C813'.54   C83-098215-9
PR9199.3.B6L87

Library of Congress Cataloging in Publication Data

Blaise, Clark.
Lusts.

I. Title.
PR9199.3.B48L8   1983   813'.54
ISBN: 0-385-15474-7
Library of Congress Catalog Card Number 82–45100

Copyright © 1983 by Clark Blaise

ALL RIGHTS RESERVED
PRINTED IN THE UNITED STATES OF AMERICA
FIRST EDITION

To Paul Bennett

Lusts

Prologue

For a frank discussion of the life and art of the late Rachel Isaacs (Durgin), I would appreciate correspondence with anyone holding letters and manuscripts or willing to share anecdotes and experiences.

Rosie Chang
Department of English
University of California
Berkeley, CA. 94720

Notice appearing in the New York *Times Book Review*, *The New York Review of Books*, *Atlantic*, *Commentary*, and *Harper's*, January and February of this past year.

Dear Rosie Chang:

A long time ago, in a country far, far away, I was married to Rachel Isaacs. Whatever I have achieved in my life happened in those five years. She killed herself in our New York apartment, about ten feet from where I was watching a football game, nearly a dozen years ago.

As you can see from my address, a lot has happened since. I was a force in her life, however, for the great years of her writing.

You could say I possess anecdotes (narratives? epics?), and some of the manuscripts. I'm not necessarily looking for anonymity, and you can keep anything I send you. What I'm looking for is more than sympathy—call it justice. My interest is redemption.

It's your story now, Rosie Chang. I'll help as much as I can—I'm not disinterested, after all. How far along are you? What attracted you to her? How old are you? (What are you doing Wednesday night?)

Ten years ago people like Judith Singer were writing vicious articles about me. Those articles triggered death-threats. Dead things were left outside my door. I tried to respond the way I knew best—in a novel—but no one was interested. What they wanted was a memoir of our marriage. I told them our marriage wasn't out of Bloomsbury; we weren't inverts or libertines. I did crazy things after that. I've had two marriages since then.

If you want my help, just write me, c/o Ajanta Woodworking, Faridpur. They'll find me.

Sincerely,

Richard Durgin

P.S. I'm curious to know your likely first sentence. Do you know it yet?

Berkeley, CA.

March 13, 1982

Dear Richard Durgin:

I had given up all hope of finding you. When I inquired about you in New York, I was told you'd left five years ago. Some said you had died (I even researched that, and you'll be happy to know that reports of your death are inconclusive, if not exaggerated).

For the past three years I have been working summers and weekends at Pomona with the Isaacs papers. I've only now gotten access to the twenty thousand pages (!) of diaries and day-books and drafts of poems and stories. As a result of that *Times* notice, hundreds of letters are waiting for me in the office. There are even poems in French and Italian dating back to her schooling in Italy.

I have done all the California research that I can on my own, so it's probably not boastful to think that I "know" Rachel Isaacs up to the age of eighteen as well as any outsider is likely to. All I lack (as you point out) is the real story. What made this brilliant schoolgirl turn out to be a great writer and not just another bright Berkeley graduate student?

Any thoughts?

Her life is a paradigm of a culture and of her times, as well as of her sex and background. Her life was uniquely complicated, yet, in a different perspective, it is still the story of a generation. (You wonder how old I am; well, old enough to have been a bright Berkeley undergraduate whose head got completely turned around by Rachel's poetry reading in 1968. I was going to be an architect—not bad training for writing a biography, by the way—but I changed to English two weeks later).

In a disguised way, it's my story too. I'm writing my autobiography in a quiet sort of way, through her life.

Enough about me. Let's get to you.

I'll just give you a "shopping list" and you can choose your responses accordingly.

I have read your novels and stories and I trust you totally as a writer. Is it simpleminded to assume that Rachel's death in some way silenced you? Your silence is partially responsible for the monster-myths you refer to, like Singer's "Dinner with the Durgins" and "The Carla Goodings Connection," linking you to Carla, or her to Rachel, or you to both of them. I can imagine your reluctance to take up the charges; nevertheless I should know the identities of friends, lovers, old boyfriends—the usual paraphernalia of a literary "life"—even if I don't mention them. In her New York diaries, near the end, there's frequent mention of a "Jack T." I've drawn a blank—any help? And did she ever mention to you the name of the father of her daughter born in high school? The listed father

is an old Hollywood friend of the family, a lifelong homo-
sexual.

The tragedy of early death is that the principal actors
are still fairly young. She'd only be forty-three, even now.
The fingerprints are still fresh, the soil still spongy, and the
dozen years have kept her alive in a ghostly half-light. If
I'm not careful, I'll behave more like a novelist than a biographer. It's my job to stay within the facts and to keep
cutting the drama back.

Why did she kill herself, Richard—that's the final question, isn't it?

My first sentence? I can't be sure I'll use it, with all the
thousands of pages left to read, but one of the journal entries is teasing me. She saw her life as an accident—old,
European-Jewish parents, their exile, their disinterest, her
upbringing in an alien California, and in Italy. She felt
sometimes she shouldn't have been born, and that her gifts
were entirely unnatural. So maybe something like, "She
viewed herself as an accident." She admired you, Richard,
far more, perhaps, than you know.

The distances involved make me feel like a biographer in
the grand manner. As though I should seal this letter with
a gob of wax, though the Regents might object. I'll stand
at the end of the pier, waiting your installments with all
the anticipation of the French Lieutenant's woman.

Sincerely,

Rosie Chang (SOF, into
running, gardening, and
MJF esoterica; free on
Wednesdays.)

ONE

ONE

Chapter One

My father was a carpenter (measure twice, cut once, that was Joe Durgin) and when he said his first and only house wouldn't collapse, it didn't. He rented it in 1939. The house was stitched to a cliff three hundred feet over the Monongahela River, pinned in place by a blade of Pittsburgh steel. No child in America mowed the ozone quite as I did, or felt himself on such tentative terms with gravity.

The house was a product of industrial lust. No basement, no yard. No form, no function. Yet it soared. There should have been a plaque out front: HERE THE INDUSTRIAL AGE DEFIED GRAVITY. HERE PITTSBURGH STEEL HELD A MOUNTAIN BACK AND LIFTED A FAMILY INTO SPACE. But Pittsburgh wasn't that kind of city, and the Durgins were not that kind of family.

The house outlasted my fear. It survived ridicule. A proud, new Pittsburgh invested its hope in aluminum buildings down at the Point, a civic center, Three Rivers Stadium. See, Pittsburgh said to America, we've got taste, class, and championship teams. Many of us remember a chaste, guilty Pittsburgh, and we haven't been back.

Forbes Field fell to subdividers. Our house was ripped from the cliff.

Is that what it means, being forty? Counting the legends you knew in their prime?

I had the back bedroom, floating in sooty space. Under me were the Homestead Works of U.S. Steel. Shift whistles blasted through my windows. Greasy orange shadows played on my childhood ceiling while the open hearth ladled out tanks and bomb casings twenty-four hours a day. I looked down on pits of baking coke and watched the sidewalks swarm with steelworkers in shiny black raingear. That was my introduction to cause-and-effect: the whistle blast and the anarchic depatterning of the parking lot a few minutes later.

After they tore our house down, the cliff started shearing. The next three houses crumbled. Houses below us in the valley were crushed under rockslides. Engineers tried to rivet the mountain back in place. They poured concrete down the fissures. The next two blocks were condemned. We got our plaque at last: WARNING! UNSTABLE CLIFF. KEEP YOUR DISTANCE. They used to laugh at us when we were the bookends, but now the whole shelf has come crashing down.

The house outlived my father. Sixty stubby little Camels a day, Pittsburgh sludge, sawdust, and torch gas pinched his lungs to a pair of cancerous little welts. He was forty-seven.

I used to think that a carpenter's inheritance was what got me off the cliff and out of Pittsburgh. I used to believe that his choice of an unwanted wind-waggling house was a matter of vision. Being a carpenter's son put me in a Renaissance relationship with writing. Artisan into artist. I believed these things even as I realized that he was an indifferent carpenter who never mastered the *Unified*

Plumbing and Carpentry Code Book. He roughed-in house and roof-frames, and he did odd jobs with pipes and wires.

You always inherit, but never what you think. From him, I inherited a mild competence with a craft. The legacy of unspendable spleen. Sudden rage, as bitter as the sea.

And yet, Rosie, all I am now is a glorified carpenter. And my father would not be proud.

My father was a foot taller than my mother. She was more than two feet wider. When they married, she was eighteen, five feet two and scrawny. By the time I was born, she was twenty-five and weighed about a hundred and seventy-five. Women in Pittsburgh either withered or ballooned in marriage; hatchet blades or the Ohio River. I first remember my mother when she was about thirty, her face and flesh tighter than a doll's, and she must have weighed two hundred and twenty-five pounds.

I remember the day my father, at six feet two, hit one hundred and thirty-seven pounds and remarked that he was getting a little pot. I was shaving when he stepped out of the shower. He weaved a little over the toilet bowl, but he wasn't pissing. He was holding the wrinkled white flesh where his pubic hair stopped and his belly hairs funneled down from his navel. "Feel this," he said. It was like a tennis ball implanted in the loose skin. I was a smart kid, I knew what it had to be. "It's a hernia," I said. "Don't squeeze it, it's your guts coming out."

I was wrong.

My mother was an eyesore. She had to rip out openings between the shoulders and elbows of all her blouses and still she couldn't squeeze her arms through. The channel of her bra straps—over the shoulders and cinched across her back —reminded me of those U-shaped valleys we read about, the hillocks of displaced flesh rolling up from the floor of a wide, elasticized river.

All that fat altered her hormones, or maybe vice versa, and she suffered an early menopause. Spikes of hair sprouted on her chin and jowls. She kept a cake of bees-wax in a saucepan under the sink, and whenever I came home early from school I'd see her stretched in front of the television set with a caramel-colored plating of wax all over her face. I could hear the hiss of uprooting all the way upstairs in my floating bedroom. To this day, the sight of butterscotch pudding makes me sick. The sad fact is, my mother had more to do with getting me out of Pittsburgh and the life of maybe seven generations of Pittsburgh Durgins than anything in my father's miter box. She was what happened to people who stayed.

And yet.

It wasn't that bad. It was great.

One of my first memories, postwar but not by much, is of a summer camp run by the Brotherhood of Carpenters and Roofers up in Cooke's Forest, north of Pittsburgh. My first weekend away from home. I'd put my age at seven.

Guides came through the open porch at four-thirty in the morning. It was cool and dark, late in the summer, when fogs had settled in every depression. On our nature walk, we were supposed to keep count of deer, identify birds, and make crude little maps. Most of us planned it to be an organized assault on peace and quiet. We'd filled our pockets with stones from the night before.

In an open field at dawn, with the trees sharply defined, colorless etchings on a wall of fog, the guide stopped and whispered, "Deer!" We tried not to cough in the damp. And miraculously, a stag rose from the mist: a perfect black outline with wisps of cloud still tangled in his antlers, and dense gray fog dancing at his legs. He stared at us, then turned, drawing out does from every mound of fog. Then the whole cloud bank rose in a torn wind that swallowed the thump of a dozen lemon-sized rocks fired in their direction.

That memory has stayed with me through thirty years. I draw on it even now for the privilege of once having seen it, and for having been the one to throw the first stone.

Until my senior year, everything was entirely normal in my life. I dated a girl named Wanda Lusiak, whose parents were from Poland, which saved her from just being Polish. She was the kind of girl who married early. With her shrewd, wifely manner she made you feel that mere petting was underutilizing her, but anything more might call out the guard. Domestic duties were what she wanted, and she was determined to marry a boy who wouldn't come home sooty from the steelworks. We wouldn't rent for more than two years, she said, and she wouldn't mind moving from Pittsburgh if it meant we could own a house. Leaving Pittsburgh was unthinkable to me—only Perry Como left Pittsburgh. The nature of Pittsburgh life was gritty loyalty. If we—note the pronoun—stayed in Pittsburgh, Wanda had her eye on the new developments in Whitehall and Bethel Park.

She was scared to death of our house. She never entered it.

I was thinking of college. Pitt and Duquesne were recruiting local talent. On the Pitt admissions forms, I checked "Veterinary Medicine" and "Accounting." My idea of veterinary medicine (if any of it was my idea) must have tied in with the suburbs. An office in one of those colonial-inspired shopping malls: Richard Durgin,

D.V.M. Cats and spaniels. Life was so easy to plan back then. You assumed you'd earn more than your father, marry a girl prettier than your mother, be happier, have nicer things, fly around in your personal heli-attachment by 1970, and retire to a life of perpetual youth and virility by the early eighties. The problem would be in coping with all that health and prosperity and free time. Wanda and I bought it. It wasn't even presented as a dream; it was just another commodity in the World of Tomorrow.

Between us there were the usual limits. She was the kind you married, but that did not interfere with the territories to be explored, most of them free for the taking. She was a brown-eyed blonde with eyelashes she had to darken. To me, she was beautiful and always had been. We'd all started school together, and no one ever moved away—that meant that you decided around sixth or seventh grade whom you were going to marry, and in the June weeks after graduation, you did it. There wasn't a time when Wanda Lusiak was not to be my wife.

I believed back then in my essential goodness, the essential purity of my motives. In all things sexual and economic, enlightened self-interest led the way. If Wanda wanted Bethel Park and built-in lazy Susans, she'd have to unbutton when I asked her to, present her delights in descending order to my rising expectations, so the whole thing could go off in the second semester of our senior year in a Steubenville or Wheeling motel.

I know how this sounds. I was a little more chaste and guilty myself when I met Rachel six years later.

So that's how I was before the world started knocking. Undifferentiated adolescent slime. I doubted nothing in my little universe. Except for my relative shortness and lack of a varsity letter, I was even proud of myself. I had a pretty girl, I had a chance to better myself, and there was even a possibility that I'd achieve more than Wanda expected. What exactly, I couldn't say.

In the winter of 1957 (the year I'm talking about, in case you're dating this), Rachel had already graduated from that Los Angeles private school with the English name (Runnymede? I forget it now), and had finished her first semester at Pomona College. She was always a year ahead of me (or light-years, depending on your perspective). Those improbable forces that brought us together were emphatically not underway. California wasn't even a concept to me. It was the place where girls' names all ended in "i." Jewish girls were unknown. The life of the mind—literature, contemplation, call it what you will—had never existed in my family's history. We were as unevolved as the original Durgins (carpenters, probably), who had pushed West with Jackson, then stopped. The gray blanket of Pittsburgh poverty, and petty strategies to escape it—that alone made sense. That alone whispered in my ear.

But, Rosie, I remember even now the softness of Pittsburgh, long summer twilight hours playing street baseball, when the greatest accomplishment in life lay in lofting a tennis ball to deepest center field over the link fence at the end of the street, to sail another three or four hundred feet down and bounce on a rooftop under my bedroom window. Pride went with the sweet surrender of a tennis ball.

If you've read my first novel, *Will You Be Coming out Again After Supper?* you know this reminiscence is the core of everything in that book. Those long warm hours of endless summer between supper and a mother's call for bath and bed. The blessed hours before the stars come out, when a cool breeze rises from the valley and even my mother shows herself to weed the garden in our patch of front yard, and the neighbors sit in lawn chairs to read their *Presses* and *Sun-Teles*. No television yet. The papers delivered. "Dragnet" and "Mister Keen" on the radio: the weeks and days of a child's immortality. Rachel wasn't terribly sympathetic to the whole undertaking. She used to refer to it as my undescended-testicle novel. Anyway, keep that book open, Rosie, because I'm older now and I can't do justice to that kind of innocence anymore, no matter how much I want to. When I wrote that book, I still thought it was Pittsburgh I was trying to escape. And I thought that I had.

Chapter Two

My high school sent ten percent of its girls on to teaching colleges at Indiana State and Slippery Rock, and a few dozen interior linemen to West Virginia and Penn State. Except for Duquesne's basketball, Pittsburgh was a city of losers, with the Pirates, Steelers, and Panthers the jokes of their respective leagues. People spoke well of Carnegie Tech, for a school without teams, but that was probably just another desperate rumor. I'd taken Pitt's admissions forms, but deep down I rebelled. Pitt had been 2–9 the year before. Penn State was possible only because the alternative was West Virginia.

In high school, I was a good student without trying, and a poor athlete who'd spilled his guts in cross-country and wrestling. I earned no letters, but made the honor roll, an embarrassing compensation. Because of the honor roll, Pitt accepted me, with the hint of a scholarship. It was considered shameful in my high school to win a scholarship for anything other than height, speed, or strength.

I checked the "Accounting" box for my father and the "Veterinary Medicine" box for Wanda: I played along. Penn State and West Virginia chipped in with acceptances, the Mountaineers with generous aid. One winter weekend I took my father's truck down to Morgantown and up to State College. They were so large, I'd never felt so lost and frightened in my life.

My father told everyone I'd be going to Pitt for Accounting, and he'd tap the side of his head at the mention of a scholarship. "The boy's got a good head," he'd say. "Don't know where he got it at, but he's gonna look after me in my old age."

I would have traded my good head for the six extra inches he owed me. A boy of my generation had every right to expect that he'd be taller than his father, and I had failed by nearly half a foot. Deficient maternal genes.

How in the world am I supposed to write this?

There I was in 1957, Richard Durgin C.P.A., D.V.M., in a steelworkers' high school in Pittsburgh, as anonymous as a toadstool and just about as conscious, and here I am today writing about it to a professor at Berkeley as a way of taming the mystery of Rachel Isaacs. Why my life and yours should cross and that we should triangulate on Rachel is a deeper mystery than anything in your life or hers, or surely in mine. Complexity like that makes the pen wilt in my hand. The unexamined life may not be worth living, but the conscious life can scare you shitless.

For a long time, I comforted myself that simple overload was the reason I'd stopped writing. Not guilt, not bitterness, not even (if I'm honest) the discouragement from publishers' row. I'd seen too much, couldn't strain for the forms anymore. But that's not it. Somewhere along the line I exhausted my defensive love of Pittsburgh and the mother lode of working-class spite that went with it. My smug blue-collar self-righteousness, as Rachel put it. She also had a title for all the proletarian novels and films and tacky affinities of my Pittsburgh youth. "Boxcar with masturbating hobo," she called them. She could be cruel.

Okay, Rosie, here's part of what I mean.

Today—April 10, 1982, in Faridpur, Rajasthan, India—as I write this, I am sitting on a porch under a ceiling fan, sandaled feet propped on blazing plaster, in 115-degree heat, with the sounds of my new life bursting around me. Semi-tame peacocks strut on the neighbor's roof. I woke this morning to the screams of a sow cornered in my driveway, unable to advance against the men with planks, unable to scale the plaster wall that separates the houses, repulsed by the fence I'd built to keep the pie-dogs from attacking my garden. And as I watched in the pink tropical dawn, they whacked the sow to death and dragged her out to the roadway to join her butchered litter. And so tonight in my new city tourists will dine on suckling pig or on fresh pork chops cut from a sow that had wandered too brazenly into the village trash heap. And I will have pools of blood in my garage and a plaster wall that looks like the site of the St. Valentine's Day Massacre, until the monsoon rains come and wash it away.

And just as I go back twenty-five years to Pittsburgh and to the first truly self-conscious moment in my life (the first time I was an individual in the universe), my son bursts onto the porch, demanding in that precise English he's picked up in the Montessori School, "Dad-dy, you must do something about Narinder Singh."

Narinder Singh, the taxi driver's son, a towering seven in his Sikh's topknot, claims the wicket toppled because the soil was cracked, not because of Dev's expert bowling.

My Hindi now is good enough for this. O Rachel, O Father, O Mother, God, how can this happen in a single life?

I've even learned more than a Pittsburgher's fair share of cricket. I dreamed once of taking a son of mine to baseball games, teaching him to be ravished by the game as I once was. Instead, he practices his bowling by the hour in the backyard cricket pitch cleared by the larger boys in a nearby compound, aided by the usual layabouts and some of my workers and the lunch-hour clerks in rolled-up white sleeves. My son! The stiff-legged approach, as though he were about to pole-vault rather than release a ball, and the vicious, scything, counterclockwise overhand release of that whizzing black pellet. A murderous game as it's played here by the bitter and unemployed. And I wonder about my errant sowing. And that brings me back, literally, to Pittsburgh.

On a day in biology class, when we were to bring items from home or the street for microscopic study, or to pluck hairs or prick fingers, I found myself dissatisfied with the shred of newsprint I'd brought and only vaguely interested in the scaly eyebrow hair I'd pulled.

"Ooo, blood!" I heard. "It's like cherry Life Savers!"

"Yeah, but watch out if there's a hole in the middle."

I knew then what I wanted to see. The boys' room was just across the hall. As a senior and third-string wrestler, I had crapper rights, waiving the usual fee levied by the eleventh-grade custodians. They charged their highest tariff for those brief acts of standing ecstasy, the result of which I smeared on a slide I'd smuggled in. Capping it with a cover-lens, I took it back to class.

I knew how thinly I'd spread my milt, yet still they churned from the depths of a jism sea. Each of them entirely me. Suddenly I knew what was meant by an inner world, a subconscious, and how untamable they were. Like dreams, like tumors. Each of them made in my image, but not quite me. I was a god.

From that day on, my version of the ultimate fiction—all the metaphysical speculations belabored by astronomers and anthropologists—would have a strongly sexual bent. Why me, in such a profligate universe? The millions of potential selves I'd just flushed and the millions more I smeared under my seat told me I was nothing but a runt-sperm who'd barged his way up the egg channel, passed on the shoulder, run a stop sign, and slammed broadside into the target while the smarter, taller, handsomer models skidded on by.

If I were to choose one moment of my life before meeting Rachel, and to say it was the moment that started making me arrogant and ambitious, made that motel-tryst in Steubenville a heartless seduction instead of a prenuptial celebration, and even left me indifferent to my father's tennis ball in the gut, then that moment in Senior Biology was it. The origin of everything in a not-quite-sexual act.

Wanda got the message, broke off our unstated engagement five weeks before graduation (but still hooked a husband by later that summer), and I found myself ejected from the open grave of Durgin history in Pittsburgh.

Chapter Three

We didn't have a college adviser. We had a job counselor who served as an assistant track coach. He'd gotten me weekend work as a bellhop at the Carleton House. For college he'd advised me to check out the Army Language School at Monterey.

A visiting counselor from one of the suburban high schools had come to look us over. She was middle-aged and well dressed in a fawn-colored suit, with touched-up hair and glasses on a silver chain. Rich bitch, I thought. She talked encouragingly of Indiana State and Slippery Rock, congratulated the college-bound athletes and encouraged me to take up the scholarship from West Virginia. Be a Mountaineer, she said, do well, and try to transfer to Carnegie Tech your sophomore year. I had no idea that colleges weren't permanent events in one's life, like marriage, citizenship, and baseball loyalty. She was counseling disloyalty, the only alternative to luck in the world I came from.

"And did you like Morgantown, Richard?" she asked. Her manner was ingratiating. Her job was to come down here and tell us that things weren't as bad as we'd heard and that many very successful people had never gone to college at all. Morgantown had been ugly and immense; no scholarship, no Hot Rod Hundley or Sam Huff could neutralize the lostness I'd felt. Then I spotted something peeking from her purse, and when she shifted haunches, it fell to the floor. I picked it up.

LOVETT COLLEGE
Calendar of Courses
1957

"What's this place?" I demanded. I couldn't lift my fingers from the glory of its page; it was like my first thrumming of Wanda's breasts. She reached out to take it from me.

"A small place in Kentucky," she said. "I don't think you'd like it."

"Kentucky?" One of those Monopoly squares, between Free Parking and Chance. Except for a trip to Niagara, and another to Cleveland, plus the usual excursions to Steubenville and the weekend to Morgantown, I'd never been out of Pennsylvania. Living in a tri-state area had made me feel effortlessly cosmopolitan.

"I like it," I said.

The cover showed a chapel at the end of an elm-lined brick walk. A beautiful blonde in a plaid skirt and blazer, wearing her hair in a ponytail, sat on a low stone wall. I'd never seen anyone in such a costume: white socks, brown-and-white shoes, pearl earrings, a Terry Moore fuzzy white sweater. She looked like a young June Allyson holding her books against an artful bosom, waiting for the *New Faces of 1957* to sweep her off her feet. A blond young hulk in a letter jacket, books wedged against his manly hip, gazed down fondly at her scalp. In one picture

all the pretty girls in my high school, including Wanda
Lusiak, were blasted out of the water. There wasn't a smile
like that in all of Pittsburgh. A smile of such total adoration that I thrust myself beside her, bumping the letter
man, one leg casually slung on the wall, an arm posses-
sively on her shoulder.

West Virginia held no such paths. No such scalps.

"May I have it back, please, Richard?"

"Just a minute."

"I have to show it later."

"Where? Sewickley? Mount Lebanon?"

"Richard. I don't like your tone."

I was already reading the preface. I was like a cancer patient who'd stumbled across the descriptions of a miraculous cure, and now had to convince his doctor:

> For the fifth time in the past seven years Lovett
> College was honored with the Southern States Re-
> gional Accreditation Committee's "Special Cita-
> tion" as the most successful college in its twelve-
> state district in combining overall excellence in
> teaching, service, athletics, and leadership, while
> fostering healthy social, intellectual, and moral
> values.

"It is a truly excellent little college," she said.

"Do they have an application blank here?"

I ripped out the whole page before giving it back. I had
seen my future in a photo, just as I had seen my past on a
slide. It was walking down a tree-lined path with a young
June Allyson, arms aching with knowledge, passions
throbbing. The path out of Pittsburgh was brick-lined,
elm-covered, passing over a bridge and ending at a chapel.

Lovett College, Lovettville, Kentucky. There were no

ZIP codes in those days. I sent away for the forms that afternoon.

When I think of California, girls like Rachel Isaacs (or Rosie Chang, for that matter) don't automatically leap to mind. I've never been west of Des Moines. I think first of Raymond Chandler novels and rows of pastel, tiled-roof houses in Santa Monica, back when California wasn't such a bizarre idea for expatriate English gentlemen. As it turned out, Ben-Zvi had known Chandler well. Chandler used to make up stories for Rachel, playing Lewis Carroll to her precocious Alice.

If I could hold on to that version of California, I might have a better sense of Rachel's growing up. Back when houses in southern California were cool and dark and vaguely Tudor, under spreading eucalyptus. Back when California represented an alien past and not a mindless future. While Wanda was plotting our life of built-in lazy Susans, Rachel was dipping into built-in bookcases with leaded-glass doors holding uniform editions of Victorian classics. I didn't want to think that people in Los Angeles read George Eliot or Thackeray, or, like Rachel, learned violin and oboe, staged backyard plays, painted and exhibited. My imagination is too parochial and too corrupted, full of old radio and early television shows, and fantasies of wrapping Annette Funicello in a beach blanket. Suddenly, tall, dark, studious girls like Rachel just disappear.

And now you tell me she had a baby in high school? At Runnymede? It's just incredible. She never told me, and I never guessed. I can't relate to California, but I resent it mightily.

She was happy in New York, that's all I know. In California, she said, people "thought with their bodies." Is that what she meant, babies instead of poems?

Ben-Zvi Eisachs (as the name had been spelled in Ger-

many) was a shlock scriptwriter by day, but at other times
a traditional Weimar intellectual. Seven generations of
Berlin Eisachses glowered behind him: bankers breeding
professors, professors breeding poets, poets breeding scientists, scientists breeding lawyers. The intellectual nobility,
a humbling lineage to marry into. He let me know it, believe me. (I met him once in New York after his fall from
Hollywood, when he was scrounging for television work.
He was a sour little man who treated me like a Shabbes
goy. I'm struggling to be objective.)

He never talked to Rachel about "the industry." She
grew up thinking he did something shameful for a living.
The first time she asked him what he did, he told her, "I
play the organ at a pet cemetery." It's hard to take movies
seriously, she told me once, when you know the hero who
looks so noble and self-sacrificing has had five wives and
insists on a "sexual-servicing" clause in his contract.

Her mother was Hilda Federman, one of the early voices
of Mighty Mouse. She'd sung opera in Vienna, had turned
to voice teaching in Paris after their initial uprooting, and
continued to teach when they arrived in the United States
in '37. She vowed never to sing in German again, and
Mighty Mouse is where it left her.

If you know Rachel's poem, "In America, Rheingold Is
a Beer," with its bitter little rhymes;

> . . . on a terrace in Paris
> watching *Regen* turn to *pluie*,
> Isolde barks at a concierge
> and Tristan takes a pee . . . ,

then you know something of Hilda's bitterness and the
ways Rachel tried to sympathize. They never talked, so
she could only do it in poems. Nearly everything she

wrote is autobiographical, no matter how "surreal" the critics say it is.

Her father had not permitted her to see a film until she was fifteen. By that she meant a Hollywood film, but still she was innocent enough to shout out in the middle of a theater, when one of the minor actors made a brief appearance, "That's Dotty's daddy!" She was that innocent. And now you tell me she had a baby in high school? Everything is possible, especially in her world. Life was a script, and the world was a prop room, despite her father's best efforts.

He belonged to a chamber-music ensemble. He was a pillar of the émigré community. By day he was churning out formula scripts, by night he was polishing Thomas Mann's English. It had to screw her up. He hated Hollywood and its values, so he tried to do Rachel a favor by keeping her ignorant of everything about it. And that kept her ignorant of America as well. She knew nothing about us! She was never vaccinated against us. She wasn't raised in California; she was raised in a cryogenic bubble. (How can any of us survive this culture without adopting a few of its less objectionable scraps and learning to love them?)

What do you know about her Italian childhood? In 1950, BZ left Hollywood in disgust and tried to become a neo-realist. Rachel described it to me in glorious detail, but how could I follow? It was all so dazzling. Her life was full of sophisticated Poles and cultured Italians—mine is chockablock with Wops and Polacks. She was placed in a convent school, but on weekends and holidays she came down to Rome and hung out in Cinecittà and became indistinguishable from any other movie-mad Italian schoolgirl of her time and place.

When we moved to New York, she put herself on the mailing list of the Italian Consulate, showing up for every

film retrospective. (Like me with sports, it was one of
those unworthy obsessions we agreed not to ridicule.) She
responded to every bit of Italian trivia as warmly as I did
to Pittsburgh and the American fifties. (Essentially, she
had no American trivia.) One night at MOMA as we were
watching a "white telephone" screwball comedy of the
Mussolini period, she cried out in that fifteen-year-old California voice, "My God, it's Fausto Giachetti!"

She had a reality confusion that functioned as art, even
as great art. She didn't know what was real and what was
in her head. She was always looking for things strong
enough to resist her imagination. For a long time, Italy was
strong enough. So was great literature. So was I. We all
failed her. She even met my mother (despite my best
efforts) and instead of recoiling in horror (now that's reality!) she wrote half a dozen poems about her. When she
learned my mother's name was Mary, that became the
source of "Mary, Queen of the World."

Reality confusion is fatal. You want to know why she
died and if I told you right now Hitler and America did it,
and maybe I did too, the details would sound like a tragic
farce, like those Fiji Islanders who died of the common
cold. She was a reality junkie, and she died of an overdose.

The most real thing she ever found was me. I had reality
coming out of the ears. I dribbled it. But I wanted dreams,
I wanted Hollywood. I wanted a key to the prop room,
and I wanted evenings with Thomas Mann and picnics
with Kurt and Lotte. No wonder, for a while, we were
mutually miraculous to one another. Toward the end,
however, she said to me, "You're right, you don't deserve
me. But I deserve you."

Chapter Four

The name of the Admissions Director of Lovett College was T. Lysander Crommelin, a southern gentleman of the old school. He was deeply aggrieved to inform me that all the places for the class of 1961 were allocated. Nevertheless, he included the forms and scholarship blanks I'd requested, and my name would be kept on file, in case anything opened up.

I was working weekends as a bellhop. A month of tips went off to Kentucky just to cover the application fee.

No one ever told me that some colleges cost more than others. I didn't know there were reasons besides geography or athletics for boys like me to think only of Pitt, West Virginia, and Penn State, or why Lovett brochures and hundreds of others never made their way to our vocational guidance office.

Freshman fees at Lovett came to five thousand dollars a year. Working full-time in a good year and doing weekend plumbing and painting, my father once made eight thousand dollars. There had to be a mistake. How could boys like me even go to Lovett? Didn't anyone realize that?

I told Pitt I'd be coming. Chartered Accountant Richard Durgin. It pleased my father, then patting his freshly sprouted potbelly. "Need someone to look after me in my old age," he said. "Accountants start at three times what I ever made."

With a loan, the tuition scholarship, living at home and keeping the job at the hotel, I'd be able to make it through my freshman year at Pitt. That wouldn't even cover my deposit at Lovett.

I read the *Official College Guide of 1957.* For Lovett they reserved their highest praise:

> Set in a magnificent region of rolling hills, ver-
> dant pastures, horse farms and tobacco planta-
> tions, and in a village of surpassing charm, Lovett
> College imparts the graciousness of the Old
> South with the academic rigor of New England.
> The discriminating undergraduate is here offered
> everything he might choose for a rich, rewarding
> educational experience.

Lovett only considered applicants from the top five percent of the finest secondary schools in America. How
about the top two percent of one of the worst? College
Board scores compared favorably with the top Eastern
schools . . . for girls, verbally. The average Lovett coed
outscored her male counterpart by nearly one hundred
points.

That told me all I wanted to know. I was tired of stupid
girls. Wanda, rest her soul, was shrewd, but dumb. I never
met a girl smarter than me, until I went to college. Intelligence, in the beginning, was an erotic charm.

The rest of the *Guide* debunked Lovett's "country
club" reputation. It highlighted the most successful depart-

ments—Theater Arts, Political Science, and the combined major of Business & Advertising. In the roll call of famous graduates, I recognized a few of the politicians, none of the businessmen, and a surprising number of actors and actresses.

Where was my head? Ninety-eight percent of men belonged to fraternities. "No student earnestly desiring fraternity affiliation will be denied it," promised the Dean of Men. What could be fairer? What could be more democratic?

I believe in transformation. I'm very American that way. It went farther than belief—it was self-evident that slow starts meant nothing. The home team always bats last. Even the Pirates were becoming respectable, after all those bitter, humiliating years.

So there was a chance for me, too, off the cliff and into the green charms of Kentucky. I cling to my decisions, and I'm fiercely loyal, no matter what the cost and the pain, to all of my mistakes.

Chapter Five

In the summers of the mid-fifties I used to live in the bleachers of Forbes Field. The Pirates were terrible. Slow, old, dispirited.

I may never see another baseball game, or read another box score, so this is more for me than it is for you. Maybe, like Rachel, team sports leave you cold and you care only for the encounters of grace and danger. Gymnastics, skiing, skating, fencing. But Rachel had her impure attachments. She was the only person I've ever met who knew the scoring rules of roller derby. She carried a Runnymede bowling trophy with her, even into our marriage.

The first time Pittsburgh became entirely mine was when I walked out of the house one summer Saturday and pieced together the various transfers and streetcar routes that would drop me at the Forbes Field parking lot. I was eight. Bliss, when you're eight, is sitting in the bleachers and pitting your knowledge against the beer-swollen platitudes of laid-off steelworkers. The sweetest words in the world come from some hunky downing his Iron City and nodding, "Think so, kid? Yeah, maybe yer right."

(It's not quite Raymond Chandler taking you in his lap.

Rachel, I must say, was gracious about some of these recol-
lections, in the beginning.)

A couple of times each summer, the Negro leagues
would come to Forbes Field. Every year the bleachers
snickered at the announcement of a game between the
Clowns and the Monarchs, the Black Barons and the Panthers. But in the summer of my senior year, I went.

I went for the love of baseball. I wanted to see baseball
where even the slowest guys on the field, even the um-
pires, were black. The National League was a well-kept
zoo; I wanted to see the jungle.

It was black, all right. Forbes Field had suddenly turned
jivey, starting with a new Homestead DJ voice on the PA
system. The stadium was as vast and solemn as ever, and
the University of Pittsburgh's Tower of Learning was still
visible behind the bleachers. Schenley Park was still green
out past deepest center field, but the atmosphere had
changed. What they'd done was make the largest major
league park acceptably Triple-A. Fat old men in double-
breasted suits were hawking menu-sized flyers cut from a
stencil. An hour before the announced start of the game,
hundreds of civilians, mostly women and children, were
strolling on the holy turf between first and third. Some
boys were practicing their windups off Vernon Law's con-
secrated pitching rubber. Some of the players were in their
undershirts, smoking and playing pepper.

The practice balls were gray and scuffed. The fungo
bats were heavily taped and in short supply. The banners
in the stands and near the two dugouts were from the
Pittsburgh *Courier*, a paper I'd heard about from jokes
("You deliverin' papers down there? Whatcha deliverin',

the *Courier?*", but had never seen. Everywhere I saw
banners that totally confused me:

PITTSBURGH'S LEADING NEWSPAPER!
WORLD CHAMPION MOBILE GIANTS!
HALL-OF-FAMER HEAT-LIGHTNIN' LOU MURPHY!
BABE RUTH'S BOW-DOWN MAN THUNDER CLOUD JEFFERSON!
ROOKIE OF THE YEAR CHOW DOG LEON WILLIAMS!
5-TIME BATTING CHAMPION LINIMENT BURNS!
28-GAME-WINNER SUGAR BEAR CISCO SUMTER!

Where had I been? I—who'd gone to Cleveland once to
see Satchel Paige, and who'd heard of Josh Gibson and the
Homestead Grays and was willing to grant them all instant
immortality, and who knew that Aaron and Thompson and
Newk and Campy had started as Negroes before passing
over—had never heard of any player on the field. I was
ashamed of myself.

Except for a couple of familiar peanut vendors, I was
the only white face in the crowd. Seats were plentiful—
there might have been fifteen thousand in the grandstands
—but fans sat clustered together, leaving empty rows between them. I had a row to myself.

The game was seedy. I'd expected a game of Titans,
where even the incomparable Roberto might have been
benched. That's why they played so shallow in the
outfield, I thought at first, and why they edged in on the
grass at third and short. They set up defensively like slow-
pitch softball. But after an inning, I knew the truth. The
Clowns were playing with only two outfielders. Mobile's
shortstop didn't have a glove. Their arms were shot.
Infielders staggered under pop-ups; catchers waved at wild
pitches and tubby batters like Thunder Cloud Jefferson
rumbled down the baselines slower than the Adcocks of

the game I knew. And what was Sugar Bear Sumter throwing out there? I hadn't thought of left-handed Negroes in the first place, but if they were, I expected them to be craftier than Spahn and faster than Koufax.

In front of me sat a mother and four teenage daughters, passing food back and forth, dipping it into jars, lathering their chicken with bottled sauces, eating cold biscuits dipped in honey and talking among themselves so loudly that I couldn't follow the game.

With those girls in front of me, I couldn't remember how Chow Dog and Chain Lightnin' and Heat Lightnin' and Thunder Cloud followed by Mushroom Cloud were doing. I was bored with baseball for the first time in my life. Either the game was too poor, or I was too white. Or I was getting too old for silly games, white or black.

And then the girl in the yellow dress directly in front of me turned in profile and called back, "You must be hungry, jest watchin' us eat. Here, c'mon, have yourself a piece of chicken."

She passed her paper plate up and, my goodness, yes, I was hungry. But more, I was amazed.

She watched my fingers take the plate. "You really ain't, are you?"

"Excuse me?"

"Colored."

"No, I guess not." I was willing to claim an eighth or a sixteenth, anything that she wanted. All of my life, Rosie, I have abased myself, or boosted myself, into belonging.

She turned all the way around now, for a good long stare, just as I put the chicken to my lips.

"Hi," I said.

She snickered. "Come on. Why you here?"

"I like baseball. Every year they announce these games, and every year I think about going. So this year I went."

"Where they announcin' these things? This place old, man."

"Here, at the Pirate games," I said. Could it be she didn't know the Pirates? This whole vast stadium, built and maintained for the annual visit of the Mobile Giants?

"But it ain't fo' you."

"They didn't say it wasn't."

"Dint they say it was Negro Leagues?"

I sensed I was gathering a crowd. I'd sensed all day I'd been watched and kept in isolation. Her sisters were whispering among themselves, and I could see the game was as forgettable to them as it was to me.

A man stepped over the empty rows and took a seat behind me.

"What's this boy sayin'?" he asked. I could smell his cigar, and something, maybe his shoulders, had blocked the sunlight behind me.

"He ain't said nothin'. Who ast you?"

I munched the chicken.

"He ain't said nothin' about the game, has he?"

Then the mother turned sharply in her seat, her eyes barely grazing my face as she focused on the voice behind me. "What game? I don't see no game. I only see a bunch of fat old niggers flappin' their fannies worse'n the girls in a Hill District cathouse."

"Mama!"

"Yes, ma'm, you are surely right there. Old Thunder Cloud looks like the march of time done run him over."

"Thunder Cloud can't outrun his farts no more," the old lady observed.

"Thanks," I said, passing back the plate.

"You got pickles in there?" the man behind me asked the girls. "I seen them jars and I jes' had to come on down."

"Peppers, real hot."

I passed the jar up to him.

"You ever taste real 'Bama peppers? Go'head—they real bad." He held out the jar for me and I reached in.

Red, hot, and still a little sweet. I had a second, after the man had fished around for two whole red ones. He belched, then I.

"Now tham's peppers, Mama!"

"What about you?" asked the girl in the yellow dress. "You like them?"

"Loved them."

"Come on. You liked the chicken?"

"Best I ever had."

She gave me a slow smile; I could see for the first time she was younger than me—maybe fifteen or sixteen—a little gap-toothed, very dark, with a warm smile.

"I'll bet you even made it," I said.

"Some of it."

"The chicken, right?"

She scowled, she frowned, she pulled her lips into a complicated pout. "How'd you tell?"

"It was so good, that's all." I'd never found compliments coming so easily. "It was especially good chicken."

"You know," said the man behind me, "Ol' Thunder Cloud so old now he got a boy just signed up with the Cardinals."

"Where they at now?" asked the mother.

"Where they always been. St. Louis."

"Dint there used to be a Cardinals in Memphis?" she asked.

I was about to pop in, primed with *Sporting News* lore: "No, ma'm, those are the Chicks, Memphis Chicks of the Southern Association"; but the man beat me to it.

"You be thinkin' of the Chicago Cardinals. They never

was no good. Detroit Black Panthers run 'em out of town.
They only had Chow Dog Sullivan."

"How come all these chow dogs?" I suddenly asked.
"There's Chow Dog Williams out there, rookie of the
year, and Chow Dog Sullivan in Chicago . . ."

"Every team gotta have a chow dog," said the man.

"That's 'cuz a chow dog always blue-gummin' the empires," said the lady.

I let my face make a gesture of "Oh, I see."

"Where you livin' at?" asked the girl.

"Homestead. Over the steelworks."

"Homestead! *That* was Negro baseball," said the
mother. "The Grays."

"Josh Gibson," I said.

"Cool Papa Bell. They was mighty fine. I wasn't no
older'n that one there when I seen Josh Gibson."

"Josh Gibson and Satchel Paige could take on the Pirates and shut 'em out nine–nothin'," the man said.

"Wouldn't be too hard." I chuckled.

I felt a heavy hand on my shoulder. "They could take
the Milwaukees and shut 'em out nine-nothin'," he said.

"What's the score? Anybody know the score?" asked
one of the other daughters. The scoreboard wasn't operating that day.

"I think Indianapolis is ahead," I said.

"How come Mobile's the home team?" she asked.

"They ain't got a home. They's always travelin'," said
the man. "They take turns."

"That's crazy," said the girl in yellow. "You think that's
crazy?"

"Confusing, maybe."

"You glad you came?"

"I wasn't for a while."

"He sayin' he wants to ask you out," giggled her sister.

"Shut your haid," she said, in that same scowl and pout. Then she turned to me. "How'd you get here?"

"Trolleys."

"I thought maybe you had a car."

"I'm saving for a '54 Merc."

"They're nice. Where you workin' at?"

"The Carleton House."

"That's a fancy place," she said. Her sister turned around with a half-smile and added, "They don't 'low no colored in there."

"Shee-it, girl, Carleton House ain't so fancy. It's filthy. You ain't missin' nothin'," said the man.

"Yeah? How you know that?"

"I put in the air-conditioning, that's how. And my wife, she used to work there. She used to come home sick to her stomach from the things she seen."

"What was you doin' there?" she asked.

"Bellhop."

"He's the one what turns the black people away," said the man, laughing (I hoped).

"Is it dirty?" she asked.

"Unbelievable," I lied. "Like the man says, it's pretty scummy. I wouldn't stay there if I was coming to town. I'd go to the William Penn."

"That so?" said the man. The voice was like a razor. "Then you really don't like black folks, do you?"

The girl turned away. A very large shoe was planted on the top of the seat next to me, and another shoe on the top of the seat I was sitting in, pushing me forward after a nasty clip. The row of women in front of me were suddenly quiet. The shoe on the chair beside me kept edging closer to my elbow, then finally swept it off the chair arm entirely.

"What I think," said the owner of both feet, speaking

now to no one in particular, "is that some people had ought to leave this park sooner than some other people."

Both feet came to rest on the points of my shoulder, first very lightly, then crashing down, grazing my back as I lunged forward. Dozens of men had gathered; some were smiling, some laughing. I walked backward down my row, staring at my tormentor for the first time. What was wrong with the man? He watched me with one eye, a giant in his forties with a peaked cap and some kind of union button, a leather jacket with a few fresh bright scrapes along the arms and elbows. What had I said? This is Forbes Field, my chosen home. You can't evict a man from the place he loves. Of all the whites in Pittsburgh, I was one of a handful who had made the effort at understanding.

When I stopped retreating, he turned both eyes on me and brought one foot down sharply, the way you'd stamp a heel at an unretreating mutt—and I jumped. I moved to the aisle, then down a row. The girl in yellow kept me in view. One eye, one arm half raised, two fingers fluttering a good-bye.

The only opened gates were under the right-field stands. It was an inconvenient exit, opening to the park, far from the narrow alleys leading back to Forbes Street and the trolleys. I joined a group of older blacks who were leaving and came out, unscathed but still angry and shaking, on a narrow side street that bordered the park, farther from Forbes Street than I'd ever been.

All my life since my senior year, I've been like this—one smile from a girl in yellow, and Wanda Lusiak went flying out of my life. If a size 14 shoe hadn't been at my neck, I would have gotten her name and strayed to the Hill District and taken her out. Already I saw myself bringing her back to our house—she wouldn't have flinched walking across our little drawbridge. Subconsciously, that's always been the test—could she go back home with me, could she look down at the clouds?

Unfaithfulness is not my only weakness.

Back home, up in my bedroom, my throat tightened, my eyes watered; I was almost crying. Oh, sentimentality! I knew my father downstairs was dying (his coughing threatened our house the way seventy years of wind had failed), and I was crying not for him, but for the shabbiness of Negro baseball. I said that the slide in biology class had started making me strange and arrogant. I was inconsolable because I'd been born too late for myths and greatness, and now I knew there was no unreceding wall of talent, no undiscovered forest of baseball sequoias. Our anemic white statistics were all there would ever be. No more Willies and Henrys mocking Cooperstown from dirt patches in Alabama.

The context is shabby, but I respect the feeling even now.

For most of my life I've been an accidental observer of a passing order. I've played out this little scene a dozen times: the last year of Negro baseball. The last years of pre-wired, pre-criminal, pre-paranoid, pre-drug, pre-sexual America. Today on a porch in India I'm playing it out again.

There's an open field behind my house where the village strews its garbage, where pigs, goats, dogs, beggars, and buzzards root by day and jackals scavenge at night. At the far end of the open field is a wall carved out by villagers who've converted its antechambers into tea-stalls and tire-patching stands. The broken wall dates to Tamerlane the Great. I've traveled half the world from my house in Pittsburgh, but the view hasn't changed that much at all.

Chapter Six

It was ordained that I would get to Lovett. First came the waiting list, then the acceptance. Then my acceptance of their acceptance, contingent on a job in the dining hall and a scholarship. They waived my deposit, contingent on the scholarship. The college of multiple contingencies.

While waiting for Lovett, I kept Pitt on the hook. It made me feel wanted; being on domestic terms with the good girl next door while secretly courting the spoiled, cruel southern belle.

In mid-August I attended Pitt's orientation for local freshmen. All of us who'd checked the pre-Accountancy box met the professor of Introductory Methods in a seminar room for coffee and donuts.

"Maybe some of you have heard the old saying, 'Those who can't, teach.'" He scoured the room with his glinty eyes and great bushy eyebrows. "I'm here to tell you I was senior accountant for the Mellon Bank."

He brought the words "accountant" and "Eisenhower Era" into sharp alignment. He advised all of us to invest first of all in half a dozen Arrow Dart white shirts, modeling his after taking off his suit coat and vest. The proper length of sleeve, the snugness of collar, the cuff links. He was a balding, mustached little ectomorph, pale-skinned but furry, with tufts of black ear hair that stood up like a bobcat's. Most of my fellow pre-penpushers already wore approximations of the regulation uniform: an honest charcoal suit ("Bond's will do in a pinch"), unostentatious cuff links and matching tie bar ("key chains and pocket watches are pretentious, unless you're a Phi Beta Kappa"). That had to be a good fraternity, I thought. I'll join that one if I get into Lovett.

The orientation continued.

We toured the nationality rooms. Then we were taken to the top floor of the Tower. It was a moving spectacle, Pittsburgh from that height and from that Gothic security. My city had always seemed to me an ethnic dead end, where all of central Europe had come to shorten its names and dump its objectionable pieties. I was moved to see their passing marked with flags and heroic murals.

I'm a veteran of cloud suspension, and I was at it again, soaring over Pittsburgh. A clear view down the river to the Point and its shiny aluminum buildings. I counted a dozen bridges, and named them. The innocent greens and sand traps of Forbes Field lay practically at my feet. Out another window and up the river, punctured by orange flashes from the open hearths and burn-off from the spindly stacks, lay those nodes of steelworks, and somewhere in the smoke on a day with the proper winds I might even have seen my house.

And that was the day of my first dizziness.

It couldn't have been worse if the top floor had become a centrifuge. I felt thrown against the wall, and my shirt was suddenly drenched in sweat. The senior guide ran over to me and had to pry me from the wall. I couldn't talk. The sensation (I remember it to this day) was of trying to bring a crippled airliner through dense fog, and just as the clouds thinned and a runway should have appeared, being confronted by the flashing red lights of the Gulf Building instead. I put my hands on an imaginary throttle and tried to climb, but I couldn't. My plane, my buildings, my life were crashing.

The guide gathered our group to the middle of the room.

"Look, guys, stay here, okay? I'm taking Richie here back down. He needs a little air. I'll be up for you and the tour will continue." I plastered myself in the corner of the elevator, hyperventilating, held up by the senior. "Don't be afraid," he said. "It happens lots of times. Some people can't take the heights. Look, we're down to twenty-five. See, you can count off the floors . . . twenty . . . there, nothing to be afraid of . . . fifteen . . . more than halfway down to the grass and sidewalks now . . . there, easy. Nothing to be afraid of, Richie. What's your major going to be? Ten . . . nine . . . what's that? Easy, easy . . . Oh, Accounting—couldn't catch it at first—good choice, man— four . . . three . . . Great. You were super. Now you wait right here, and I'll go back up and bring down the others. Don't go 'way, Richie, that's a good boy. Wait . . . right . . . here." He probably assumed I was also deaf.

When the ornamental brass elevator doors closed on him, I was gone. I never ran harder in cross-country, over those walks and across the grass past the Heinz Chapel and down Forbes Street to my old, safe trolley stop near the Bureau of Mines. I was half a mile away before I dared to turn and look at the Tower behind me. If it fell, I'd be safe. Not even the gargoyles would scratch me.

Rosie, as I sit here today, my body is dry but my hands are sweating still. I have to think there are messages your body sends that are responding to past *and* future possibilities. Rachel believed that, too. When the past and the future clamp together in one fused moment, they can kill you. When they just graze you like a bat's wing, we can call them poems. They came together one day for Rachel.

On the day I received my final Lovett acceptance with the scholarship, my father was brought home bent double with pain, sweating, and coughing up great ladles of rust-colored phlegm. My life in the city of cliffs and inclines was ending. My body was saying: Don't climb too high. I became an acrophobe.

But my brain was saying something else. It said: You are destined for something great. You will open your bedroom window, spread your wings, and soar over everything, down the Ohio to the verdant pastures of Kentucky. I could feel that golden girl of the elm-lined walk in my arms.

If Lovett hadn't come through, I would have stayed with the Carleton House and waited for the Army to call me up. Maybe they had a cure for this new disease. I could hardly mention it at home, with a father who was dying and a mother who was incapable of sympathy for anyone.

So there you have it, Rosie, a little portfolio of senior-year memories. All those Pittsburgh things that are probably gone. Forbes Field and the Carleton House are torn down and so is our house, and the Negro leagues and Pittsburgh trolleys have disappeared. And my father is dead, who was just little older than I am now; and my mother, who that year was exactly my age now—they've all gone with no one to mourn them.

And of course Rachel is gone, for whom sizable chunks of the literary world continue to mourn. And the anonymous Wanda Lusiak Ponchuk: the Homestead life span never did keep pace with the twentieth century. Everyone who made my life secure is dead.

That's why I started writing, once I found the switch: to avenge myself on all that silence and to speak for the population inside me. How can you be only forty and have seen so much? Traveled so far, in every sense, with the worst, probably, still to come?

And so I have sailed the seas and come to the broken deserts of Rajasthan.

I'm not trying to be contentious, Rosie, but there's only one thing that does stay the same. I saw part of it on a slide in Senior Biology in an eerie moment of other-directedness, just like I saw that stag and recognized him. I've put my faith only in it, whatever "it" is. Let's just call it blind, undiminished life. Let's even capitalize it. It's the only thing Rachel Isaacs didn't have and couldn't get. Let's call it Self.

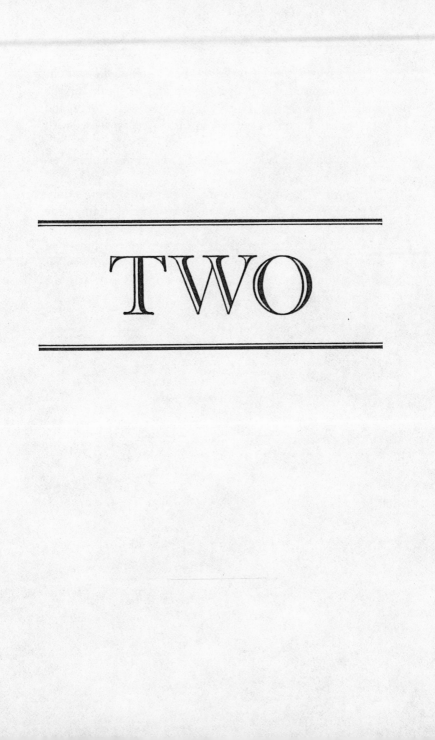

TWO

Dear Richie:

Bravo! You are a biographer's dream. You were worried about "the long lay-off"—well, don't be. I'm getting to like the guy. If you and Rachel had taken a compatibility test, you might have blown the computer. You're right to steer me onto her Italian childhood (it's where I'm weakest, though I'm going over there this summer. I love that "Fausto Giachetti!" bit. Patient research discloses that Fausto G. starred in just about every Africa epic that Mussolini ever financed).

In her papers are some poems and stories she wrote in French. I showed one of them to a French professor, who thought it might even be early Apollinaire. What it reminds me of actually is Flaubert's *Salammbô*. (Did she ever mention reading it? I know she visited Pompeii at nearly the same time.) In it, a wealthy Roman lady is taking her bath at a seaside resort. Heat and luxury and scented bath oils and African slaves give the whole scene heaviness and authenticity. Then suddenly, Vesuvius erupts, and they all perish in the rain of ash and brimstone. The last stanza is very "Grecian-urn"-like, with the modern poet presenting herself as a tourist at Pompeii looking at mosaics. Well: What can I say? Most impressive for a twelve-year-old. The nun who read it declared it "decadent and pagan."

(I make quite a bit of this, as you can imagine. The eruption is so close to the Holocaust that it seems a prefigurement. Innocence and catastrophe are her major themes—wouldn't you agree?)

The things you mention about Rachel in the first part are all new to me, for which I am grateful. Her parents barely survived her death, as you probably know. BZ's will left her papers to Pomona and the royalties (which so far have exceeded half a million dollars) continue to enrich a public radio service in southern California.

I have no idea what you're going to spring on me next. If there's anything a biographer learns quickly, it's that the line between autobiography, biography, and fiction is a matter of emphasis that must continually be redefined: I am writing a biography of Rachel's life, incorporating your autobiography and a little of my own—and together we might be writing a novel.

Yours,

Rosie

Faridpur, RJ
July 1, 1982

Dear Rosie:

I think I'm lucky that you took an interest in this and lifted it from me, and the Judith Singers. I wrote a novel about all this—now lost—called *Missing in Action* about a modern marriage between two decent artists, that ends tragically. In the early seventies, Bloomsbury lay fragrantly on the air and everyone was rhapsodizing on the Nicolsons and the Woolfs and how sensibly they'd coped with madness and inversion. Christ! I was trying to write about a contemporary American couple who were not psychotics or sexual cripples, but I never found the key to an editor's heart. "Why did she kill herself?" If I told that, I'd be a princeling on publishers' row.

I didn't know that French poem you describe, but I do know a few of her Italian anecdotes. I met her lover of those Padua years, a painter named Marco. He came to New York for an Italian Consulate exhibit.

We were mildly involved with the New York painting scene in the mid-sixties (hence the "Carla Goodings Connection" —God!). Because Carla became famous for her "cockshots" (I'm even in one of them), it doesn't prove to me that she's necessarily lesbo, or nympho, or that she's necessarily my friend, or Rachel's. I always thought she was friend to both of us. When I met Carla, (and, yes, committed infidelities with her), she was doing her "Museum Guard" series, which made her known (before "cockshots" did the rest). Rachel didn't like Carla's politics (this is a twist on Carla the "tough broad proletarian" and Rachel the lily-pure aesthete); Rachel felt too much irony —in the form of pity—was directed against the guards. That's why she wrote her series of "guard monologues" in a blues-y dialect; she thought the guards represented a culture as valid as the high European.

Don't think of her as a big proletarian; she was merely fair. She hated sentimentality wherever she found it. Remember her name for my carpenter's-son self-righteousness: Boxcar with masturbating hobo.

We've left the world of my first novel behind us now. Turn now, Rosie, to a copy of my second novel, *Smoke*, if the Berkeley Library is sufficiently endowed. I called it

Smoke to honor the tobacco money that so conspicuously endowed my college. By the time I got to the end, I was also describing the smoke of Vietnam villages and the smoke of ghetto riots. The link was in blind, self-congratulatory wealth.

What I'm saying is, the first book is a fifties novel, all about innocence and ambition and joining forces with the American dream; and the second novel is typical sixties stuff about the dream turning to nightmare and spitting you out the bottom. Maybe that's all I was destined to write.

Sometime in the sixties I went into a closet in order to concentrate on writing long sentences with a minimum of punctuation, and when I came out and looked around, my wife was dead and everyone was on drugs and I couldn't sing the music and everything was out of my control. The seventies were just a long unraveling. I'm waiting for the eighties to get under way. I'm glad you think we may have a novel here. I confess I no longer know what a novel is.

Baffledly,

Richie

Chapter Seven

You're the biographer, Rosie, and you want to keep the dates straight. Okay, it's September 1957. The place is Lovettville, Kentucky, about twenty miles southwest of Lexington.

The kid who left Pittsburgh that September could have become anything. I was a toadstool, and even that is boasting. I was still a caterpillar, crawling around the underside of things. Even compared with my fellow Lovett freshmen, I was something alien and unevolved. I had six toes and body odor; I lived on grubs and grasshoppers. Rachel was in her second year at Pomona, getting ready for Italy. We were planets apart.

I took the bus to Lovettville: express to Cincinnati, a local to Lexington, and the special Lovett van to the campus. I had the family suitcase and my father's gift of a new typewriter plus the charcoal Bond's suit I was wearing. Seventeen sleepless hours after starting out, I was dropped downhill on Clay Street near the freshman girls' dorms. This was the farthest west and the deepest south, the hottest and the sleepiest I had ever been.

The path uphill to my dorm led through the trees of the

lower campus, past the freshman girls' dorms to a series of steps, then up to the crest of College Hill. The temperature might have been ninety-five degrees. My Arrow Dart and new tie were stuck to my neck, and cutting in.

The girls of the class of '61 were being moved into Pusey, Blodgett, and Ramsey halls by their parents, old boyfriends, and opportunistic upperclassmen in their cut-off blue jeans and fraternity sweat shirts with the Greek letters stenciled on the front. I felt bad for those old high school boyfriends.

I'd never seen such girls. I had never even seen such mothers, whose slim, bleached blondness rivaled their daughters in youth and beauty. Invest in a Lovett girl and enjoy a child-bride for life. (The Lovett brochure had assured me that I had a better than sixty percent chance of doing just that.) This may seem strange, but I had never seen parents hugging their children, girls kissing fathers on the lips. They all seemed infantile. They were all infinitely desirable.

(I'm a confirmed hugger of children now. Most evenings, after supper, Dev and I come out here to the porch and I hold him on my lap until he falls asleep.)

As I watched from under a tree, unable to move, I felt like some poor Roman scout who'd stumbled on a glade of prancing Druids. (The educated fool in me says like Actaeon spying on Diana—they seemed so self-involved with their beauty and flirtatiousness, they couldn't see me anyway.) The idea of young men kissing their mothers on the lips sickened me. Maybe I'd enrolled in a school of perverts, and this is how I would have turned out if my mother had looked like Doris Day.

Those girls carrying in their racks and trunks of clothes, and all the electrical contraband, were the gaudiest females I'd ever seen. Farewell forever, Wanda Lusiak, despite the fact I still had her signed senior portrait in my suitcase. (She really was gone forever. She'd gotten married to Stan Ponchuk two weeks before, a man I might still have to avoid if I didn't want a crowbar buried in my skull.)

If I were to write my campus novel again, I wouldn't bother with Lovett's evils. I would concentrate instead on my selfishness, and my innocence. I might not have been classic Lovett material, but that's no excuse. I should linger on the unloading of the station wagons behind Pusey Hall. My reactions. I could have emptied most of the cars in a single trip, even with the contraband these girls were smuggling. (I'd even left my electric razor at home, since the approved dormitory list included only a radio, a clock, and a phonograph.) But my help would not have been welcome. The fathers were already inviting the polite upperclassmen to dinner, casting their daughters into their weird embrace. The fathers stared at me, muttering, I thought, "I don't like the looks of that one, honey. Stay away from types like that."

An emotion overcame me as I watched them. It wasn't love, and it came over me as suddenly and surprisingly as the dizziness at Pitt a few weeks before. It was fierce jaw-wrenching hate, and I clenched my teeth so hard my head started shivering. I didn't exactly hate the girls or their parents, but I suddenly hated wealth and confidence and good looks—everything that my previous life had denied me. I was alone in the world, and the sudden awareness froze me. It's bitterness, Rosie. My oldest, trustiest, most murderous companion.

It came as a vast betrayal that mothers didn't have to become sexless, half-witted, wax-coated lumps. And that fathers could be helpful and courteous and look as young as college boys, and joke with their wives as though they loved them, call their daughters "Princess" and see that they got settled, and even launched, romantically speaking. Girls could bleach their hair and not look cheap. Mothers could too, without sending "available" signals. These girls and even their little sisters could smoke in front of their parents, showing less furtiveness than if they'd sneaked a stick of gum. Many of the cars were equipped with horse trailers, and my female classmates stood for long, tearful minutes stroking the muzzles of their favorite mounts.

"She'll be a-waitin' on ya, honey."

My first Lovett words. Father to daughter. Daughter who looked like a wife, laying her hand on her father's hand as he lit her cigarette, father who held her like a boyfriend and kissed her just as deeply. My head was reeling as I climbed the hill to Sawyer Hall.

Chapter Eight

Brendan McIvor had already rimmed our room with empty vodka bottles hung from molding hooks. Jonah Jones's *My Fair Lady* bubbled from his phonograph. Two trunks still stood off to the side, and his suitcases rested in the lower bunk. Short and tanned, hairy but balding, with shrewd, darting eyes, horn-rimmed glasses and a harsh Chicago accent, he was a roommate fashioned for me on some jokester's match-up list. I was disappointed with the accent; I liked the strength of Kentucky's southernness. It was my exotica.

"Hey, roomie," he winked, then turned his back as he gave a pair of chino khakis a few solid whacks with a wire hanger. He had suspended several new, blue, button-down shirts and the pants from the center light fixture. At first he looked a little sheepish, but he had a gracious smile as he lashed at his new clothes. Then he took out a small emery board and began sanding down the elbows and collars of the new shirts.

It appeared pathological. He swayed with the music.

"Just lifting the threads, man." He worked on the elbows, thinning them to the point of rupture. He'd seen all he needed of me, and had turned away, perhaps in awe. Without looking back, he asked, "Where'd you get the suit?"

I told him—Bond's.

"Smart," he said. "You expecting to take in a funeral or something?"

He was in a Lovett sweat shirt and Madras shorts, and low-cut new sneakers with holes sanded over the little toes. No socks.

He explained later that afternoon: "The thing is, be casual." Casual was his religion. Everything had to be clean, but well worn; rumpled, not wrinkled. The code of casual radiated to all facets of campus comportment: courses taken, mode of study, choice of booze, fraternity affiliation, teams, music. And especially, dating. For us freshmen, to be seen with the right kind of girl from the right sorority was more important than settling down too early. To be seen doing anything was better than doing alone (right? wink, wink). She had to be blond, with long straight hair that moved one way in a convertible and other ways on the tennis court. She had to come from a city on sizable water and have a sailboat to prove it. She had to give a good time (wink, wink) but keep her reputation. She had to be smart, and keep good notes. But all the girls at Lovett were smart and blond, and most of them had convertibles, sailed, and played mean tennis. I'd never been on water, never held a racket; I felt sick.

Most of all, he said, she's got to make your fraternity brothers think you're getting it off her, even if you're not.

Well, that was Brendan.

Twenty years ago, Brendan seemed like a visiting deity, down on a visit to shape me up. He'd made up his mind to go to Lovett at about the same time I'd made up my mind to marry Wanda Lusiak. There'd never been a time he could remember when he wasn't going to Lovett. Back in seventh form of his prep school, he'd noticed that the coolest guys invariably went to Lovett. The guys he modeled himself on, the guys from the top families who landed jobs in the best ad agencies.

He'd already picked his major, his courses, his professors, his sports, and his fraternity. This, I reflected, is what is meant by research. He'd already ranked the pictures of girls in the *Freshman Directory* (the "Baby Book"), narrowing the two hundred pictures of replicated dewiness to half a dozen he'd start calling, based on their looks and addresses. In one afternoon I learned the names of the Right Suburbs in the upper South and Middle West —where to come from in Louisville, St. Louis, Cleveland, Detroit, Chicago, and Milwaukee. Other cities probably had nice suburbs (even Pittsburgh, he cheerily conceded), but they weren't near enough water, and he wasn't about to surrender his dreams of a fourteen-footer.

And so, even before I'd properly gotten over the surge of raw hatred and self-pity, Brendan was telling me Lovett stories, like an old alum.

"Don't buy your safes down at Pop Townsend's," he cautioned, patting a suspicious bulge in his wallet. "He'll act really friendly and sell them to you with a wink and real man-to-man advice, and the next morning the dean of men will call you in and ask what the hell you're doing, trying to screw a Lovett Maiden."

Our girls were called Maidens. Part of the southern heritage.

"If you want sex real quick and don't mind the consequences, lay twenty bucks out for a 'Week-Ender' down at the Pizza Palace. The weekend waitresses come from the County Home for Unwed Mothers. Watch out for the guy that runs Stripes and Blazers. His prices are high, and he's queer. Don't let him get you in the back for a measurement. Anything else?"

By this time I'd torn off my moist suit and soaking shirt —they should have been sent out like a baseball uniform after a St. Louis doubleheader—and had changed to a dry undershirt and what Pittsburgh called "dungarees." Brendan warned me against wearing them on campus. Wrong image. Not casual. Too hoody. He was a Chicago guy; he pronounced "hood" to sound like "who'd." I was sitting up on my bunk, where the room's heat collected. I held my hands out, palms up, and shrugged. No more questions. Finally I asked, "Fraternities, maybe?"

"Okay. The big question, Richie. The old numero uno. Biggest decision you can make, and that includes your major or the girls you date. It even decides who you can date. What have you heard?"

I trusted the brochure. "Anyone desiring affiliation will not be denied it."

He cracked a grin. "Were you on any teams?"

"Wrestling and track."

"Oh, God, Richie. You make it *hard*, you know? Outdoor track takes you right out of spring drinking. And who the hell watches wrestling? If you're a hardnose, lacrosse is the sport. Very classy, very Ivy, snows the girls and gets you a letter faster than any other sport. Now, your heavy jock types—football, basketball—they go to the Zoo, the Betas. Fancier sports—soccer, lacrosse—they pledge Sigma Chi. Gentlemen drinkers, big-money types, big spenders—Phi Gam. Raunchiest parties, with a pipeline to Covington—Phi Delts and SAEs. Campus politics and slight weirdos—DUs. That's it."

I was counting: six. "Isn't there another one?" The brochure had said seven. He started counting off on his fingers. Embarrassment and consternation darkened his face, like a father counting his children and coming up short. Even I could appreciate the gravity of the situation. Then he laughed out loud, slapping his forehead. "I knew them when I was twelve years old. No wonder I forgot. Yeah, there's seven all right. I forgot LSC, the all-time fag house. Let's Suck Cock."

"Pardon?"

"LSC—Lovett Social Club. Let's Suck Cock, for short. I mean . . ." And now his hands were outstretched, palms up, and even he was lost for words. "Losers," he managed. "To give you an idea, there's only two sororities that allow their girls to date in the Social Club. And they're called the Kennels."

So that's what they'd meant by "earnest desire."

Brendan saw himself as Phi Gam material, with luck. They had the best contacts on the outside, the best parties on the inside, the best files, and good faculty contacts in Business and Advertising. They held their best jocks back from varsity sports, and used them in the intramurals. Less "L-Men" than the Betas, but first place in the IMs, which was smart. If you had a girl and a blanket and a flask and wanted to take in an IM football game, you wanted to make sure your team was going to win, right?

I could see the handwriting. I wondered if LSC even entered a team.

"What if . . . you know, you don't pledge?" I asked.

"Don't make Fiji, you mean? It's possible. I have a back-up. SAE probably."

"I don't mean that. I mean what if you don't go through Rush at all?"

Every now and then you can ask a question that's never been asked before, and the effect can be unraveling. Brendan frowned, shook his head, and tried to chuckle at my joke. "What do you mean?"

"I'm serious. Just not go through with it. Or maybe wait for a year."

"Be a sophomore pledge?"

He was slicing a few stitches from the belt in the back of his new khakis as he tried to answer. "You mean wait a year? Like waiting after the honeymoon to get laid? Your sophomore year, man—" And he stared out the window, hunched in his disappointment with me, as though I'd failed to grasp a thing. "Your sophomore year, that's your greatest year. That's when all the shit's behind you. You get to run Hell Week, and the freshmen call you 'sir.' All the shit-sessions, all the housework—you put up with it this year so you can pay them back next year. Why would I wait? Why would any sophomore go through freshman shit?"

I could appreciate the arrogance of my question. What I meant was, why do any of us go through this? I hadn't heard of housework and shit-sessions, whatever they were. It sounded like Pittsburgh all over again. Why does a place that charges so much and boasts of its morals stand for things like that? Just looking at the two of us, at Brendan's blond good looks, his vodka bottles and rumpled clothes, and at my knobby little body, like someone who'd been lifting weights in a closet without mirrors, you knew he'd get whatever he wanted and I'd end up with that unmentionable thing at the bottom, the Social Club.

When we started going through Rush a few nights later, no one else on my floor even kept his Club appointment. Common courtesy might be misinterpreted. The Club president was blind, and the only brothers I talked to were sanctimonious divinity students. And that wasn't the worst part. The worst part was that Brendan as usual had been right.

It was apparent from the way the Rush chairman held his cigarette—down near the filter and stiffly perpendicular —and from the way he unfurled from the couch with his knees together, keeping his spare hand over his lap, that he was not just gay, but actively promoting it. And there were others, I could tell from their voices and glittering eyes. One either survived in the Club as a virtuous wimp or a wicked witch. But they also had half a dozen Phi Beta Kappas, a Filipino, and the whispered presence of Lovett's only black. And they took no votes on membership. "If you're good enough for Lovett, you're good enough for us," the president explained. No other fraternity on campus was permitted by national charter to take in Jews, blacks, and Orientals, and some even balked at Catholics. In practice, T. Lysander Crommelin's personal taste eliminated the more obvious minorities. The Club scooped up the lame, the disabled, the unpopular, and unpalatable.

It was dishonest of the dean of men not to admit the price one paid for the earnest desire to affiliate.

Even Brendan failed at Phi Gam, and was taken at his second choice, SAE. I failed at DU and went immediately to the Club, where I became the second pledge of the evening. The first was an albino Baptist from a one-room school in Tennessee. Striking as he was, no one in the dorms had seen him before or knew his name.

An hour later, my secret horror came to pass. There was one boy in the freshman dining hall where I worked whose obnoxiousness had already earned him a crown of watermelon, a slab of ice cream in the face, salt in his tea, and sugar on his chops. His name was Malcolm Roudebush, a hefty, red-cheeked lad with long wavy hair that stood like dingy meringue. He affected the speech, the clothes, even the waddle of a border-state barrister running for county office. At night he held up the dinner lines by demanding of the servers, "How do I know this silverware is clean? What disinfectant do you use? How many rinses?" And at breakfast he held up the line again, requesting of the dim-witted girl who dished up the grits and sausage, "Give me that last melancholy strip of bacon, my good woman."

At the second morning's breakfast he'd asked me, his waiter, for a side dish of stewed prunes, complaining loudly, "My bowels haven't moved since I arrived in this outpost!" He seemed to be on such intimate terms with his bowels that I imagined some impeccably dressed smaller self, in the same tweed jacket with the row of variegated pipe bowls peering over the breast-pocket rim, picking up and moving, just to please him.

Well, Malcolm Roudebush became our third pledge of that disastrous evening.

And yet, Rosie; he had a reckless courage. In the midst of his difficulties—wiping the ice cream from his face and glasses, muttering "Unpalatable!" to the sugary meat and salty tea—he kept his dignity, and I felt a terrible pity. I was probably closer to Malcolm in the general esteem of the Lovett freshman class than I was to anyone else. Fittingly, Malcolm was now my brother, our third pledge on that calamitous night. Every other fraternity bagged its legal limit of twenty-seven pledges. By evening's end we had come up with five; one infamous, and four toadstools. After Malcolm's pledging we waited an hour, and our albino Baptist returned to his room for prayer. I never saw him again, though we carried his name for the remainder of the year. The two of us waited another hour. Then Jon and Don, who'd discovered each another on the same floor of the same dorm, and persuaded their respective roommates to switch places, rounded out the pledging for the night, and the year.

No one seemed to mind our skimpy numbers. What we lacked in bodies, said the blind president, we made up for in character. We had character the way certain girls have personality. I suffered through a long night in our room with the vodka bottles, thinking of packing my bag and returning to Pittsburgh. Several unpledged freshmen did just that, rather than face the temptation of Social Club membership. Around four o'clock that morning, Brendan and some of the other pledge classes came staggering back from their celebrations. The SAEs had all been given the Week-Ender Specials. The brothers were the greatest guys in the world. "Where'd the DUs take you?" he asked, then saw the anemic black-and-white ribbons of the Social Club. "Oh, God," he mumbled, "after all I told you."

He didn't talk to me for a week. I'd brought shame to the room.

I look back on my first two years in shame. How awful I was, how awful all of us were! Baptist morality made carnal beings of us all. Out in front of Pusey, Ramsey, and Blodgett halls loomed the statues of Gideon Ramsey and Hosea Blodgett, marble sentries whose parted lips seemed to twitch with admonition to Keep It Clean, and whose stony eyes glared the impure back into the fold. The Body Is the Temple of the Lord! those statues howled into the fertile Kentucky night, beards dancing on their opened Bibles. The body, the body, whimpered the broken response.

And in our freshman year at five minutes to one o'clock
on the verandas of those dorms, we grappled like savages
for flesh, for heat, for combustion itself. Or maybe for
none of those things: maybe it was all for making an im-
pression on classmates and upperclassmen— "Old Durgin
really had her going there, didn't he?" Or for the right to
join in the aching chorus of freshman boys winding their
way back up "Blue Ball Hill," moaning in feigned agony,
"Oh, my balls, my balls!" That's what the rules were for.
The girl could be forgotten till the next encounter.

And back in those rhythmically rocking bunk beds in
the middle of a Friday night, you traveled with the foam-
flecked shade of Gideon Ramsey down the curfewed cor-
ridors of Ramsey Hall, smacking goatish lips over the
moist and fragrant forms of three hundred recumbent
Maidens arrayed for their nightly bed checks.

Everyone but the true libertines (who were invisible to
me for my first two years) had a stake in keeping sex
dirty and unattainable. We carried that need with us from
whatever high school we'd attended, that urge to exult in
sex, to make up stories, to fantasize. Even those pure little
darlings who'd been kissing their fathers and patting their
horses good-bye had staged a "Talent Show" a few hours
later at the Freshman Mixer. The girls of Ramsey Hall had
won the talent prize. Had they already known the snicker-
ing connotation of "Ramsey," or had their advisers taught
it to them during that first night's supper? While we were
up in Sawyer dining hall drawing numbers and wondering
who'd get a head start with the finest faces in the Baby
Book (Debbie Warner had reduced us to putty; a hundred
dollars was raised at dinner for anyone who drew her
number and turned her over to the winner of the Debbie
Pool), the freshman girls were already auditioning, already
simpering in close harmony:

We are Ramseys,
Ask for us by name;
We don't want your pansies—
That isn't why we came.

Our shape is nice,
Our fit is tight,
You won't think twice—
About tonight.

We're not pre-tested
No sirree!
But when molested—
We go, "Wheee!"

Are we to be blamed for thinking they'd also learned back-seat imperatives in the mountain hamlets of southern Kentucky, before the collective restoration of their maidenhood? Pusey girls, just possibly, had been assigned their residence on the basis of a disbelieving gynecological examination, and Blodgett girls—the very name suggestive of a lugubrious cruelty—promised an embrace of pain and pleasure so intense that sturdy young Baptists from the pastures of Kentucky were brought to their knees even in picturing it.

"It" —that inevitable collision of passion and impediment —had nothing to do with reality. The girls were pure; they were the border-state aristocracy, keen on stud and lineage. Keener still on knowing their worth and not devaluing it, on recognizing scrub and banishing it.

That didn't stop us. It drove us. Most of us were trash and knew it. Evenings in my freshman year, I would listen as the would-be ravishers gathered in our room (Brendan being a prominent nodule in the sexual relay of the freshman class), elaborating histories and pooling reports on the pre-Lovett sexual careers of Pusey Hall's little buttercups. You'd think we had nothing else to do, and you'd be right. All the interesting girls, the ones I later came to know and even to love, were omitted from our freshman fantasies. We ignited only on centerfold looks.

That herd of awkward, itching adolescents, of which I was one, could drive themselves mad on rumors, jacking off as stories everyone knew, or thought they knew, got told over and over. "Her? Yeah, went to my high school. Faster'n shit back then. Whole football team used to climb on. Gotta have a T-Bird, though. Her old man's loaded."

It was safe to speculate that the old man of any Lovett student was loaded. With obvious exceptions.

Those slippery little darlings, then, just days removed from Daddy's clutches, bloomed as demons of sex, vile and corrupt, in the tales of their unauthorized biographers.

And so ended my freshman year, Rosie, at the college of multiple contingencies.

Chapter Nine

The first half of my college career was concerned with a major (Economics), clothes, fraternity, and comic attempts at establishing a social life with girls whose legs and shoulders were in approximate balance. On a low level, I did the things most fraternity boys were supposed to do. I pulled a float at Homecoming, hired bands, turned up for the various intramural competitions that we chose not to forfeit, and even served as a Rush chairman to help restore the membership to the strength, if that's the word, of earlier times. As a scholarship student, I was supposed to do very well, and in my freshman year, feeling myself the academic flagship of our tiny fleet, I had done adequately.

But the sophomore slump did me in. It was as though I'd absorbed a ferocious pounding to the body during my entire freshman year without its showing in my face and footwork. I worked at the hotel again during the summer and made fifteen hundred dollars, enough for the Merc and a year's spending money. My father still survived, though his morning cough brought up blood, and a roll of flabby skin sagged across his upper chest, over his ribs and nipples. "Death-tits," he called them. His stomach was hollowed out. His hips were gone.

"Tell you what, Richie. You better finish that fancy school real quick, see. I'm aimin' to take it easy soon's you get a fancy job." His notion of what Lovett could do, based on its tuition costs, translated to a Senate seat or Cabinet position.

So I had driven to Kentucky in my Merc for the sophomore year, to take my place in the fraternity house, wearing my pearl-clustered pin and hoping that a good batch of pledges might lift the sorority ban on our dating. This time I had a trunk, two suitcases, and the proper jackets. I was a Homestead dandy, the kind of Social Clubber that some sororities might even make an exception for. It should have been (as it was going to be for Brendan McIvor), a perfect year.

I began it beaten. I had a seven-thirty Statistics class, and after the first week I couldn't get up for it. Between classes I dashed back for half an hour in the Union, and held a table through the class break, then through the quiet class hours when only the serious bridge players or senior seminars offered their indifferent company. I was the sophomore who liked to watch them, the kid without a girl, friends, or even a book to dignify his idleness.

I was fascinated by everything about those girls—their cashmere sweaters, their tartan skirts with the oversized pin, the rows of Salems inclined at identical angles. And on the worn pinnacles of those sweaters, the double clusters of sorority diamond and fraternity pearl, the trophies they'd worked so hard for. The moment a girl got pinned, we assumed she'd given her body. We whimpered inwardly, then busily redefined her as a little wobbly and wifely. Another cow cut from the freshman herd, leaving the bachelor bulls to bellow in the dark. When students gathered at the next class break, some would come over and ask, "Where were you, man? Henderson popped a quiz."

I don't know where I was. I'd never had a period like it, though I've had many since. I had lead in my shoes and aches in my back, and my assets were pouring through my fingers like a drunken sailor's. Around Halloween I asked my friendliest professor, "Is it too late to turn things around this semester?" He made some phone calls and told me it was.

I went on probation. I petitioned to hold on to my scholarship, borrowing credit from my father's cancer. In the second semester I achieved the minimum performance that would lift the probation. And so I finished half of my college career with a straight "C" average: no distinctions, no liaisons, no friendships, no convictions, no prospects, and, worse—no ambitions and no security. By that summer my mother was a widow, stranger than ever, and now she depended on me.

My father had slipped below a hundred pounds, rebounded twice, and died weighing a pasty hundred and five. He was forty-seven. I wrote the obituary notice for the *Press* and *Post-Gazette*, and discovered in the process I knew nothing about him. I'd never known his parents, and my mother didn't remember their names. I had to leave that line out: "Son of the late ⸺ and ⸺ Durgin." He had a married sister somewhere in the Southwest, and a brother who'd shown up once when I was a child, but had been afraid to step inside our house. My mother thought his sister's name was Elsie, but she couldn't be sure.

I didn't think other Lovett students had things like this to cope with. The old self-pity. Why, oh why—me? I felt deprived by my father's life even more than by his death. When I finally put down everything I knew about him, it came to this:

> Died, Joseph P. Durgin, carpenter of this city, born in Pittsburgh, June 18, 1911. Loving husband of Mary (Sigsby) Durgin, father of Richard Durgin, student at Lovett College, loving brother of Elsie of Phoenix [I guessed] and Phil [I invented] of Atlanta [I utterly fantasized]. Cremated. No flowers. Contributions to the strike fund of the Brotherhood of Carpenters and Roofers.

I don't remember making a formal vow, but when I left the cubicle at the newspaper office, ashamed of the dribble I'd turned in, I must have decided that to die in such a way, to leave so little behind was somehow unforfeitable. I would hold him accountable. His life was a waste, unless it had been to spawn me.

I sat on the trolley burning with the same recognition I'd felt that day in biology class and hadn't felt since—that had to be it! No matter what the indifference of my record to date, I was destined for redemptive things. From his ashes, I would fly. I remember that trolley ride back to Homestead as another turning point in my life.

Until that day, I'd been like a man searching vainly for his car in some enormous airport parking lot—just scuffing along, trying not to look foolish, and not having the slightest idea of where he's left it. Forgetting even what it looked like. Then suddenly I'd spotted it, and every part of my body aligned itself with that goal, very subtly, of course. You don't want to look foolish and slap your forehead; you don't want to repudiate twenty years of sleep-walking. But suddenly I knew where I was heading, and I knew the shortest way of getting there.

I knew I wanted to be famous. I wanted to ram my father's life down everyone's throat. And that was the slight mid-course correction that lined me up with Rachel Isaacs, all the way in Padua. She was making her own correction at exactly the same time. All we had to do now was to keep walking straight.

My mother gathered her various insurance and death benefits and rented a small house on Mount Washington, overlooking the Point. She had a taste for inspiring views, but she now confessed that our old house had terrified her for twenty years. "He made me move in there. He kept me there. I wasn't like this when we moved. He made me be like this—" And she broke down, sobbing and cursing my father's name. She lost about sixty pounds the first few years she lived alone. By the time Rachel saw her, she wasn't nearly the eyesore she always had been. I think Rachel felt I'd been exaggerating all along.

Then came my junior year. The first of eight golden years in my life. Two years at Lovett, two at Iowa, and four of marriage in New York. Everything I've achieved in my life happened then. I haven't done too well with my life ever since.

There were two reasons for the dating ban on our fraternity. The official reason was that our racial policies ("our non-racial policies," we strenuously denied) had brought Negroes into our fraternity in the past and could well do it again. This could place a Lovett Maiden in some jeopardy. But we knew it was more hypocritical than that. We knew we were being discriminated against because we were wimps and creeps. It was feared that our general loathsomeness would contaminate anyone who associated with us. In Lovett ideology, the purpose of fraternities was to foster individuality. It ran against official pieties to hold any group collectively responsible for the actions, good or bad, of its individual members.

We were free to date unaffiliated women, or in the Kennels. In my years at Lovett there were about twenty independent women, most of them attached to the Art or Theater departments, who lived in Garnett Place, a converted frame house half a mile out of town. Garnett was a co-op dorm, run as a self-governing unit.

Garnett was the home of Janet Bunn. And it is of interest to you, Rosie, because Janet, unlike poor Wanda Lusiak, was in the ancestral line of Rachel Isaacs. We were Neanderthals to Rachel's Cro-Magnon; saber-tooths to her Bengal tiger.

In September of my junior year, I still had to finish my English requirements. I was barely surviving in Economics. I needed something that would keep me above disaster. The class I chose was creative writing.

(Wouldn't it be nice to say, "The rest is history"?)

The center of Bohemian activity was all downhill in the Theater and Art buildings, and of course down the road at Garnett Place. The sixties were still a year away, but the Garnett girls had anticipated the future while recreating a functioning Beat America: folk songs, undergound movies, poetry readings, candlemaking, and macrame. Avocado plants grew on every window ledge.

(I can date the birth of my self-consciousness from the growing of my first avocado, and the transferring of my old baseball loyalties to something nobler by faithfully carrying that tree from Lovett to Iowa and even to New

York. I date my liberation from the time, years later, when I actually cut up an avocado and ate it, and threw away the pit.)

You might think that those of us in the Social Club would also have known about such things, and would have copied them in our own wimpish way. You'd be wrong. You'd have to understand how America, or fraternities, work. We were "the American alternative." Stupid politics breed stupid opposition. We saw ourselves as virtuous competitors, not weirdo dropouts.

The women of Garnett and the men who hung out there were a talent elite, the Sigma Chis of taste and special breeding.

When I think of Rachel's life at about this same time— her senior year abroad, living in Florence with Marco—her poetry, her languages, her sexual sophistication, the whole thing can make me sick, or wondrous. We were about three years from our bloody little collision. In separate little universes, we had made slight course corrections. We had turned to face each other, though the curve of the earth still intervened.

In the English Department there were a couple of senior poets and short-story writers whose work appeared in the campus magazine. They were considered geniuses; they'd gotten Fulbrights for graduate study in Europe. (They have prospered; their critical work is known. Have you ever noticed that the precocious poets turn out to be critics, and the best young critics end up being writers?) They spent their weekends in Vanderbilt, where some literary giants were teaching. They went up to Ohio just to see the offices of *The Kenyon Review*. They saw John Crowe Ransom playing bridge. They traveled all over the South and Midwest, attending poetry readings and lectures. They managed an air of importance and urgency. They knew they had done something with their twenty-one years on this planet that resembled a work of art, just like the actors and painters.

I knew I couldn't do anything clever with my fingers or my body, but I longed to do something important with my life.

Two weeks into my junior year, I told the fraternity I'd be moving out and taking a room in the village. The waste of two years hadn't just come from my father's cancer or in bucking the Byzantine social system. The only real problem lay in Economics. I didn't have the right imagination. I was finally learning disloyalty. Cutting the losses, getting out.

In my new rooming house were several acting students. They hung out with the painters and the writers. Many now are famous, or were, five years ago. They spent their waking hours in the theater, then came back to candles and illegal wine, to chop vegetables and fry them in spices on their hot plates. My rooming house smelled like a Chinese restaurant. The Garnett girls who visited them wore black leotards, and pulled their long dark hair back in buns, or let it hang loose. They were pretty, even beautiful, but so far outside the orbit of permissible blond attractiveness that I'd never noticed them before. They rode bicycles and carried their books in green sacks like the actors and poets. And when I looked up their pictures in old copies of our Baby Book, there was no similarity to their high school portraits. Something had happened to those dimpled, perky little faces. They'd mutated. Now they used eye shadow and wore small gold earrings.

And I was changing with them. Just a year before I had stared at those unapproachable sorority girls, ashamed of myself for not having at least an approximation of one for myself. I wasn't even allowed to approach one, except for a classroom assignment. Even then, the more upright ones would turn away and suggest to the space they'd vacated that I should ask someone from a different sorority, and we both knew the ones she meant. (You wonder how all this could happen on an American college campus in the very recent past, and all I can say is: the same way the twentieth century happened. Where was I? Where were you?)

So I lusted for them, tuned in to their conversations (so regally indifferent to anything but cute boys and cute clothes), stared at their snowy cashmere bosoms, suppressing an urge to bite down hard on those weighty clusters of diamond and pearl. It could drive me crazy, knowing that some Brendan type was getting under that sweater every night; it could keep me rooted at a table, out of any classroom. We'd all started out the same, anonymous together, and already, class had told. Brendan had his, and I had none.

Now, as a junior with a car, living off-campus, stashing wine and six-packs against village and campus ordinance, I was an upper-class shark myself. I could cruise the dorms if I disguised my affiliation. You couldn't immediately tell that I belonged to that same blighted society as Malcolm Roudebush and the notorious Jon and Don. I had put that world behind me. Never again, to be awakened by Jon's morning call from the bathroom, "Ah, the glorious crack of Don!"

And suddenly I realized I didn't have to disguise anything. I was what I was, and no one who mattered cared.

Where had I been? Where had they been? The Garnett girls were beautiful! And that's where the writing course (sorry for the long excursion) and Janet Bunn and Garnett Place entered my life. I was coming out of my father's inheritance (I thought), that search for a sour security, and going toward those surging little corkscrews waiting to be born.

Chapter Ten

All candidates for literary sainthood should have one last chance to redeem themselves.

Of that period in a woman's life between adolescence and menopause, what can I say? Writers have the talent to involve others in the drama of their lives, and Rachel has involved millions. For a period of five and a half years, she played to me exclusively. I consumed the drama. Front-row center. Rehearsals and opening nights.

The origin of the drama lies in a simple proposition. Culturally, this is a European century. Intellectually, it is a Jewish century. The collusion of ancestries imposes a special burden. She was not parochial, but there are ultimate curvatures of the earth and skull about which even a genius is blind.

She admired the great exiled minds, the Morningside Heights intellectuals who'd pulled back from the edge. They gave her the tools to go on, and she did. She went to the bottom, gave it a voice, and she died. It's easy to blame something down there for killing her. It's no lie to say she was Hitler's last victim, and I'll never dispute the fact that she identified with all the victims. But it's not the whole truth.

The point is, she was an American. Maybe it's hard to accept, but it was America that killed her. Not Vietnam, not the assassinations, not all the turmoil of the late sixties. It was something so small that I can't even mention it without sounding trivial. You want to know, but what could you do with it? It's tabloid stuff, Rosie.

For a long time, America was what she used to keep Europe safe and distant. I was America for her. Can you imagine what treasures my mother showed her on her only visit to Pittsburgh? Her albums of Green Stamps! The catalog of things she was saving for! All the little doodads around the house that she'd munched for, all those years! (You know Rachel's poem "How Many Books?" No critic ever thought crudely enough to understand the kind of books she was talking about. My mother inspired that poem.)

Rachel, whose unvarying breakfast was grapefruit and tea, at first was charmed by my daily bowl of cereal. "Protestant flakes," she called them. She was "charmed" by the "H" and "C" faucets in our apartment bathroom. She burned herself on "H" the first time—her parents had European fixtures, where "C" meant hot and "F" meant cold. She once wrote her father (you've probably seen the letter), "I fear I have fallen among people who say 'Christ Jesus' instead of 'Jesus Christ.'" She, who was vegetarian, used to stare at my nightly slab of beef, with its dab of melting parsley butter. Pure steak pit, Pittsburgh elegance. She was less charmed as the years wore on, but I don't think my dietary habits had much to do with it.

It seems to me there are some areas where fiction and poetry simply can't venture. The brutality is too vast, and irony is too indelicate a tool. A major artist with the compulsive theme of the Holocaust must eventually find a new language and a new form, and I don't know if an American writing in English can hope to do it.

I have critical prejudices (yielding to them, I've given up writing). Great fiction, I believe, is healthy and aggressive—it extends reality. A novel should be a living cell of the entire social and individual organism. If we perish and future generations uncover only one artifact, and it is a good novel, they should be able to clone our century from it. Not a profound thought, but one that pretty well accepts things as they appear, even confirms them. By those standards, I would except Rachel from greatness; the work is too defensive. Her ancestor, understandably, is Kafka.

And about the time I used up all my areas of common experience, Rachel started going public with her uncommon ones. I learned quickly enough what she'd meant in calling me a "synthetic writer." I converted what little I knew to fiction, and when there wasn't any more cheap raw material left inside, I closed down the furnaces. Those oceans of little corkscrews? They just weren't words.

Her basic proposition is probably true. Up to now, this has been a European century. But now I'm looking out on Tamerlane's broken wall, and I wonder if the rest of this century won't belong to the children who escape that wall, and the poverty and the ignorance, and who learn about America—and Tamerlane, too—and watch the jackals feed on village trash and watch the peacocks strut and the pigs get slaughtered. They will extend the common experience, push back the horizons the way Rachel did.

She would approve of my diet now. And she and I would be reduced to the same level of ignorance. This place where I've decided to make my stand is the great equalizer at last.

Okay, Rosie, I'll be brief. This is what I know of Rachel, before I met her. This is all she told me.

If I said to you that Rachel was a child of the movie industry, you'd probably agree—born in Santa Monica of a screenwriter father and the voice of Mighty Mouse, what the hell else could she be? (Until the family left for Italy in 1950, she'd never even been east of Pasadena.) But Hollywood had nothing to do with it.

She was a child of the European industry. She was the daughter of her father's marriage to German expressionism, and his mid-life fling with Italian neo-realism. She was the little convent girl who watched De Sica film *Umberto D* and she became the woman who knew Italian cinema of the thirties and forties as thoroughly as any child of fascism. She went to movies those three years in Italy. She would go with her father to those giant hangars at Cinecittà and sit through screenings, translating for him when necessary. Rossellini was "ravished" by little "Rachele" and promised to write a *Miracle on 34th Street*, especially for her. A little American girl in Italy: he rattled off names—Judy Garland, Margaret O'Brien, Shirley Temple—names she'd never heard of.

Out in Hollywood in the late forties, he'd been an informal promoter of the new Italian cinema. In 1948, he'd been sniffed by the anti-communist vigilante group he called the Arrow Cross Gang. They accused some of his unproduced Westerns of espousing miscegenation, of his gangster scripts sacrificing action for bits of social commentary. The new Italian movies he screened for friends and sympathetic directors condemned the social order, mocked piety, and didn't flinch over child and wife abuse.

Italy seemed just the place for him. But what he hadn't understood from his isolation in California in 1950 was that the Italian films he loved were already three and four years old. Even more repressive things were happening in Italy than in America. Italy was sincerely committed to cultural suicide. The Christian Democrats dismantled neorealism, piece by piece. Films, like Fiats and Olivettis and Sicilian blood oranges, were seen as sensitive exports; nothing that might taint the image of a wholesome, prosperous, Catholic Italy was allowed to get out. Laws were passed against the use of amateur actors and against location shooting. Disgusted by McCarthy, sick of Hollywood, BZ knew nothing of this. A cynic like Ben-Zvi, mustering his last frail breath of naive optimism, is a man worthy of some pity. Even from me, who hated him.

Ever since arriving in California, even as he churned out the garbage that shamed him, he'd been planning a masterpiece. His *Citizen Kane*. His autobiography in film. He was a child of the European century, and he wanted to take his revenge on all of it. He'd been a student in Berlin during the 1919 riots (even I, child of Pittsburgh apprentice builders, had learned of the Freikorps and the Spartacists, Liebknecht and Luxembourg, fifty years later in New York City, from his daughter); he'd been a financial lawyer in the twenties during the inflation, when anyone with money invested in film. (There's a comic image in Mann's *Disorder and Early Sorrow*, which you may remember. The family servant—a surly upstart with his ambitions pinned to stardom—climbs a tree in the front yard, hoping that a film director might see him. We might think it absurd, but that's how it was in Berlin in the twenties;

"the times" created such absurdities.) Ben-Zvi, friend of Mann and of the filmmakers, was created by such absurdities. His daughter was too, and she was finally destroyed by them. BZ invested in film. His friends respected his "bourgeois values," his practical criticism of their projects. The writers and actors used to sit in his apartment, reading their scripts aloud for his opinions.

I must have snickered, back then, early in our marriage. What could anyone mean, even Rachel, by "scripting" silent films? I hadn't understood the paradox. "Does film talk?" Rachel had answered. "Of course it's silent. If it weren't silent, it would be drama. Silence creates character. Dialogue can only give character a little more personality."

(I think of the best of her poems as exquisite silent movies. Even the Pompeii poem you mention sounds silent to me; "Neighbors," which is my favorite, should be acted out in black and white—and silence.)

Anyway, BZ had seen it all, known all the young faces, and with Hitler's rise collapsed his life and fled to Paris, then Hollywood, where the crafty old faces welcomed him. And except for the self-respect he managed to preserve, and the masterpiece he still intended to film, his creative life had ended.

His autobiography could have been glorious. He would use actual footage of German films, German riots, the War, undercut with California gothic. It was ambitious. It was unworkable, even in Italy, in 1950. But a few years later, I used to feed on those European film autobiographies—Fellini, Antonioni, Truffaut—they seemed so literary, so daring.

So he'd come to the right place too early, or maybe too late; with the wrong idea, or perhaps too strange an idea. He spent three years in Rome, paying for Hilda's opera tickets and Rachel's convent school by making his savings stretch on the Italian black market. When he returned to Hollywood, television was killing the industry, and people thought he'd died or emigrated to Israel.

I know this may sound grotesque, Rosie, lowering Rachel to my level, or attempting to raise myself to hers, but vindication for our fathers motivated both of us in our writing. The Italian Christians may have destroyed BZ's film career, but they gave Rachel her poetry, and the fire and the urgency to see it through.

Up in the convent school above Florence, down in Rome for the weekends, she found her home. At the age of ten, in Italian and in French, she found her calling. At the same time in Pittsburgh, I was trying to lose tennis balls over the link fence at the end of my street. I was living my first novel. She was already writing her first poetry.

Here's something you might be able to use.

The neo-realists shot their films in silence, and dubbed them later in the studio. One day, Rachel watched a day's shooting down along the Arno. It wasn't the illusion of "peasants" sneaking up and killing a slack German guard that excited her—it was the fact that it all happened in silence, or in unedited background noise. It was silent films, all over again.

She grasped the metaphor immediately. She imagined the world in perfect silence, with the babble of her classroom pared away. She went back to her school and sat out in the sloping backyard where the cliff sheared away. There she wrote of the Arno valley a thousand meters below her, the trains curling in the distance, the Cinzano umbrellas at the station just two switchbacks below her, and she added her memories of deer nibbling grass by the tracks (she too had deer, Rosie, city girl that she was) and the times she'd uncovered possible Etruscan relics on her school outings. All without words. The poem lay in the coordination of image and feeling; the language could always be added later, back in the studio.

(She wrote most fluently in Italian, but French, she knew, was the language of serious poetry. She never tried English. English had become her Yiddish, her *mamaloshen*, a shameful dialect she shared with her parents, hardly fit for poetry.)

She remembered the agony of being consumed by poems without language, merely the urge to print the scene before her. It was a painterly, a musical, a photographic urge. She forced herself to internalize the vision, preserve the mood, for some eventual Later. Then she would add the words.

"I have the poem," she'd often say to me. "All I have to do is write it."

Where is that train going? And who is in it?

The idea that words had meaning apart from things presented itself as a kind of liberation. ("When words mean things, then I write fiction," she said. "When words are feelings, I write poetry.")

Does it make sense? I confess, at the time, I used to hate things like that. Poetic smugness. Prosy proles. That's the kind of girl she was, at eleven. The Pompeii poem you describe doesn't surprise me at all, not any more.

In the five years that Rachel and I were married, I had no concept of second countries, of countermyths, of otherednesses. There was Pittsburgh (which you were born with) and Lovett (which changed you). And you resolved the tension by carrying your transformed Pittsburgh self to New York City, where, legend had it, you prospered. In a pinch, like the sainted Beats, you went West, or to Mexico. If you went to Paris (a terrifying concept to me), you did it like Hemingway and Fitzgerald, always as an American, shopping for low-rent settings. Whatever you did, you didn't let those other places get to you. Most of all, you didn't let them *fuck with your mind*.

Rachel was happy in Italy, and Italy did a job on her. She loved those neutral, passive months of learning a language, a recess in the act of living. She learned six languages in three years: Latin, Greek, French, Italian, Spanish, and German. She was on good terms with the past and the present, and with every point on the compass until east and south threw themselves on the intractable barbed wire of Russian and Arabic. She's the only person I've ever met who could get enraged over languages she couldn't read. Simply for being there. For being, as she would say, too utterly Hungarian about it. If she had stayed in Europe, she would have sailed through every language, become a lawyer or a diplomat. Instead, she was forced to stop with words; she achieved linguistic lift-off, but never escape velocity.

Maybe I'm projecting all this from the perspective of twenty years, and from my own life, deep in the heart of a supreme otherness, but I know that her Italy and my India are much alike. The only difference is, I was thirty-six when I settled here and started dropping the shells of successive selves. She was only ten. Until I came to India, I had never been east of New York, west of Des Moines, south of Lovettville, or north of Niagara. Whenever Rachel would tell me of her childhood, I'd try to respond—it was fascinating stuff, even to me—but it was all unreal. It

wasn't till I crash-landed here in the deserts of India that I
started understanding her.

This is where it's taken me, so far.

She'd never been allowed to think of herself as an
American, or a Californian, or a child of the movie industry. Ben-Zvi had contempt for all three. Like any cultured
survivor of the old Hollywood, he'd succeeded by stran-
gling his intelligence. He wrote every script as an autobiography (so he could face himself in the mornings), then,
when he loved the script sufficiently, he'd light his Sam
Goldwyn cigar, put his feet on the desk, and start cutting
and slashing, ridiculing his own creation, twisting everything he'd written until all that was left after the chips and
shavings and amputated bleeding chunks was a studio-
certified Hollywood hero. "Behold, Moloch," he says, in
another poem of Rachel's. They were his monsters. His
irony was taken as Old World craftsmanship; only Rachel
knew his rage.

When he came back broken from Italy, he had to beg.
He didn't have the big script, and he'd lost his authority,
even in the family. Rachel was fourteen and lost, back in
California, after the six languages and the discipline of a
convent school. She didn't feel herself at all American by
that time. For her first year back in Santa Monica, her father kept her in a lycée run for diplomatic kids. She
thought of herself in exile; nothing she did seemed real, or
with consequence (thanks to your research, I now know
what she meant). With her father's eclipse, she started
seeing movies ("It's Dotty's daddy!") and started hanging
out on the sets, getting summer jobs down at the lots,
warming up to some of the technicians, bringing some of
them home. I can imagine more scenes out of *Disorder and*

Early Sorrow —Rachel, the perfectly cultivated teenage girl, the girl her father had tried to protect, throwing it all away on some surly Jimmy Dean type. And one of them must have gotten her pregnant. I can imagine all of that, though she never breathed a word of it to me.

So that's the way I make sense of her first seventeen years. For the first ten years: shame. For the next three years: golden achievement. For the last four: apathy. She went along with the shame—her father was authoritarian, and she was raised as a dutiful, accidental, European daughter of a dying tradition. America was a further accident—something Europe did as a hobby. But when they moved to Italy, the rules changed. She was allowed to think of Italy as something to be proud of. For her it was ideal. The languages gave her a mission. She tasted success and praise, and relief from guilt and embarrassment. She experienced a movie industry she was allowed to respect. Facility with Italian even placed her at an advantage with her father.

When she finally returned to Italy in her sophomore year of college ("home," as she thought of it), she felt all problems would be over. Nominally, she lived in a foreign students' dormitory; in reality she shared studio space with Marco. It should have been perfect. What attracted her to Italy was not pasta and exuberance; Rachel's Italy was classical and severely intellectual. She admired the irony, the angularity, the wit and bite of Italy, and Marco was its embodiment.

She spent her junior year writing poetry (in English now) and taking whatever lectures amused her, living the existentialist life of the streets and cafés, not sleeping, not eating, criss-crossing the continent with a backpack and

cheese and wine and a lover. She and Marco would scour
the villages around Padua for the incongruities of a passing
piety—the religious relics discarded by old churches, sold
off by the Communist children of black-shrouded widows.
Marco was a collector of pop debris; it all came back to his
studio to be rearranged, repatterned, with a few movie cal-
endars and political posters, against a backdrop of peasant
brass beds, mangled Christ heads, lurid Sacred Hearts, ro-
saries, coffee cans, opera tickets, and sentimental souvenirs
of the Ethiopian campaigns. Marco thought of it as terribly avant-garde, politically daring, and so did Rachel, for a
while. Then she saw it more as spiteful and impudent, the
work of a clever child, a mischief maker. His work didn't
go that extra step; it didn't fall over the edge. It wasn't
quite undescended-testicle stuff, and it was too clever for
boxcar with masturbating hobo—but it was something
worse, given Marco's Brechtian ambitions. It became in-
group chic, decorous Milanese irony.

Something happened to Rachel in her senior year, something Durginlike, a rebellion of the flesh and sky. She was
still in Padua, still with Marco, still happy in Italy and
thinking herself Italian. Yet before the year was out, even
before her official graduation, she would be back in Los
Angeles, living at home and taking her final semester at
good old Pomona.

And then she would study graduate school bulletins, ig-
noring the schools of either coast who would have fought
to get her. She told her parents and her college counselor
she was American after all, and she wanted to get acquainted with her country. "What's good and central?"
she asked, and the counselor said, "You mean like Iowa or
something?" And she said, "Iowa? Show me where it is."
"Here, somewhere," she said—it was an exclusive private
school that thought only in terms of Berkeley or the Seven

Sisters—and together they hunted down the midwestern campuses. She applied to all the Big Ten graduate schools, disguising her accomplishments (by then, she had published about a dozen poems) and her languages, and Iowa offered the warmest acceptance. She arrived there a year before me.

To understand what happened in her last European year (she never went back), you'd have to read her poem "Neighbors" the way I did once (earning her unaccustomed respect). She wrote it one day in Marco's studio, looking beyond the heaped-up trash he was preparing for a still life, out the french window, across the alley, to the open balcony of a facing tenement. It was a working-class district. She was staring directly into a typical kitchen: fat wife boiling spaghetti, uniformed husband coming in, lifting the lid and walking out, a daughter staying around to help serve. A crucifix on the wall. A balcony, where the man stood for a few minutes, unbuttoning his shirt and letting the breeze dry his sweat. Absolutely nothing, in short, out of the ordinary.

A perfect silent scene. The idea that "Steam is already cooling, when it appears to us as steam," occurred to her. She wanted to write a poem about that deadly invisible space around the spaghetti lid. Not the steam exactly, but the vapors. Not the crucifix exactly, but the aura.

She'd remarked on the scene to Marco, who looked up. "So?" he asked. Marco was an intellectual Communist; he responded only to exploitation and degradation. He naturally pitied the wife and the worker, and he despised the Church. He prayed for a Communist victory.

"That's not it," she said.

It was a hot day; the windows were open, and the vapors of conversation almost carried across the alley from the kitchen. Marco thought she was responding to some-

thing poignant or dramatic. He apologized in advance, in
the usual way. A hard life, lack of capital, whatever, makes
people animals. "He didn't strike her," Rachel said. Marco
went back to work; Rachel went back to her poem.

So?

She remembered a moment that had disturbed her a few
days earlier, when she'd been walking to market. The perfect student: string-bag, bread, wine, some tomatoes, some
hard cheese, an eggplant. A hot, fetid day, and in the
market area the gutters were green with discarded lettuce
leaves, rotten vegetables, pierced blood oranges. She was
happy in the colors and the odor; she had an intellectual's
love of mindless profusion. Then suddenly a shadow had
fallen over the whole scene and she'd prickled from a cold
tongue of air pooling at her feet and licking up from, or
down from, where? It was like a premonition, and it made
her shiver. When she looked up she saw nothing but high
steamy clouds. She was standing at the foot of a high row
of steps. On the steps were students reading out their
manifestos, others exhibiting some artwork. At the top of
the steps was the largest church in the area—a beauty that
she'd often toured—and she realized in an instant that the
cool air, crypt-cool, had been flowing undetected down the
stairs, pooling in the sidewalk, waiting for her to step in it.
It had gripped her, even paralyzed her, and she'd had a vision
of nerve gas. No one else noticed it, they moved freely. So
it wasn't nerve gas, she thought. It was just gas. Just for
her.

And so she had stood shivering in the sun on a hot au-
tumn day, with something odorless and tasteless swirling at
her feet and climbing up her bare legs, settling under her
skirt. When she could, she had hurried back to the studio.
She'd just had a poem; all she needed was to write it.

Then, a week later, she'd been watching the family

across the alley. And she had that same feeling of cold, dead air, as though she'd been dropped in a soundless envelope. She couldn't hear Marco and she couldn't hear the family she was watching, and she doubted that anyone could hear her. They were all neighbors, and dead to her. She felt like a ghost. And when she thought back to the church she could feel its front wall crumbling down on her, and the rows of pigeons rising slowly from it like vultures from a carcass.

Marco kept working, and she started writing her poem. I've read comments on that poem as a "salutation" to solid working-class Italy. If anything at all of the "mature Isaacs" is seen in that poem (she still signed her name "Eisachs" in those days—"Isaacs" didn't occur to her until she returned to California), they see a charmed, momentarily "unarmed" Isaacs, overwhelmed by a kind of spontaneous tenderness. Strangely enough, considering my insensitivity to most poetry, when I read it a couple of years later, I understood it immediately. Call it the equivalence of disparate experience—the fact that I'd made the same journey in my own way, from the biology class, Lovett, my dizziness, and my drive to vindicate my father's wasted life. I understand Rachel now as I never understood her in life. I see us gripped in the same mythic patterns, carried along like rivers in flood, wiping out all flimsy distinctions, once we enrage them. I understood Rachel. I always understood her.

The "neighbors" weren't the family across the way, or the lover at her elbow. This was a poem for neighbors who couldn't be. It was a cry for the loss of community and loss of neighbors, in the midst of excessive neighborliness. The laboring wife is lost behind her "aggressive steam," the husband is "garlic statuary." For the first time in her life, Rachel was looking at the Italians not as her long-lost people, and at Italy not as her home, but as a kind of captivity.

In other words, Rosie, the missing neighbors in that poem are Jews. Rachel was not Jewish simply because she was born into a Jewish family in Los Angeles. She was Jewish because she had to invent it all over again for herself, just as she was American because she had to invent that for herself, too. She rejected the accident of her birth; she had to convert it to an act of will. What she saw that final year in Padua was that Europe had everything but a consciousness of her, everything but a history and a conscience she could relate to. And there was no way Europe could regain it—it was gone forever. No matter how "good" the people were, how sympathetic, how guilty, they were spiritual amputees. The mutilated crucifix on that kitchen wall is not a commentary on twisted Catholic values; it's a sign to her, suddenly, of a chronic, unhealable condition of the European soul.

Anyway, that's the way the poem spoke to me. Until that day in the marketplace, she'd never seriously considered herself an American, or a Jew. It had always been something to be apologetic for, or ashamed of. But now she forced herself to go back to Los Angeles and even embrace it. To be American and to be Jewish (and to be free of being Jewish and American) required her to be an American, in America.

That poem about an Italian working-class family cooking its spaghetti in a Padua flat was the most American and most Jewish poem she ever wrote.

Chapter Eleven

I'll spare you some of that vast realm of Wolfean sentimentality—the Young Writer Discovering His Métier—but I probably believed in the Divine Inspiration theory back in my junior year at Lovett. I was born to write in the same way as volcanoes blow their tops: a torrent of molten talent was pushing upward and had been pushing for nineteen years. Yes! Now I'd say it was an accident. My father's death had freed me from having to succeed on his terms. It exposed the true object of pity: not him—me. In that golden junior year at Lovett, I would have been a success at anything I tried.

His death gave me a mission, and a career. Rachel's death took it away. But her death has given you a career, and I'm feeling strangely like a version of my father.

Lovett had no famous writers on its staff in those years, but it did have a man named Sturbridge Foster, who knew precisely what he was doing. He offered two writing courses: one for credit on an introductory level (the one I signed up for) and a senior seminar for no grade or credit that met twice a month on Wednesday evenings at Garnett Place. Those chosen few were the green book baggers, the guitar strummers under the trees, the hitch-hikers to Vanderbilt and Kenyon.

I tried to write poetry first—squiggly little cummings-ish lines about God, and dying, and my father—and failed. (Remember, Rosie, this was the fifties. New criticism had taught me one thing: with a father named Joe and a mother named Mary, I was in good Messianic shape. My life might possibly be a spectacular one, acclaimed but painful.) Then I wrote a miserable sports story, then a sur-vivors-in-a-life-raft story, then a western shoot-out story (none of which Foster read aloud, none of which he even graded), and then, sometime near Thanksgiving, respond-ing to an assignment that would be graded and was ex-pected to be "full length," I closed my eyes and started composing from life itself. Pittsburgh, my parents, and myself. As I wrote, I could feel all the advice and criti-cism, all the anthologized stories we'd been reading and discussing in class pushing my pen, correcting my errors even before I committed them, pulling me into the next paragraph even before I could invent it. My knuckles ached, I wrote all afternoon, evening, all night. I didn't eat, and I finished the thing, seventeen pages, when the sun came up. My first university all-nighter. My fingers trem-bled, my face was flushed; I felt myself somehow anointed. I knew I had done something new in my life; I had linked up with a past and I'd cleared out the future. (I'm enclos-ing my only copy of it, Rosie, pretty much the way I wrote it that night. Of course there were some rewrites, but minor ones. It won *Atlantic* magazine's undergraduate talent search for 1959.)

We read our own stories to the class. Stur Foster brought me coffee, and I began. I was still drawing energy off the story, though my eyes must have been red and twitchy. I could not imagine an aspect of the world that was not touched upon in that story; it was an evolutionary leap from anything I'd written—even anything I'd ever thought before.

Well, it's pretty good. Only pretty good. I've carried this battered *Atlantic* with me ever since 1959. It was an emblem to me, it was Excalibur to me, it paid for part of my senior year, it got me a scholarship to Iowa. It got me an editorial listening, it probably got my first book published, and, most of all, it started me thinking seriously about myself from the beginning. I don't know why I carried it here. (I remember, when I finally left the States, coming across it and almost throwing it out. And at the time I couldn't. It's a sign to me now, that I can.)

Here's the story, and I'll take up this narrative when it's over.

The Birth of the Blues

As a real young kid, no more than four or five, Frank Keeler wanted recognition for the difficult ideas he was beginning to articulate. The first idea of his life—a truth— was so vivid that it gathered the clouds from the heavens and forced them into a funnel point just over his mother's head. It was Pittsburgh in 1944, and there were dark clouds enough for all the truths of Tolstoy. He was helping his mother to weed their Victory Garden. She was a squat, manly woman with white flabby arms and chin hairs, though she must have been only twenty-nine or thirty that year.

"Sometimes," he said while working his way down a row of radishes, not knowing what he was pulling until a pinkish bulge in the tuber betrayed him and he quickly tried to replant the evidence—"sometimes you pull out radishes, I bet, when you're trying to pull out weeds."

Phrased, it disappointed. What he meant (and remembered meaning) was the darkening of doubt in what had been the bright skies of certainty. It had to do with guilt. Though he was no stranger to the casual butchery of earthworms and caterpillars, this time he had murdered without meaning to. It had to do with a cruelty of nature that the weeds no one wanted looked just like the vegetables that were winning the war and keeping him from being murdered in his bed.

Taken to its extreme, which was the only way he took anything, the equivalence of opposites is a horrible concept.

"Sometimes you sure throw out the baby with the bathwater all right," his mother joked. Perhaps he hadn't heard properly. It could have been a song or she might have been talking to herself, which she often did. He must have heard it wrong. But she asked again, making no mistake about it, "That it? The baby with the bathwater?"

From weeds to radishes is natural. Even a child can follow it. From there to moral choice and guilt is a scream for help. Reassurance arrived in the form of a metaphor that he received as literal, wondering if in fact babies were often thrown out with their bathwater; if normal precautions might not reduce, if not eliminate, the number of wet babies squirming in soapy puddles; if mother love might not be invoked on the side of soapy babies everywhere. Obviously, it couldn't be. Luck alone accounted for his survival. An unexpected callousness had been exposed; the world was incredibly brutal. He wanted, for a moment, no part of it. Black clouds were boiling overhead and he thought, Messerschmitts! And he hid his head and held that posture in the rain until his mother pried his arms away.

A freak storm destroyed several small towns just north of Pittsburgh that day.

The configuration was set for life: Dark clouds giving birth to Truth and Destruction; his own contribution dismissed (or worse, rephrased as one of his mother's "little sayings"). Oh, the dark terrors, the dread that could be rendered by "from the frying pan into the fire," the swift curtailment of liberty pardoned in "When in Rome . . . ,"—all so much bathwater, so much craving for greener grass. The proverbs never quite matched his meaning, never approached the intensity of his premonitions. His mother had been stuffed with sayings and Depression recipes; she was profound on any topic dealing with turnips, disappointment, or forbearance.

His father had only one saying: "Nothing succeeds like success." He used it when the Pirates were getting pounded by talented opponents who were also getting lucky. It meant that everything was either stacked up for you or against you. Its analogy was "The rich get richer." It was a justification for being poor, for losing, for not trying, for taking what you could get. When Frank got some education years later, he saw it as crude Darwinism.

What can we say about intelligence when the child's highest utterances were clichés even before he formed them? He came to think that his originality would always be blunted on some higher and preexistent logic. Someone would always be there ahead of him. That's how it was and how it would always be; you had to admit you weren't exceptional, you couldn't jump over your mother's sayings, you couldn't invent new clichés.

Years later, he read Hamlet. *The melancholy Dane struck him as no hero, basically a winner, one of the rich and gifted, who was mildly incompetent with his tools.*

Keeler's hero was, alas, Polonius. A man elevated by the bureaucracy into what should have been secure employment.

Even as a child, he devalued anything his mother could understand. His father could read, his mother couldn't. Her "little sayings" were the farthest extensions of her thought. They were also its everyday currency; how like the educated are the very, very foolish.

She would stand in the kitchen—another early memory—melting something over the gas. Keeler would watch, fascinated. It was a caramel-colored, stubby candle, melting like a thick slab of frozen butter in its own battered saucepan. He liked the slow process of transformation, like blueing in the washtub, the tab of orange worked into the bowl of margarine, and this third thing, whatever it was.

But when it had finally melted, looking like burned butter, she smeared it over her face, wincing with the heat. When her face was entirely plastered in the stiffening caramel-colored paste, and when it had hardened, she pulled it off. It hissed not only with heat but with the hundreds of hairs pulled off with it, and when it was all recollected, a twisted heap of cold beeswax back in the saucepan and wrapped in old aprons under the sink, his mother's face was pink and smooth and he was asked to feel it.

"Hot," he said.

"Smooth?"

"A little."

She sighed, made sure the pan was hidden. "Ah well," she said, "don't let your father know."

Keeler wanted to forget everything he'd seen.

"Let sleeping dogs lie," she said.

The boy could picture them, fierce and mangy, sniffing out the saucepan under the sink, tearing open the aprons and wolfing down the cold wax with its old skin and stray black hairs. He came to associate her strange ritual with the yellow wax always with stray dogs; the lingering odor for years after was the odor of dogs and of some terrible unnatural operation that left his mother's cheeks hot and smooth.

Keeler's father was a carpenter by trade, but after hours and weekends he did other things: non-union work like plumbing and house painting and simple wiring. By day he was strictly a framer and roofer, and with the suburbs spreading all over the South Hills, there was construction enough to keep him busy.

He had all the skills to put up a house single-handedly if you weren't too choosy. He'd done it for other people, but the Keelers continued to rent. For Joe Keeler, owning a house was a dubious venture. New houses were always a little unfinished, and if he peeked into a wall or a window sash he would begin to price out the cost of repairs, calculate the builder's profit, and work himself into a rage. He was usually in a rage, and he hated builders. He hated the idea of anyone making a profit on his money. He even withheld what he considered an equitable amount of labor from any job. Renting, he practically got the duplex free after deducting for continual improvements. Renting or buying, his father told him, was six of one, half a dozen of another, and maybe because by then Keeler was seven or eight, he understood. His father was easier to understand anyway: Measure twice, cut once—that was Joe Keeler.

When he was ten, Keeler started going out on jobs with his father, nightly and weekends, carrying his tool kit or miter box, holding ladders and spreading drop cloths. Keeler's father was lean; his pants always bunched around the belt loops as if there were clothespins holding them up. He had to keep a leather punch for adjusting his belts, al-

ways well beyond the last notch, and sometimes he had to cut off the unused part of the belt or else lap it back through the first two loops.

There were no subtleties in Keeler's life, no surprises. His father coughed like a dying man because he'd been secretly dying for a long time. In four years he would be dead, as anyone would have predicted, of lung cancer. The only time he'd gotten fat was a few weeks before the growth was detected. He'd had to let his belt out a notch to accommodate a painful little paunch just below his navel. "Gettin' fat in my old age," he'd said (he was forty-six), "and sometimes it hurts like hell."

His father enjoyed smoking more than any man Keeler had ever seen. He smoked with the total absorption of a wounded soldier on a stretcher whose cigarette is held for him by his buddy or a medic. With every draw on the cigarette his breath shunted like a child's who'd been crying. On the rare moments that he took the cigarette from his lips, he would pinch it tightly to keep it from rolling, then set it on the nearest table edge. Every table and countertop featured charred parabolas, as regular as sawteeth, along the edges. The minute his father set down one cigarette, he absentmindedly lit another. That was the hardest thing coming home to after the funeral, all those black defacements. He smoked the butts right down to stubs that disappeared in the center of his lips. When he extracted them he had to use two fingers, as though he were about to whistle for a taxi. All of this endowed smoking with a deep sense of ritual and mortality in the boy's mind; smoking was a calling, like carpentry, built on long apprenticeship and certification under fire. Keeler's grandfather, a drunken, arthritic old man who'd burned his toolbox rather than pass it down to Keeler's dad—the Keeler family was a

study in a long career of spite—had perished in a smolder-
ing easy chair, a smoker's death.

Keeler's father, younger and less careless, was to die a
more protracted smoker's death. Keeler was fourteen
when his father finally died. This earlier death, the one
recorded here, happened two years earlier.

The apartment they were looking for was near the town
center of a suburb called Mount Lebanon. His father
rarely ventured beyond downtown; Keeler himself had
crossed over the bridges to the south side only for annual
trips to the county fair. This trip was to be by the number
38 trolley to the end of the line. Whenever Keeler thought
of Mount Lebanon, he thought of skies permanently blue
and lawns as green as Forbes Field in June and of every
house painted white and never flaking, as though they had
been dipped in cream.

The village center, where the trolley made its loop, was
—on a wet, windy Saturday in March—as dark and dirty as
any other place in the city. A theater and an upholsterer's,
shoe-repair shop and a grill, bakery and the tracks. Keeler
and his father had ridden out on one of the old trolleys,
the cane-seated, yellow ones that managed to look like
raised and elongated roadsters, with their wide running
boards, two saucerlike headlamps, and an elaborate
wrought-iron cowcatcher in front. His father had remem-
bered as a boy watching these same trolleys tearing
through the countryside, following the riverbeds and
mountain flanks all the way east to Johnstown and
downriver to Weirton and Wheeling. Riding a trolley to a
different state struck Keeler as a kind of freedom he would
never see; he had to be satisfied to be still able to ride one

of the heroic old cars to Mount Lebanon. They were only in service on weekends and during rush hours, and they were to disappear completely, scrapped or sold to museums, in another year.

They walked downhill, Keeler holding his father's heavy box with both hands, and shifting the burden by a modified swinging from side to side. At the base of the street they found the building, an old five-story apartment house with gilt numbers above the door and a name in gold leaf painted on the transom: ALHAMBRA. *It was the sort of building with a long waiting list.*

The inside walls were a cream-colored stucco meringue. The wood trim was dark; the whole thing must have been put up in the Moorish period of the mid-twenties, when buildings were all named Babylon and Araby. There were real paintings in the common hallways and big chandeliers outside the stairwell on every floor, looking as out of place as the pictures he'd seen of chandeliers in the Moscow subway. No scrap papers, no empty bottles, no greasy paper sacks of undisposed garbage in the hall. This was Mount Lebanon. Their business was in Apartment Five, third floor. Some plumbing, the woman had said. Then maybe some plastering and painting, if she liked the work.

The woman who answered the door didn't go with the old wood and stucco and watercolors in the hall. She was in her thirties, barely, with short black curls that fell over each other in layers, like skirts. She had one long set of eyelashes already attached and the other, like a smashed centipede, between her fingers. One set of shaped fingernails had been lacquered with the kind of red in the deepest crevice of a rose. Her eyes were black, velvety, but she wore no lipstick. Her cheeks were rough and blotchy. She was building herself from the rafters down, in defiance of sound carpentry principles. Below her eyes,

everything but the nails was in a state of disrepair: a clut-
tered work site held together by a faded wrapper, like a
tarp.

"About time," she said. "I see you brought a helper.
Well, you're going to need all the help—just look."

While Keeler's father paused to light a cigarette, Keeler
took in the sights. First, the shallow tubs out on the
kitchen floor, the mop propped against the sink, and a
puddle of alarming dimensions. But far more wondrous to
Keeler was the sight of the half-formed lady, from the
pink slippers up: her ankles were chapped and veined, her
shins shiny except for small nicks and scrapes—shining the
way his mother's cheeks and chin would shine after the
layers of wax. Perhaps some women bathed in wax and
came out looking like apples. Lugging the box, he followed
his father to the kitchen. She said from just behind him,
"This gave out this morning."

A fine spray shot out from under the sink. Even Keeler
knew that a twist on the main shut-off valve was all that it
needed. His father pinched the cigarette and balanced it on
her countertop. Then he reached under the sink and
stopped the water.

"Better get this mopped up right away," he told the
woman. "If your linoleum has leaks, it'll seep right
through."

"I'm busy," she said.

"Frankie—"

The woman walked out through the dining room,
which was enclosed by heavy doors with leaded glass
panels, then down a corridor to her bedroom. Keeler
wrung the mop by hand and started in at the puddle's
shoreline, pushing it out toward the walls, then spreading
the deeper parts back over it. A process like painting in
reverse: every coat thinner, tending to a final disap-
pearance.

The first time he saw her, it was accidental. The bath-room was in his line of vision at the very end of the corri-dor. When he looked up from his mopping, she was lean-ing over the sink to hook on a brassiere. It was all over in a split second, but Keeler replayed it, stunned, for several minutes. By then she'd put her wrapper back on. His fa-ther was sawing through a rusty pipe.

Just in time, Keeler spotted the old cigarette, beginning to smolder. Her countertop was plastic and the burn was very light yellow. He rubbed it out.

She stood by her lavatory in the same pink slippers and bathrobe, leaning forward to inspect her face. He could sense somehow that she'd forgotten all about the men in her kitchen.

God, if he hadn't been mopping! If he'd just looked up ten seconds earlier and seen the whole thing! He'd never forgive himself, seeing his first naked lady, and it being in Mount Lebanon. Right now she was safely under wraps, but anything could happen.

She turned on her taps; the pipes coughed. His father from under the sink grunted, "Damn fool." From far down the hall, the lady turned. Keeler applied himself quickly to unnecessary mopping. She was on her way to the kitchen now, eating up the space between them.

The transformation had spread to her second eye and both cheeks. It was as though her eyes were speaking, as if the top half of her face were two feet closer and ten years younger than the rest of her. Her eyes were soft, loving, densely lashed. It was as though only part of her were in focus.

Her voice, as he expected, was cruel and shallow. "Can't you see that I'm trying to get ready . . . to go out?" She was standing over his father where his legs issued from under the sink. From down below came the magnified ex-

*ertions of his father, coughing with a smoker's snarl; even
his normal breathing was like a lion's purr. He held a section of an S-trap in his hand and he swirled his fingers in it,
extracting grease and hairs, entwined like brick.*

"Well, what do you propose to do?"

*He offered her a glimpse of his finger, wedged in the
pencil-thin opening. Then he reached up and placed the
section of pipe on her counter. She didn't look.*

*There was no mistaking that she was getting ready to go
out and that she expected all the help that electricity and
plumbing could give. Keeler had never seen his father on
his knees in front of anyone, especially not an angry
woman, and the effect was exciting. It made Keeler look at
the woman from the floor up, undoing her decoration, and
it made him respond to the perverse intimacy of all the
layers of her dowdy clothes, so at odds with the top six
inches of her face. It made him think of flesh, alien tex-
tures, and the way flesh must feel in the richer suburbs of
Pittsburgh, so different from his mother's hot waxy stub-
ble. And his father stood up, very slowly, lifting the cigarette out with two clamped fingers, letting his eyes drift
upward, insolently, as he stood.*

*She didn't like that. Keeler felt, at that moment, that if
he had not been there, his father would have attacked the
woman. Or she would have clawed him and screamed.
And in all his life, he'd never seen his father turn his head
at a woman, whistle, stare, or even tell a dirty story.*

"Please, just leave," she said.

"Then you won't get nobody to fix that there pipe."

*"I really don't care. I have ten minutes before my
fiancé comes, and I want you out."*

*He flipped over the sides of his tool kit with his boot,
and Keeler sealed it. Then he ground out the butt.*

"Suit yourself. When in Rome."

108   LUSTS

"What do I owe you?"

"I dint do nothin'."

"If you'd been on time, you would have finished."

"I don't make appointments, lady. You still got an hour's work there. That piece was totally froze out. I gotta cut a new section and solder it in."

"Come back tomorrow then. I'll be in at two o'clock." She said this like a big concession. Tomorrow was Sunday, and Keeler's father had never gotten up before two o'clock on a Sunday except to catch a Steelers game on television. He never finished dressing on Sunday; some days a shirt but no pants, other days the opposite. It was March, between all sports seasons.

"Too busy tomorrow. Come on, Frankie."

"Here." She held out money, two coins. *"For the boy at least. He did the mopping."*

His father didn't stop him from accepting the fifty cents.

Yes, definitely, the woman had affected them both. A woman couldn't show a man into her apartment, dressed like that and adopting such an attitude (while being already half-beautiful and giving promise of completing the job) without becoming for Keeler the prototype of all beautiful women. For his father, the most perfect bitch. Together, father and son, they were consumed by lust. One beginning to die, the other too young. And they left.

Down the stuccoed halls, with Keeler carrying the tools, they lumbered, down the staircase like an elephant with bells on. When they got to the first floor, a short Italian man with shoulder pads of hair lifting up his undershirt squinted up at Keeler's father and asked, *"Plumber?"*

By way of an answer, his father lifted his hand in the general direction of the street. It was his ambition to own a panel truck some day: JOE KEELER GENERAL CONTRACTING, *it would say. For an instant, as his father pointed, Keeler could see that truck parked out front. Light blue, it would be. Something self-explanatory for nosy janitors.*

"What makesa you t'ink, hah, you can come inna the front, hah? There'sa the back for pipple like you."

From inside the super's apartment the opened door revealed two young men as thick as their father, only taller and blonder, with wives, children, mothers and grand-mothers, and a tricycle being pedaled around a dining table. The Keelers followed his pointing finger down to the basement and up through a bulkhead that opened on the back alley. The flesh on Keeler's fingertips was begin-ning to split.

They were walking now back to the trolley loop. It had turned dark, with bits of freezing rain stinging their faces. His father growled behind him, coughing and spitting.

"Fixed her good, huh? She won't have a drop of water till Monday. If then."

Keeler was working on one of his agonized generaliza-tions: the whole exercise had seemed to him a demon-stration of some great truth about pride and discomfort and, in his father's case, laziness. Now she wouldn't have water, and his father would miss out on at least ten dollars. And he would miss seeing her again, in her Sunday clothes.

"That sure teaches her to act smart with me, huh? Cut off her nose is what she done." He seemed to be laughing, but laughter—with those two gluey pits he called lungs—ended up half killing him every time. Nose, nose? Keeler had heard something about cutting off one's nose to do something equally stupid, but it wouldn't come to him. Nothing would come to him. His father stopped, bent double in the classic posture of a man being sick, but it was the cough, first lowering him, then bobbing his head like punches. Keeler rested the toolbox.

*He stood a few feet above his father. Ahead of him lay
the trolley tracks. None of the old trolleys was waiting,
but one of the sleek new ones, with silent, effective fans in
the summer and a row of solitary window seats up front,
had just turned off Washington Road onto the loop. And
below him he could still see the Alhambra, where they'd
been forced to exit through the basement by the garbage
cans. There'd been a handpainted sign over the bulkhead:*
TRADESMEN AND LABORERS. *The sign was wondrous to him,
a definition of himself he'd never considered.*

*His father stopped coughing once they boarded the trol-
ley. He took a window seat and fell asleep as soon as the
trolley started moving. When he couldn't smoke, he usually slept. Keeler had the whole car, the long corridor up
to the driver, practically to himself. Somewhere on that
trip a kind of fire rose up in him, and he said in a voice so
loud it surprised him, "I'm going to do things with my life.
No one is ever going to tell me where to go. No one but
me is going to tell me what to do, ever."*

END

(You know, Rosie, I wasn't going to send this. I read it
again for the first time in maybe ten years, and I saw
things I'd change, but I still like it. And that depresses me,
the way I used to be depressed after touring museums with
Rachel. I'd look at portraits five and six hundred years old,
or at objects crafted thousands of years ago, and feel—hey,
where's the progress? Where's the evolution? In five hundred years, I expected some physical changes. But those
milkmaids in Vermeer are absolute contemporaries. And
they are dead. And I could feel their deaths as a crime and
a mystery, not a historic inevitability.

(And I read this first story of mine and think of the

ignorant kid who wrote it and wonder how he did it. Shouldn't I have evolved after such a beginning? But I couldn't write it again, and I couldn't write it as well.) I don't think Rachel ever read it. You're one up on her.

Stur Foster was a meditative man, born ten miles from Lovettville, but educated entirely in the East. He'd stayed in New York for a dozen years as an editor. He'd known them all—Wolfe, Fitzgerald, Hemingway, Max Perkins—and then sometime in the late Depression his parents died, leaving him orchards on a hilltop in central Kentucky. He came back, built a house, and started writing a series of local histories. The war sent him to England, where he wrote and edited dispatches. Back in Kentucky, he wrote his war memoirs. Everything he ever wrote was perversely modest. ("The sign of the editor," he told me. "Everywhere and nowhere.") He was an omniscient voice, never a personality. By the time I knew him, the histories and the memoirs were all out of print, but they lingered in that literary half-light of goodwill and respect that's nearly as negotiable. In the early fifties he won a prize for a biography of a local nineteenth-century politician who seemed to have combined good sense and sound principles. That man's name was Warren Pusey, and he had ended his years as president of a local Baptist Seminary in the town of Lovettville. From that association came an offer to Stur Foster to teach whatever and whenever he pleased in the English Department of Lovett College. By the time I met him he was about sixty (a child of the century like Ben-Zvi, only Kentucky-style), short and silvery, with that slow, folksy delivery Southerners affect in New York and Washington. That way, their wit and sophistication are kept eternally amazing.

"Richard," he said after my reading, "come down to the Union for a bite to eat."

"Why?" I asked cagily.

"You should have been writing all along. That story is a triumph."

"Oh, I think it's too long. And I can't take that kid at the end too seriously."

"I do," he said.

I shrugged my shoulders and tried to behave graciously. I was wondering when he would ask (as the students always did), *Did that really happen to you?* I was ready to volunteer enough information to indicate that I had known deep bitterness, suffering, and humiliation in my life, but that I also had one hell of an imagination. He asked instead, "Do you mind if I show it to the editors of *Askance?*"

"What would they want with it?"

"I really can't say. I only know what they should want, that's all."

This was the only time I ever wanted a different Stur Foster: some hot-blooded enthusiast, someone to wring my hand and weep joyfully at the crowning of a bright new talent. If I had known the publishing mythology—I was about as sophisticated as the boy in my story—that I was having lunch with a literary superscout who stood in the ancestral line of Hemingway and Perkins, I might have crafted my modesty less sincerely.

"I also wonder if you'd think of reading it again at the Literary Society next week."

What could I say? That really was an Opening Night.

"I think they'll be surprised."

"Who's they?"

"Oh, the senior writers. It's good to prune them back in

the fall with a sharp reminder . . . that they're not alone out there."

A week later I entered Garnett Place for the first time. It was like stepping behind stage and seeing all the actresses in the evolving drama of my downhill life suddenly at home, half-dressed, going about their work of preparing dinner for the Literary Society meeting and for the small crowd of professors and other students who showed up for it. Among the seniors were all the campus poetical celebrities, the young men who looked ten years older than me, with wire-rimmed spectacles, beards or mustaches, and old work clothes. And I recognized the girls who frequented the rooms of the theater majors in my rooming house: the girls in leotards and peasant skirts, with the gold earrings and eye shadow and no other makeup. They were all Garnett girls and they had made the food, prepared the salon of their quasi-dorm, and gotten themselves finally fixed up, to hear poetry from the expected sources, and a story from Richard Durgin, a junior. My name had been on posters.

Janet Bunn, also a junior, read the introduction. "Richard Durgin comes to us from Pittsburgh. He's a junior in Mr. Foster's Introductory class, and he's a member of LSC." Nobody snickered. And the girl was a vision to me, small and a little plump, in purple tights, skirt and a black sweater, with long brown hair gathered in a clasp. No makeup, teeth a little prominent in a way that seemed to emphasize soft lips and a mouth you could watch for hours. It was an anchored sort of face, with large green eyes, a substantial nose, angular cheeks, and that very independent mouth. In ten years that face would achieve its unity; for a junior in a pretty-girl's college, it was too strong, just as the eyebrows were a little too thick.

(She looked like someone's sister. One look at her and a host of male and female variations suggested themselves. She was attractive, but you could easily imagine improvements, greater or lesser appeal along the same general principles. But with Rachel, there was no possibility of siblings. She had condensed all contingencies. Like a queen bee, she had stabbed the life from any possible duplication.)

"Richard? Don't be frightened—"

She'd been holding her hand out for several seconds. I'd missed my first cue from Janet Bunn, and I started reading my story too speedily until, from her front-row seat, she made the universal "slow down" gesture. Unlike my fellow beginners in Foster's class, this audience laughed where I'd intended, and it mumbled its "yeahs" in the appreciative, San Francisco coffeehouse manner known only to the initiated.

When it was over, when I transcended my nervousness to look up from the page and render that child's bold announcement to the empty trolley that he would never be humiliated, the small group was standing and applauding. I had never been so confused and gratified by anything I had done—not even lofting a tennis ball over the fence at the end of my old Pittsburgh street. There was nothing like it, no way of describing it, and the next morning I showed up in the English office to declare my new major. And that evening I showed up at Garnett Place as Janet's dinner guest. I took her to a campus movie, an Indian film by the name of *Pather Panchali* (how these things come around to whack us, twenty years later!), which seemed to be the thing that serious, artistic, independent people did with their Thursday nights.

Chapter Twelve

Only in Pittsburgh with Wanda Lusiak could I say I have shared the assumptions of my wives and lovers. The older I've gotten, the farther apart we've started from, and the wider the gap has grown. At Lovett, the gap between an ignorant fraternity boy (me) and a sensitive mature woman masquerading as an undergraduate (Janet) was already unbridgeable.

After all, a hundred points in the average SAT scores count for something.

Her assumption, and the assumption of Garnett girls in general, was that college was a time of growth and experimentation. Growth and experimentation were ideas that struck at the heart of the Lovett experience. Rules against having men in their rooms, against late hours, against liquor, and against sexual expression simply did not apply to serious people.

The assumption of fraternity boys like me, even defective ones, was that rules existed in order to compress the possible thrills. To bend and test and tease, but not to break. In fact, the rules that separated the sexes served the very necessary role of inflaming the senses, of turning even

the Baptists among us into snorting bulls of copulative
fury. The freshman girls' dorms down on Clay Street at
the base of College Hill were just across the street from
my rented room. And I would watch the ritual at 1:00
A.M. Friday and Saturday and at 10:00 other nights, of
moaning couples rubbing against each other till their knees
buckled and the boys hobbled away. A world not entirely
unknown to me, in my earlier manifestation. Then I would
leave my room, walk to Garnett with a bottle of wine, and
pour it for the girls who came down to let me in.

I thought I was quite the lover, quite the suave fellow,
the lucky one. But I was corrupt to my core. I didn't do a
thing in those last two, perfect years without a sense of
being observed, being approved by Brendan McIvor or
someone like him. *Hey, see what I'm getting!* (And Janet
wasn't interested in giving other people the "right" im-
pression; only the other girls at Garnett knew about us,
and they didn't care.)

And this is the boy who was to find love? Who was to
pursue a decent woman for once, who would try to understand *Pather Panchali?*

I remember late one night in Janet's room, the happiest
night of my Lovett career, talking to her of our freshman
year, the earnest depravity of Brendan, of me, and our
friends, sharing with her the dirty secrets of our local
celebrities. (Ah, the biographical impulse, Rosie, and the
twisted forms it takes!)

The world will always yield its mysteries, given pa-
tience and the proper friends.

"You took out Burley Grimes?" she asked.

"She was my number to the Freshman Mixer. Brendan
McIvor relieved me of her." Burley had been named for

the expensive leaf that paid for her Jaguar and vacuous refinement. She'd scared the hell out of me, that first night on campus.

"How did you know Brendan McIvor?"

"The only way," I said.

"Interesting," she said.

I reached across for an explanation. It was about two o'clock in the morning; most of the Garnett girls and their admirers were still sipping wine, reading, peeling into early preliminaries. "Come on, out with it." When a girl says "Interesting" in the way Janet had, its only meaning is sexual. She held out her glass, which I filled, then turned out the light.

"Did he have a big, you know, cock?"

"It was uncircumcised, as I remember." Actually, for fear of seeming too engrossed, I'd spent three years trying to outlaw the image of that enormous thing, that "boar hawg," in Kentucky parlance, that was the anchor of Brendan's authority in all things sexual. "Yeah, I guess you could say so."

"There were rumors," Janet said. "They said he could injure a girl."

And then we began a conversation that lasted till dawn, when even the bolder admirers of Garnett women feared detection from the rounds of campus security. I remember it now as something extraordinary: past and present and maybe the future all sliding together. Janet Bunn—you were magnificent! It turned on the intimate attributes of Lovett girls. All you ever wanted to know about the secondary sexual characteristics of prime Kentucky breeding stock.

Burley Grimes had been in Janet's suite. "She had a cute little ass," she offered. "She slept in those pink shorty pajamas, just like you'd guess she would."

"Boobs?"

"No boobs to speak of. Not like Connie Stickney. Remember Connie Stickney?"

"Very well. How could I forget?"

"She was very serious about getting surgery. She used to cry herself to sleep because she could never be sure why boys liked her."

"We feel her loss even today," I said. She hadn't returned after our freshman year.

"She was raped twice that year. The University expelled her before she could bring charges."

I probably joked about it. I was slime—what can I say? None of us took rape seriously, all of us would have assumed, if we'd known about it, that Connie Stickney got what any five-foot-two blonde with D-cups deserved. Since it had happened when she was out on dates and not when she was walking through the woods, a certain amount of hanky-panky was assumed, and there had been no investigation.

Half an hour later, we'd gone beyond Stickney's amazing boobs. Janet, an art and philosophy major, had induced many of our classmates to pose for her. Out came the sketchbooks, on went the light, and we lay near-naked in bed, feasting on the freshman bodies and faces that had evolved into local legends.

What a night that was!

"Too bad you weren't a photographer," I said, knowing at once I'd gone too far in my prurient appreciation. If she did have photos, I would never see them.

"This is the hairiest girl on campus—Mona Thwait. She's so hairy she can't wear two-piece bathing suits. She can't even wear shorts."

"That's sexy, somehow."

"So I see. You think gorillas are sexy?"

"I think she's very pretty. A little downy on the upper lip, maybe. And there's a kind of dark outline on her cheeks and arms." Then I thought, perversely, under the circumstances, of undressing Mona Thwait, an otherwise petite, even buxom, olive-skinned girl with dense black hair. I could picture nests of squashed black hair under her arms, the delicate downiness yielding to chest hairs along the nipples. My God, Mona Thwait, that little girl in my sociology class, was sitting on, hiding, warming an erotic treasure chest!

(Mona Thwait does not enter this story at all, despite—perversely, of course—being more responsible for my being here in India and being a father than either Janet or Rachel. If you've done your research, you'll know that five years ago I was invited to return to Lovett for a semester, after Stur Foster's stroke. At Lovett I still had some currency, though in the East I was barely hanging on as a second-language instructor in a converted warehouse in downtown Newark. And so I went back to Lovett for the first time since graduation, taking over an apartment in the remodeled Ramsey Hall—now for single faculty—thinking perhaps the bad times were over and they'd make me an offer and I could settle down with a pretty young thing and bask in the glow of my local reputation and her total adoration.

(I did find total adoration—her name was Leela, as you perhaps know already—when I finally gave up trying to look for it in the usual places, and it was that conjunction of vicious sex and unexpected downiness that did it to me, all over again.)

I wonder how you'll respond to my life after Rachel. At least I can tell myself that this Pittsburgh and Lovett stuff is grist for your mill, too. In some roundabout way it must have affected Rachel. I want to keep Rachel out of this as long as possible; I want to keep her still young and brilliant and talented. So long as we haven't met and married, she's still alive. And I'm not guilty of anything. The intellectual drama is already in high gear, but the moral drama hasn't even started—do you understand, Rosie? During my senior year at Lovett, she was already settled in Iowa, in a room on Dubuque Street, sharing a kitchen with a girl in Religious Studies (Maxine Rosenbluth; you might look her up, too). She's filling her journals and writing letters, but not much poetry. And she goes to the library every night, she dazzles her professors, she has no lovers that I know of, and she makes a little extra money working for the Italian Department in the language lab. And one night about a year and a half from this night I'm describing at Lovett, I too will go to the Iowa Library and spot this girl from my Dante class—the smart girl that I figure has to be Italian—and I'll take a step toward her, and that will be it. . . .

I feel as soon as I take that step, I'll be killing her all over again.

Do you know where I'm coming from, Rosie Chang?

"She really does excite you, doesn't she?" Janet grazed me at that moment, and then pulled my shorts down, to giggle at that achingly taut, terra-cotta member. She lay, seallike, her chin on my thigh, staring a little cross-eyed at that rigid red popsicle standing between us. "I'm surprised you didn't ask me about Debbie Warner," she said.

"Oh, God, Debbie Warner . . ." And my poor bowed branch straightened and Janet ran a moistened finger down its back seam. "I'm trying not to be vulgar," I moaned.

"Would you like me to tell you about Debbie Warner?"

"I'm not responsible for the consequences."

Debbie, when we'd dared, had been the star of our foulest fantasies. On a campus of golden girls, Debbie had won all the pageants. Even in high school she'd become Miss Teen Kentucky, and in our junior year she became Miss Kentucky, after one year as a runner-up. Debbie Warner crossed over from beautiful, which she surely was, to desirable, and once you made that connection to your—and her—essential lewdness, you couldn't even think of her as beautiful anymore. The typical Lovett girl, except for those at Garnett Place and the Mona Thwaits, was tall and slim and straight, with pleasant, regular features, well toned, tanned, a little broad in the shoulders and narrow in the hips; female golfers in later life, tennis sharpies, divers and swimmers. Very few—Janet being one—were shapely, or even ample. Only Debbie Warner managed it all: the sweet, regular features of a Lovett high-WASP, country-bred suburbanite with the body of Moonbeam McSwine; some improbable dislocation of intention that allowed a demure face to strike a terrified truce with its own libidinous nether regions. And you knew the face was losing. Each year, the sweetness turned just a little harder, and by her junior year even her dimples were calculating.

"She used to rub her body down with baby oil. Girls used to ask for the privilege—we were as amazed as anyone. She had the first of those front-hooking bras . . . my, my . . . not that she needed one—"

"She's not flat. Don't tell me she's flat."

"Firm, my dear. Hmm. She liked to stand around topless, doing stretching exercises. How much more rubbing can this thing take?"

"About two more strokes."

"She'd put dance music on and do a strip—ever hear about that? There were about five Theta pledges—the girls who sang that Ramsey song on the first night, remember them?—and she used to teach them dance routines—*oops*, here, I'm holding it; think of Ernest Hemingway or something, okay? I'm going to let go, slowly . . . there. Okay? Anyway, you know where they practice?"

"I don't want to know."

"The SAE house."

"So that's how you heard about Brendan McIvor's boar hawg."

"Did you know about Tammy Sargent?"

"I don't even remember her. Janet—watch it, Vesuvius—were there really any girls getting laid? Christ, the stories we used to hear. And the stories we used to believe. There was Ellie Johnson. There was Karen Pfister. There was—"

"Janet Bunn?"

"No, ma'm. Never."

"That's good."

"Who was it? No, cancel that. Skip it. Forget I asked." That wasn't cool.

"He's not here anymore anyway."

"Graduated? Goddamn upperclassman."

"No."

"Transferred? Lucky guy."

"No."

I dropped my voice. "Dead?"

"Christ, Richie, no. Don't be stupid. I'm not answering any more."

"Well, what else is there? You can't be anything other than here, graduated, transferred, or dead."

Her look told me everything. It said, Yes, you can. Mentally, I was going over the options, like Brendan McIvor ticking off the fraternities. I even thought the unthinkable, but didn't know how to ask it—a girl?

"Try fired," she said.

Let's say, before reporting my response, that if Lovett's faculty had been ninety percent young females, just half a dozen years removed from college themselves, and if the males of Lovett, far from being the pimply drones that we were, had been hearty variants of the same choice stock as the females, and if the admissions director, instead of being T. Lysander Crommelin—an aging androgyne—had been perhaps his legendary daughter, banished forever from Lovett after a miscegenetic alliance with a Kentucky basketballer—then I might have had a woman's perspective on the faculty. Maybe not just a woman's: I might have had a normal tolerance for those inevitable mating urges. What could be more natural, for girls so much more accomplished than the boys (you've seen what I was like, and I like to think I was one of the better males on campus) to give themselves cheerfully to the only available men? The Garnett girls existed mainly for the faculty: professors, not football players, were the final competition. As in any truly petty despotism, the victims—in our case, the women, with their wretched curfews—probably achieved greater freedom than their swaggering watchdogs.

"What do you mean, fired?" I naturally demanded, knowing already the question was stupid and that a new frontier had been opened. I'd thought the archetypal bachelor bull on the Lovett campus was a senior Sigma Chi with a football letter, a Jaguar, and admission to a good medical school. It had never occurred to me that, for discriminating girls, even Brendan McIvor was just another jellyfish washed up overnight. The sperm whales, the men with taste, money, authority, and experience, were the young professors. They were the ultimate ring of sharks, patrolling the freshman dorms.

She, of course, didn't answer. And when I thought of

professors, I could only come up with blanks: the baggy-suited, one-tie, stained and shiny pants brigade with bratty children and shrewish wives, who stalked the campus with swinging arms and proudly weathered briefcases, or the bespectacled skulkers with freeze-dried hair, bald spots looming like tawny yarmulkes, who mowed across campus staring at their feet, thumbs seemingly pasted to their thighs. But when I thought a second time, the campus proliferated with likely candidates. Even the Economics Department had its fiery young Madison Marxists. English reportedly had a young man who'd roamed Mexico and the West Coast as a beatnik and could provide an annotated scorecard to *On the Road*. Down in the Art and Theater departments were young men who'd never taken stock of their nominal location in central Kentucky. For them, it was always San Francisco or the Village, and the blue work shirts and patched blue jeans they wore had already caught on with the campus poets and actors.

"Anyhow, there are more important things to talk about," she said.

"At least tell me his name."

"You wouldn't have heard of him. Really, what could be more boring? Let's get back to your request show. I can tell you why Karen Burchart dropped out of school."

"How common is it—girls and professors?"

"Seriously? I can tell you it was the most uncommon experience of my life."

"It's the most serious question of my life. It's like learning there's a new continent off the coast of Oregon or something. It means I have to start thinking of things all over again, from the beginning."

(I'm reminded of something Rachel said, in a more serious context. Concerning the Holocaust. It's not that such a thing happened. It's that it happened with so many brilliant people around, in the midst of so much awareness, so much self-knowledge. Not that we're capable of murder—just that we're incapable of stopping it.

(That's what killed her.)

What shocked me was not the existence of faculty incursions but my failure to detect them. The shock was learning how complacent I'd been, and how far I had to go before catching up with Janet. And by the time I caught up, where would she be?

I wanted to shout out, "wait for me!" It could be my motto. Give me a chance, I can learn! By Durgin-family standards (the ones I'd been operating under for twenty years), I was a roaring success. I was a Homestead golden boy. But I couldn't quite silence the suspicion that Joe and Mary Durgin were not my standard-bearers. I may have lapped the Homestead pack, but I was still choking on the dust laid down by Janet Bunn. And later with Rachel? That's what this report is all about, isn't it? That gap of talent and imagination and intelligence and taste and decency—or is it just a matter of class?

Meanwhile, I'm still at Lovett, in the spring of my junior year. The new decade is crashing around us. It's the sixties. A little later, in the fall of my senior year, the Pirates won the Series on Bill Mazeroski's incredible home run. After that, Kennedy won the election. Sex in the White House. Peace Corps or graduate school for guys like me. My decade was coming up. Every day in the bright spring of 1960 seemed precious and portentous.

In the spring of my junior year, Janet and I and some of her friends in the Art Department decided on a prank.

More than a prank, less than a protest; we conceived it as political theater with a cause in mind. Dawning on me finally was the shape of an idea: sexual hypocrisy, not the idiot fraternity system, kept us mediocre. Anything we could do to weaken the palsied Baptist grip was a blow for freedom, just like the sit-ins going on all around us.

(Stupid politics gets the opposition it deserves.)

A freshman girl had been expelled for returning late to Ramsey Hall. She had no excuse, meaning she had not bothered to concoct one. She merely stated she'd been out with her boyfriend and they'd lost track of time. She forced them to expel her.

The girls at Garnett were incensed. Janet saw the enemy clearly—he was just outside our windows. Gideon Ramsey, Hosea Blodgett: the marble sentries implanted outside the cognate dorms. For years, bolder girls had crammed cigarettes and tampon tubes into those hollow mouths, but the effect had been merely impudent, when not fatally cute. Lovett in the fifties could go no further.

We went out and measured the thigh bone of the seated Gideon Ramsey. Then we measured mine. He would be eight feet tall. Then we measured my humble organ at its most expectant, added a couple of inches for effect, and determined that Gideon's heroic member should wave some fourteen super-Baptist inches in the breeze.

Around three o'clock in the morning in delicate May, three girls and I sneaked down to the pot shop and extracted a massive terra-cotta penis with a sharp iron screw protruding from the bottom. I drilled through the Bible while the girls stood guard around me, and screwed the heavy organ into Ramsey's lap, there to sprout through the opened Bible and to erupt from the top of his clenched, massaging fist.

Tacky in retrospect, but at the time the most ambitious undertaking of my short creative life.

I spent the rest of my life's shortest night with Janet, and we couldn't stop giggling at the perfection of the scheme and its carrying off. By the dawn's early light, Gideon could be hailed proudly whipping his massive boar hawg with the fevered intensity of a deviant half-wit. Gobs of cloudy glaze streamed down its sides. I'd wanted to wake all the girls in the lower campus, to shout, to sing, to break windows and present myself as their avenger, their liberator. Oh, it would be a glorious decade if this was the way it was going to start!

Chapter Thirteen

Just tying up the loose ends, Rosie.

Wasn't it Vonnegut who said that being fifty means learning the world is run by guys you went to high school with? Well, guys from my high school don't run a thing in this world, but you can get a preview—ten years early—of what guys I went to college with are doing.

You probably wondered if Malcolm Roudebush, he of the freshman-year debacle, could possibly be Senator Chip Roudebush of Kentucky, aspirant to anything going. Same guy. Same scourge of the campus. No personality change or face lift, either.

By our senior year he'd mastered a winning line of logic. "Who profits?" he'd ask. A rejection from a girl launched him on a twisted course of reasoning. "She turned me down, Durgin! Who profits from this rejection? Surely, not her. Not me. Obviously, other men who are attracted to her. Why did they put her up to it? What inducements did they offer?" For failing papers, the same logic applied. "Why would he want me to fail? What possible advantage is there? My paper obviously challenged him in a frightening new way. But, Durgin, tell me, who stands to gain from my failure?"

And he usually had an answer.

It wasn't until his senior year that he saw a way of converting his defensive reaction into an offensive weapon. I was present at the inception.

For all his tweedy clothes and pipe bowls peeking out of his pockets, Malcolm was still an innocent. Daily rejection was his habitat. Maybe even his camouflage. He reminded me of a chimpanzee puzzling over a watch; he could hear people ticking but he didn't have the slightest idea of how they worked. Half the time I wanted to say, "Malcolm, face the fact that you're both obnoxious and stupid." Other times, I felt for him. I could almost believe there was a core of decency about to surface.

Which brings us back to that fabulous spring of our junior year, and the launching of Malcolm Roudebush. It was pure applied research. First, he had consulted his father's Yale *Alumni Magazine* and found that an inordinate number of otherwise mature professionals were called Chip. It was an identity he had to have.

"God knows we've had our differences, Durgin," he said to me in that booming, press-conference voice one May morning shortly after the infamous and still anonymous Penis Caper. I was visiting the old fraternity house, where I was still headwaiter. "But I've always defended you."

It was, and is, his special genius to flatter his detractors by an act of simple inflation. Enemies, indeed. Revulsion elevated to principle, even policy, to be analyzed by his special line of thinking. Defended me? Against whom? For what?

And yet, unbearable as it was to be with him, I started missing him the moment the pipe fumes parted. He was neither creative nor eccentric in any self-conscious way (and he was not higher than the Lovett male norm in intelligence), but what he was, I think, is brave. I know no one who has withstood so much derision, so many insults, mean-spirited and spiteful attacks, and survived under them. (Except for me, and he has survived at a considerably higher level.) Five minutes with Malcolm and you wanted to throttle him; eight hours later (if you were me, discussing it with Janet down in Garnett Place) you were laughing about it, and even wishing you had guts enough to invite him down to share a bite. And you realize you'd be crazy to do it. He'd ruin your meal, your reputation, your evening, and you'd never be allowed back, even in Garnett.

He was carrying a nine-by-twelve glossy wrapped in tissue paper. It was a familiar Roudebush pose: chin in palm, one finger grazing a cheek, pipe in mouth, a pose for Karsh or Bachrach. He looked twice his age. "We decided to commission a portrait, Durgin." Always the plural; the natural committeeman, with regal aspirations.

"It catches your suave insouciance, Mal," said I.

He frowned, both at the name, which he despised, and at the word, which he probably didn't understand.

"Chip Roudebush is not a vintage wine, you dolt. The name must convey warmth and approachability, to go along with strength and character."

"Not to mention bulldog integrity?"

"Precisely, my good fellow."

"Chip Roudebush?"

"Exquisite, isn't it? I tired of E. Malcolm Roudebush in prep school, and Ed is far too common. I considered holding the 'Ward,' however." He looked a little perplexed, maybe even lost. "You have a certain talent in these things, Durgin. What's your opinion?"

He'd never asked anyone's advice; he must have been terribly lost.

"What the hell are you talking about?" I asked.

"The presidency, of course."

"The Club presidency? Are you out of your mind? The brothers despise you. I'm your only friend, and I can't even stand you. Why do you think we sent you to Lexington for all of Rush Week? Hasn't it sunk in yet?"

"Durgin, Durgin, poor simple Durgin. Of course I'm aware of differences within this organization. That's why I'm talking of the Lovett presidency. I expect the dear brotherhood will search their hearts and find sufficient reason to support me unanimously for the campus presidency. And I'm appointing you, Richard Durgin, with your special gifts, to write up my bio and my platform. We're simply going to change this college. Make it good, and make it snappy—it's due at the paper tomorrow. I was so busy with the portrait it slipped my mind."

And so it came to pass that "Chip" Roudebush, the most detested, shunned, and ridiculed presence on campus, threw his porkpie hat into the ring. He did not quite radiate the common touch, nor did he need to. The Betas and Phi Gams nominated their most egregiously well-groomed alcoholics; the SAEs countered with an unbeatable Brendan McIvor, the DUs with a twitchy Phi Beta who (as of my last issue of the Lovett *Alumni Journal*, the only link to the past that still reaches me here) is at this very moment serving his class interests in Washington, wreaking his revenge on the twentieth century.

Malcolm noted that the opposition would cancel one another out. Fraternities voted like bitter ethnicities, supporting their own when possible, and hurting, when possible, their nearest rival. If the Betas copped the presidency, along with the captaincies of the major sports, or if the Phi Gams took it along with all their T-Birds and party bona fides, then they'd also skim the cream of next year's pledges. The idea of LSC ever running a candidate was so preposterous that the fact of it being Roudebush was swept aside. Even with a president in its midst, we would still scrape the bottom.

Who profits? Chip Roudebush, that's who.

Roudebush would win, the same way our only black coed took the Homecoming queenship. He may have lost other elections along the way, but his victory at Lovett was prototypical. From what I've read, his success in the Kentucky House, the Congress, and now the Senate (and who knows . . . ?) is due to an innate capacity to divide the opposition. His "formidable brilliance" melts away under his "southern graciousness," in the words of *Time*.

I read last year that he'd married his college sweetheart. This interested me, since I knew he'd never been permitted to date at Lovett—even as campus president. The story went that, sometime in the late sixties, he'd been holding hearings on an education bill in the Kentucky House. A lobbyist from a liberal reform movement testified so movingly before his committee (calling him an arrogant, scheming, posturing son of a bitch in the process) that he'd invited her to become his principal secretary and, later, his chief of staff. This earned Roudebush high marks from the women's movement, despite his voting record.

That was in 1969, and such things were possible. It's taken me a long time to catch up with the post-Lovett careers of my two favorite people, Malcolm Roudebush and Janet Bunn.

And what of me? Fully a million like me in the spring of 1961, when I graduated; several thousand just like me in their ambition to create some permanent monument to their own uniqueness—in language, film, or welded iron.

In the fall of my senior year I heard about the Writers' Workshop at Iowa, and I applied. Again, I would need a scholarship, and again, I didn't get it. To fail at a scholarship meant the Peace Corps. Even an acceptance minus scholarship was slow in coming. Iowa seemed as necessary to me now as Lovett had been, coming out of Pittsburgh. Then *Atlantic* announced "The Birth of the Blues" as the winning undergraduate story in their national competition. Oh, what a mellow year it was! Straight A's at last, Janet's company, wine and cheese in a grove of trees we'd discovered, Malcolm's effective presidency (he pushed the fraternities on liberalizing their exclusion clauses), a healthy and normal-looking pledge class, and four hundred and fifty dollars in one check for a story! After that, the scholarship to Iowa. Lovett had never known such a success, outside of a few spectacularly endowed actresses like Debbie Warner, who leaped from Lovettville to Broadway, then Hollywood within a year or two of graduation.

"I'm very happy for you, Richie," said Janet as we walked down the slope, headed for our private *Weinstube* under the sycamores below the old Humanities parking lot. Beware when anyone expresses her happiness for you. "You'll like Iowa, I'm sure."

"We'll like Iowa," I emphasized. The scholarship seemed generous, the tuition low, and she'd been admitted to the graduate school in Philosophy. But I could see it coming.

"Richie . . ." She looked down at her sandals; she refused the wine. "I know we've talked about Iowa. But it was so unreal back then. I should have told you a long time ago, but I don't want—"

"Don't want what?"

"To go, that's all. I don't want anyone making plans for me."

I probably snickered. That's what men did, make plans. Where in the world would anyone want to go but Iowa? With me? That's what girl friends did, went where their lovers told them.

"Don't want to go to Iowa, or don't want to go anywhere . . . with me?"

"Don't make it hard for me, Richie, please. I don't want to go to Iowa, definitely. Or anywhere, right now . . . with you, I guess. Or anyone, really." She brightened just a little at the end.

"I'll marry you," I bargained. That's what people like me did. If they escaped marriage at high school graduation, they certainly went through with it after college.

"Richie—don't you hear what I'm saying?"

"What did I do?"

"Oh, God, it's nothing to do with you. We have beautiful memories; don't spoil them, okay? They're only memories. I can't take anything out of this place, don't you see? That was Lovett, and Lovett's not the world. And neither is Iowa City, Iowa. Sitting around taking courses while you become a famous writer isn't my idea of the world, either."

I pulled on her hand and we sat, staring out through the trees to the open football field, the bright cars depatterning from the fraternity parking lots far below. She accepted my wine; we even killed a bottle.

"You're lucky," she said. "You hold on to things. Lovett gave you something. You know what you want."

I stopped myself from saying, approximately, "But I want you. I want to hold on to you." If the truth were told, I wasn't hurt at all. I had trouble maintaining the mournful, bitter-swain facade over the liberated lonesome traveler within. Wolfe hadn't married. Neither (I thought) had Kerouac, my favorites at the time. My two halves had been warring: the loyal, early marrier, the grim wage earner and competent handy man with his solid, frumpy mate-for-life—that half against the mutant: the fatherless and practically motherless self-made writing messiah, the male version of Debbie Warner.

"I'm not all that lucky," I said. "But I understand." A courageous, Cyranolike moment, I felt.

"David called me last week. I can tell you now."

"David?"

"David Frye. He's left his wife. He's gotten a Fulbright to Florence, and he wants me with him." She opened her purse and showed me tickets on the Italian-American line.

"David, the fired instructor," I said.

"I should have told you everything. He has never been entirely out of the picture."

"Those mysterious weekend visits home. The painter in the picture."

A sigh, a giggle borne on the breeze, a squeeze of my hand, and Janet was gone. In two weeks, so was Lovett. In six years, even the Social Club, my passion, and my agony would disappear. A very American story: clip the wings, and the center holds, all too well.

An era passed. The next two generations of Lovett students arrived from high school with radical ideas, pot on their breath, pills in their purses, and fully formed social and political ideas. The Social Club, still appealing to the inept and unlovely in a time of radicalization, became more openly deviant. Sometime in the winter of 1969, when the country, the world, and even Richard Durgin, a recent widower, were concerned with bare survival, local police raided my old Kentucky home where Jon had rhapsodized over the crack of Don, to find the bathhouse atmosphere so totally degenerate that the house was taken over by the college and converted to its new alumni center.

I'd thought my last contact with that formative experience had been cut. I'd be wrong about that, too. In the leisurely, mocking ways of fate, I'd be brought back to Lovett fifteen years after graduation in order to be slingshot one last time, out here to the opposite side of the world, and back to the oldest profession I knew.

I like to think that sometime that summer, while I put in my last stint as a Carleton House bellhop in Pittsburgh, two young American women and their two older artist-lovers, one Italian and one American, might have brushed shoulders in the Uffizi, on a *terrazzo* in Florence, or perhaps even on a terrace in Paris. The world has become too small for me. I'm just the guy who got caught in their headlights like some lumbering forest rodent; one of them already enshrined as a literary immortal, the other on her way to plotting first ladyship of the land. For some incomprehensible reason, I wasn't wrong to have fought for Lovett, to have held out for it. Just look at what it gave me, before things started to be taken away.

Rosie, I must describe one more thing. I am writing this on the old, betel-juice-stained steps outside the barred windows of the village post office.

As I walked this morning down from my house to the post office to mail off this package of Lovett memories, a strange thing happened. I cut across the cricket pitch and over the open field where the buzzards didn't bother to move (this morning there was a dead dog to occupy them), then walked along the wall, taking my tea, buying my morning *Times of India*, then scuttling through the old village gates by the clay mosque. It's Friday, the Muslim sabbath. The village roads are unpaved. There's no electricity. It's May, hot and dusty, and the monsoons are still a month away. The carrots are as red as strawberries, and the potatoes this year are sweet enough to eat for dessert. And the mangoes are at their firmest and juiciest, heaped in the bazaar and ready for me on my walk back. Dev loves them, and they are for me now the staff of life.

As I was walking here with these bundled pages, a young man approached me, speaking adequate English. Not many in this village speak English.

"Sa'ab, come see my factory," he said. In this country, unlike in America, I always say yes. I run my life these days as though I had been assured by an unimpeachable mystical source that I will live till eighty-one and that I need fear nothing. He is a man my age, in a peon's khaki uniform, smoking a hand-rolled biri. He takes me two alleys over, to a courtyard with peacocks and cattle. There are no lights, no fans, and once inside, my eyes start watering in the half-light. But there is the smell of fabric—a common smell in India; the smell of export earnings—and a quiet hum of pedal-fed machinery.

"See sa'ab, all for export. Here for America. Here is for Holland. Here is for Germany. Here is for Italy."

My eyes are adjusting now, and he shows me several light canvas jackets. I can see a row of village girls and women, all daring now to turn and smile at me. Next to each machine is a tall stack of round badges. On the floor next to each girl is a box of blue canvas jackets, children's sizes. I am holding some small boys' jackets. They are decorated with official baseball insignias: New York Mets, Houston Astros, Dodgers—names I have not thought of in five years. Other jackets are being sewed with European soccer badges, with washing instructions in the proper languages. The women are rocking with laughter, and the man is giggling at my obvious stupefaction.

"What you think, sa'ab? Good, aye? Good job. You have a small *baba*, I am knowing. Please take this for him, my compliments."

And so, Rosie, my eyes seal to tiny slits back outside and I tell my benefactor that it's the smell of the waterproofing chemicals and the change of light, but I am crying. Crying and laughing, and smiling my way back to the post office, where this package is properly sealed and waxed. It's the biggest package the old man has handled this month; some unemployed men come over to watch and offer advice on the ways to squeeze more stamps on the cover.

"Chang," the man says, "you are writing to cheena-man?"

"Cheena-lady," I say, "in California."

They pass the package around the office so that all can say they have touched an object destined for America.

Treat this accordingly, Rosie Chang.

THREE

Chapter Fourteen

Berkeley, California
July 20, 1982

Dear Richard:

Your letter written from the post-office steps came before the much-handled bundle of pages. In fact, I had a week of wondering what kind of miraculous package I was about to receive. I pictured baseball badges and mango juice and even the dried, dusty tears of the author.

What I got was a surprise. I'd expected news of the marriage; I got instead a novel-despite-itself. Lovett's not as dead in you as you thought, and if the marriage is anywhere nearly as detailed, I may have to rewrite my whole book.

I've taken advantage of the past two months, doing more research, as you suggested, with the Italian connection, with Carla Goodings (who sends her love), even with Maxine Rosenbluth (the old Iowa roommate, prior to your arrival), who doesn't quite confirm the absence of boyfriends in Rachel's life during her first year at Iowa (your rambunctious senior year at Lovett). Sorry. There was a persistent Italian hydraulics student named Mario. There was, inevitably, a professor. (You're right, of course, about the true predators in any university situation.) And she did write more poetry than she perhaps ever showed to you. Because of all the Italian she was studying, she wrote a series of poems (never published, though I am editing a volume for U/Cal Press) in the voice of Beatrice. Beatrice answers Dante in the same *terza rima* as the *Divine Comedy*. She fears her unworthiness of his great love. They are "immature Isaacs" only because they have not yet articulated her final theme. For anyone else, they would be a crowning achievement.

Richie, I want to speak very honestly to you, because I can still read the bitterness in your book (if that's what it is). I'll never know Rachel the way you knew her. I saw her only at that poetry reading in Berkeley in 1968, and it screwed up my head for five years. I even begged my father to let me go to China to serve my people, and learn my heritage before it was too late. I could read the headline: BERKELEY GIRL BECOMES RED GUARD! Anyway, it doesn't help to translate other people's obsessions into your own terms, especially when they're writing poems and you're a cloud-headed architecture student, glowing with Maoism and Hermann Hesse.

This is what I want to say—she loved you. Did you know that, or have you forgotten it in order to get on with your life? Believe me when I say that in my own way I know her, and she's very much alive for me too. I can understand your fear of entering that last stage of her life. I've read of biographers who break down when they write of their subject's passing. The last thing in the Isaacs papers is a letter to her mother saying she won't be able to come out to California, citing the pressure of finishing a book. (Poems, stories? She doesn't say.) The last manuscript is of a poem, untitled, unfinished. It's as though she put down her pen to go wash her hair or something, and never came back. I can understand your waiting. I want to knock on that bathroom door and say, "Will you be much longer, Rachel?" And there are comforting noises coming from the tub.

I think you are excessively hard on yourself. You seem to remember nearly all of Rachel's insults, and all her skepticism over your work and background. But there are other letters, and there are journal entries that I would like to share with you. I wish you were here so that I could show them to you. She loved you, if she loved anyone. She doubted her ability to love (whom the gods bless with wit and facility, they deny great passion), and I think you've overlooked a dimension of her work that I find deeply moving. It is not her imagination of the void or of the horrors of the twentieth century. Those qualities are there, and they will of course stand. What I see is that more of her letters and journals and drafts of poems are directed to you, Richard Durgin, than to the murdered hordes of European Jews. They are love poems, in a curious and unique way. To her, you were a force of pure, miraculous ego. She'd never seen the naked ego struggle in the world before, and she appropriated your struggle (as she saw it) as an allegory of modern resistance. From innocence, she felt, would grow resistance.

I have some other things here—questions, mostly, and if you don't answer them in your sweet-and-sour way, I'll get around to asking them directly. If you do, I won't even tell you what they were.

The researching impulse never lets up. I inquired about your second marriage, and got nowhere. Are you sure (asks the biographer stupidly) you were married three times, and not just twice? There was a research librarian at Lovett five years ago, when you were invited back as writer-in-residence. Her name was Leela Mehta. You mentioned in passing that you have buried two wives—does this mean you are living with your and Leela's son in her former village? And that you are living, otherwise, alone?

I think of you as part of my life, Richie, and I am profoundly sorry, if that's an adequate word. If there's anything you need from me to help you with your writing —any dates, names, laundry lists, or rent receipts—please let me send them to you.

Love,

Rosie

P.S. I can't resist telling you that Senator Malcolm Roudebush was divorced last year and that his ex-wife has made a name for herself as a feminist journalist covering the Washington underworld. I'll send you a copy of her latest broadside under separate cover. I feel that I know her, too. This part is fun.

Dear Rosie:

We've named this Rosie Chang Appreciation Day in Faridpur. I thank you for the support, though in many ways the worst thing you could tell me is that she loved me. As you suspected, it is easier to deal with things the way I've recreated them. I think of Leela's love for me, and of my total involvement with Rachel, and her amused tolerance in return. Things are a whole lot neater that way.

The name of her last poem was going to be "Sauterne."

We talked about it before she took her final bath. She saw herself as a cooking wine, something to be boiled away and lost in a broth. "I too have traded flavors." A husband can tell, somewhere in his apartment, when his wife is making love, or when she's deep in a poem, but apparently not when she's opening her veins.

Okay, here's my Deep Philosophical Commentary:

We plan our lives along gentle curves, and I guess that's the safest way of anticipating the unknown. But our lives are really a series of breaks, falls, bubbles, and crashes. Life refuses to assume a predictable shape. Nothing in my life prepared me for this—"Ajanta Woodworking" and speaking more Hindi than English, watching my admirably dark and handsome son practicing his cricket, yet somehow I have to accept it, intellectually as well as spiritually. If I had a way of doing that—encompassing a vision that large and finding a form to hold it—I might start writing again. I left Lovett free and hopeful in June of 1961, and it's not so much my day-to-day diminishment (graying, balding, sagging) as it has been a series of sharp, sudden, unforeseen breaks that brought me here. What is the art—what is the name—for such a contingency?

When I think of the stuff I've sent you so far, it has a shape. It's neat and predictable. I still could have turned out "all right." I could have "matured" and "fulfilled my promise," as they liked to say back in the fifties. I'm about to go through the shocks all over again, and I don't know how to frame them, or even prepare you (let alone me) for the things that happened. Imposing shape on chaos is your job. There's a character in one of Rachel's stories—her first story (one which you haven't read, since I have it here)—who reflects on the science of biography. He calls it "the pathetic encumbrance of our divine particularity."

It's terrifying to think that if I am to exist at all, it will only be in your version of Rachel's life. One voice in me says, "Does that really matter?" That's the voice from here on the deserts of India, the answer of the wind blowing over billions of anonymous bones and heaps of trash and the broken walls of the lame emperor, now housing the tea-stalls and tire patchers, framed by a small grove of gul-mohar trees where the Sikh taxi drivers sleep and cool their engines—you understand?

But an older voice (for me, at least), the one that accounts for all the misery and the only real pleasures I've known in my life—the voice of the stag in the fog—says, "Well, yes, dammit, it does matter." It matters more than anyone's "life," because she's dead and I'm not. Even though it's an act as aggressive as rape to inflict myself on her readership, I'm still here, and her story has to include mine, no matter what it does to the shape of her life.

Carl Sagan wrote (in a book I picked up in New Delhi last year; I still read, Rosie) that we'll know our universe is collapsing when effects start preceding causes. A biography before the subject's birth. Criticism before poetry. A peace conference before the war! We'd be living in a world of scholarship, before creativity. And I think sometimes of the price I used to pay (and pay in a different way now) for living in a world of time, rather than space. Have you thought, Rosie, that it's not space, it's time that separates us now? You live in a world of communications, ribbons of interstate, jet travel, long distance. It takes me three days and a month of planning to get from here to Delhi, two hundred miles away. I think of Delhi as two thousand miles. I have no phone, see no movies, read a paper once a week, and can't tell you who won the Series last year. I live entirely in space now, with time out for an occasional book, but I'm losing that kind of intelligence. I've returned to a kind of timeless space. The urgency to conquer time has left me. When things collapse around me now, it's not the time-space continuum; it's just Tamerlane's wall.

I thank you for the love at the end of your letter. It stirs me more than anything else you could send.

Yours,

Richie

Chapter Fifteen

I am thinking of the hands of workingmen. All the clusters of scabs, of nicks and slashes, the untended sores, the cracks deep with grease and stains.

Cuts, scratches, scars. Like boxers, they don't notice the pain, can't locate the source of specific injuries, and are unastonished by the violent toll their wages take. Like boxers, they bear no grudges, except to promoters and managers—never to opponents. My father's and my uncle's hands were the real meat-hooks of legend, slabs of amorphous, hairy bone, fat, and muscle, with five squashed, spreading, prehensile stubs of thickened scar tissue, tipped with pinched, ridged, pruned yellow nails.

When I was younger, despite my inelegant body, my hands were slim, the fingers long, and the nails overhung the fingertips. As a child I used to think of my fingernails as landing strips of an aircraft carrier, and the blunted fingertips as waves plowed back. No matter how dissolute my life had been, my hands resisted the conversion into slabs of violent labor.

And now? Well, I recognize the stains, spreading through the road map of my palms. And the splinters of the soft, hand-planed wood have left shadows and little submarines under the surface, where they ride the festering swells of pus trying to float them out. The tale of the splinter is the story of Richard Durgin and Rachel Isaacs, too. I look at my hands today and I'm ready to begin the strange story you've waited so long to hear. I will write all day and evening, just as I once did at Lovett, and by morning I will again have Rachel and Richard together in his bed—how's that for a promise? (The day is long, it being a Hindu holiday. The rains have come, and everyone is a little feverish. The mangoes are no longer edible, and the cricket pitch is awash in red waters. Fishermen are netting where the trash heaps had been, pigs are safe for another three months.)

I want to set the scene in Iowa in the months before I met Rachel. You'll recognize the names, of course—most of my classmates in the Writers' Workshop have gone on to establish their names in American letters.

I was living in an uninsulated garage, stoking a dentist's furnace and clearing his drive. Living on pure adrenaline, ambition, and cans of spaghetti (the cold green walls were streaked with congealed tomato sauce, just behind my hot plate). I was writing every day, reading a new book every day, devouring stories, giving opinions, finding a community of souls (despite rampant jealousy and envy) as innocent and as hungry for expression as my own. A thick manuscript, one of the dozens of the early versions of my first novel, was always with me in its binder inside a Harvard book bag. My old *Atlantic* publication stood up well, though it had been over a year and nothing new had followed (no one told me that an opened door could be slammed in your face). Most of my friends, despite better education in the East, and wilder adventures, were slightly older, married, and still unpublished. Many had seen military service.

The Writers' Workshop drew from the dominant pools of American talent: from eastern Jews and Southerners, New York and Vanderbilt, with Chicago and Berkeley, Texas and North Carolina forming natural satellites. The groups were mutually antagonistic. "What the fuck is this guy saying?" my friend Larry Goodman would ask, in those freewheeling discussions of sensitive, recollective, Mississippi-childhood stories. "The world's going to end because some spade kid knocked on the front door? You shitting me, or what?"

"Well, ol' son," drawled amiable Ben Lewis, an all-too-recent defensive end with the Crimson Tide, "I don't rightly locate where your hostility is coming from. You fail to see this story rests on a deep historical tragedy."

"You fail to see this rests under a toilet seat."

"Ol' son, you don't want to rile me up now, do you?"

Whereupon the class would divide, approximately, into blues and grays, urbans and rurals, radicals and reactionaries (with liberals afraid to speak), and, as our softball teams later enshrined it, Jews and White People.

Those were the vivid encounters. But now I remember the others, the eccentrics, those without a community. There were some foreign-born American writers, somewhat older, somewhat detached. They'd come to English after two or three other languages; they'd come to America after wars and internments; they'd come to writing after military service, engineering, diplomacy, law, journalism or medicine; and they'd come to Iowa and marriage to young midwestern girls after lost years in port cities and resettlement in New York, after marriages to silent, frightened women who'd died, or left them in the Old World, or whom they had abandoned over here. And still, they were only thirty or so. There was a Polish-born

Israeli, a Swede, a South American, and a Korean. There
were always a few Canadians and one or two Englishmen.
They rarely took part in discussions, and when their stories appeared on the worksheets, the general response
would be respectful and a little frightened. Their work
was so pure, so mature. They were more than literary;
they were Literature. We would court their criticism for
our own stories, but they rarely volunteered it. And when
they did, we couldn't use it. But I remember those con-
frontations to this day.

You realize, of course, I'm describing my own house
critic, Rachel, though she wasn't ever a part of this scene.

Let's call him Pavel. Or even Paul. He was the Israeli by
way of Poland and Russia and Argentina, then Brandeis.
He was an engineer, but he'd also been a fighter pilot. He
was probably in his late twenties, graying, wiry hair, and a
stubby body that suggested quick hands, desert warfare,
and soccer fields. Eyes that told you he'd survived being a
Jew in Nazi Europe, an Israeli, an exile and an immigrant.

If called on, Paul would respond, "Yes, it is a nice
story."

"What do you mean, 'nice'?" the teacher asked. My
teacher was Philip Roth, only twenty-eight that year, himself a presence.

"I mean, Mr. Roth, they are likable people. Yes, I like
them. They are nice people with nice problems. I wish
them happiness."

"Is something wrong with happiness?"

They were playing a game. I knew it, the author knew
it. We could only wait till the cards were dealt, the pot
called.

"Oh, perhaps I might wonder why such a charming
young lady is so unhappy in this story. I may wonder why
these young people are all so sad. I think maybe I am so
stupid I have missed something—I am slow in under-

standing, you know. So I read again, but still they are eating, they are healthy. He has a job, they have a nice apartment and a car. But she is crying at the end. And he has
threatened to leave her. All of this is very mysterious to
me."

"Don't people have a right to cry? Don't people leave
one another all the time?"

"Yes, they do that. Every minute of every day someone
is leaving someone else and someone is crying. It is all very
sad, I am sure."

"So it's a realistic story, right?"

"Oh yes. Very realistic. Perhaps, however, I am not the
best reader for it."

By now the author, protected by anonymity, would be
shitting bricks.

"Yes, I am a poor reader. That is the reason I don't
speak out—people would only laugh at my ideas. All I can
say is that this story, and the story last week about young
men trying to lure a young woman into their car for sex, is
very well written and amusing, but—" And he would be
holding his copy of the story slightly above his desk top,
holding it delicately by the fingertips the way European
intellectuals sometimes held their cigarettes, and he would
let it drop. "I don't think it is very . . . important, perhaps?"

"Bruise or Amuse, that it?"

"Oh, I have quite enough bruises, please. All I want is,
perhaps, that it speak quietly to me, one intelligent person
to another, about what matters and about what lasts. This
—I am sorry . . ."

Though I was writing consciously for my friends (and,
for the most part, earning their praise), and though we all
exempted the various foreigners from really having anything to say to us (like gays, women, and exotic minorities,
they were thought to have a corner on closed markets, to

be praised, and discounted), I was a frightened young man. We were all frightened. None of us knew if we were any good at all. All it took was a Roth, a Paul, or one of the women or one of the Ivy Leaguers (not very good writers, but unforgiving critics) to say "So what?" to one of our stories, and we would die. If Rachel had been in the Workshop, and if she'd said of my novel, "Undescended-testicle stuff," I'm sure I would never have finished it. We wanted criticism to concentrate on form and language, to suggest cuts and splices. If comments were to lapse from the purely technical, we wanted them to be political or psychological. Moral criticism left me squeamish.

But there was no place precisely for me. My New York friends may have shared with me a working-class child-hood and uneducated parents and may have been, like me, the first of their family to finish high school and seek any-thing higher than a secure place in the municipal civil ser-vice, but they had come out of something grander, they reached toward something, and they had models to follow.

They had New York to write about. They had frequent and superheated sex with Puerto Rican and Italian girls to write about. They had their guilt and their mothers to write about. They had history and a remembered language behind them, they had the urgency of the Holocaust to spur them, and they had the better part of a community still left to understand them. They had been inoculated. What I had was the bitterness of lost possibility. I had class consciousness without politics. I was aggrieved. I was lum-pen.

(Much later, I saw precisely who I was, and it shook me. You remember *Portnoy's Complaint?* You remember "the Monkey"—the Appalachian sex maniac? You re-member all the hot broads in all the other New York novels and stories, and the evocation of their steamy, dirty, piggish-Catholic sluttiness? That's who I was! If I'd been female, that's exactly what I'd be. Good for only one thing. But there was no one in the Workshop to take the side of all those Carmens and Bubbles and Ginas and Betty-Lous, to show that they were just as consumed with curiosity, just as hungry for respectability and recognition as my friend Larry Goodman had been. Wanda Lusiak and me—what specks of lostness we were!)

Everyone else seemed to have a corner on sensitivity. When you are the first of your people to come close even to articulating it, it's hard not to look like a fool. Or appear sentimental. I tried a follow-up to my *Atlantic* story with another "Keeler" tale, this one incorporating the death of my father and the moment at Pitt when the room started spinning—and the workshop clobbered it. Paul the Israeli liked it, but it was frankly unbelievable that a boy like me should entertain such fine feelings; a spinning Pitt had become a giant pathetic fallacy.

I conceived a strong desire for a Jewish girl friend. All of my Jewish friends had small-town hash-slinger wives; there must be a pool of bright, cultured, witty, Jewish women waiting for a bohunk to cherish. I kept my eyes open.

Anyway, that's how Iowa did its teaching. It can be assumed that each of us was the best writer his blighted campus had ever seen. And except for a few precocious freaks whose careers are documented, we weren't really that good at all. At Lovett in my senior year I'd thought myself among the immortals; a year later at Iowa I was so ashamed of my work I disowned it. Thank God our names never appeared on the worksheets. "Wasn't that a Pittsburgh story?" Goodman asked me. "Aren't you from Pittsburgh? So wasn't that your story we did last week?" "That piece of shit?" I defended myself. "You actually think I could write something like that? Thanks a lot."

Here's how Iowa taught me to write:

I would read my drafts aloud in Paul's slightly accented voice. "Yes, very nice. But does it matter?" And I would read it in Goodman's biker-snarl: "What's this guy trying to say?" I'd throw a few "oh yeahs?" at the end of my sentences, and then some crushing "so whats?" And when the story seemed tight enough, when I could answer back, "Yeah!" I'd try a new tack, a quivering countertenor at the point of breakdown crying out before each sentence, "Oh, Doctor, I just can't tell you how—" to cut down on pleading, on self-serving. I'd go down the list of usual criticisms: Is it jerking off? Is it sentimental? Is it boring? Does it stack the deck? What are its politics? Its psychology? Its importance? Does it bruise, does it amuse? What have I shown that has never been shown, what have I told that has never been told?

Nothing? Scrap it!

A year later, a dozen stories were out in the mail, and when one came back, new envelopes were already addressed. It was a marvelous time, that second year in the workshop. I was teaching a freshman literature course. I was still shoveling the dentist's walk, my rent was only ten dollars a week, I held fast to the same circle of friends, drinking from midnight till three every night, sleeping in, attending workshop classes and one Dante course in the English Department (we had to show some competence in academics; just look where that Dante course took me), reading the reviews and quarterlies in the library, and reading, as a solemn pledge, one new novel every day. The deepest shame imaginable was admitting "I haven't read it," or, worse, "Never heard of it."

The greatest pleasure (apart from tearing open a long white envelope with a university seal, requesting contributor's notes), lay in discovering new talent in obscure places. No story fell to earth in the English language between 1961 (fall) and 1963 (summer) without Richard

Durgin's collaring it first. The satisfaction lay in making improvement, in knowledge and technique, week after week, in finding new ways of freeing my childhood for stories. Rejections from *The New Yorker* got warmer and warmer. We like it, you're talented, but this isn't quite right for us. In those days, that was music.

By twenty-three, I projected, my novel would be finished. By twenty-four, published. Another by twenty-five; five before I was thirty. I'd retire from any teaching job. Live by the pen. The bravest and most avenging word in the English language was "free-lancer."

Sitting there in Iowa City in my dentist's cold garage, I would endlessly list my stories and their eventual destinations. I would title those novels and their dates of publications. (In high school, I'd done the same with baseball statistics. It was natural to me, part of planning the gentle curve of my entry into a Hall of Fame. Rachel caught me at it once. She saw it as nouveau riche, the whole notion of keeping tabs on one's writing-neighbors, checking up on every story, having a finger in every pie.) I had my titles plotted till my eightieth year. Just trying to be helpful to my eventual biographer. A rich and orderly life, like Thomas Mann's, led like a bourgeois, as Flaubert had advised, in an era of low mortgages.

I went to the library and read through the *Book Review Digest* one year at a time to learn contemporary reactions to every book that mattered in this century, in order to learn what Mann and Lawrence and Faulkner, and Lowry and Durrell and Kerouac had had to endure, just to prepare myself.

I breathed a world of fame, in short.

Are you still with me, is it all very touching—or disgusting? Is this what Rachel meant about the naked ego?

I'm describing book writing in America as I understood

it; the Iowa branch of the fame factory. A continuous circle of literature, snake swallowing its tail, all of us desperately knocking on the same doors, pissing on the corners of the same territory.

(Something just occurred to me, Rosie. I should be saying, "*Behold, Moloch!*" shouldn't I? I'm no different from Ben-Zvi—the man I've hated for over a dozen years. Are all my assumptions equally false—that he was a bitter, defeated, hateful little man who resented me for robbing him of Rachel? And that I was a hard-working, heroic, dedicated knight-errant who saved her from a lifetime of defensive withdrawal?

(No wonder we hated each other. We were the same person, Ben-Zvi and me, and we would have split Rachel right down the middle in our murderous possessiveness.)

I'm just days now, or maybe hours, from meeting Rachel.

Around midnight, the novel manuscript again put away in my green book bag, mind freshly crammed with the latest work from *Shenandoah* or the *Arizona Quarterly*, I'd head uphill to Kenney's Bar, where the writers hung out, and over pitchers of beer and schooners of popcorn, Goodman and Grossman and Newman and I ("the new, the good, and the gross," Roth had called them), would batter each other silly with opinions, with trivia, with judgments. We found all the soft spots in allegedly great stories. We were merciless, unforgiving, our shit-detectors were turned so high that even faulty syllables could set them off. "Bad rhythms, man, the sentences don't sing."

Chapter Sixteen

We have come to that night.

It was winter, that's all I remember, early in 1963. That night, I didn't reach Kenney's Bar. I'd spent my three hours reading stories and reviews as I always did, and I'd begun my long mosey through the library, toward the exit and up the hill to the bar. I had redeemed my day by writing—the binder was imperceptibly thicker. (We were convinced, back then, that missing a day of writing could take two weeks off your life.) I'd spent two hours reading Canadian stories from *Prism* and *Tamarack Review* and had added a new country and new gossip to my tangled shelf. I was full of names and up on the poetry wars in Vancouver and Toronto. Many contenders, all named Brian. I cannot think of those cities, even now, without pain.

At one of those long wooden tables I noticed a girl in a bulky gold "Hawkeye" sweatshirt, studying. Her hair was thick and black, pulled into braids. What caught my eye were the bright, white quadrants of her scalp, luminous bursts of skull-white that seemed almost painted on: let that stand as an intimation of something special in Rachel Isaacs. She was writing furiously (I was immediately jealous), lifting her pen only to shake it and to relax her fingers, since the ink could not come out fast enough.

(Incidentally, Rosie, I wonder if you might already know what she was writing that night. It stops me dead, when I think that you might be tracking this in your own patient, scholarly way. While I gaze at her scalp and make that one, final adjustment that will put me in her arms, you probably know precisely the word where her writing stopped—she is about to lose her pen, after all, so a change in ink will reveal it all. You are there, even at this intimate moment. And you're all of what? Ten? Twelve? It's all too amazing. The universe is collapsing.

(But can you do justice to her, no matter what else you know, without also picturing her in Indian braids, a Hawkeye sweater, and knowing that she could write faster than a typewriter, faster than ink could fly?)

Then I recognized who she was: "Rachele" (with a nifty Italian pronunciation) from my compulsory Dante course. She was the girl who knew Latin and Italian and everything else. She was the girl with the deadest-white skin I'd ever seen, the blackest eyes, and the shaded pouches underneath them that suggested late hours, vulnerability, danger. (Later, I learned, they were the outer signs of allergy. And the white skin, so easy to term consumptive and alabaster, was really the opposite: an extra layer of skin that blood vessels couldn't penetrate.) For an entire semester I'd assumed Rachele was Italian, with a perfect American accent. A sickly, brilliant Italian girl. A little off limits to me, since she seemed slightly taller. (When she put her tongue in my ear, she had to stoop.)

Taken individually, all her features were ample—nose, lips, large eyes, full bust, the gold earrings such as you see on small Hispanic girls in New York—but together they functioned in miniature. "A Japanese doll," some have

said, of dramatic features erupting from that page-white
skin. Maybe it was the hint of delicacy (even mortality),
along with her gracious European manners, the soft voice
that made you strain to listen, that led me, and others, to
think her smaller than she was. (She was a Rubens, with a
Modigliani face.) Then one day in class I'd seen her absentmindedly running a thin gold chain between her lips,
and she was holding the chain by a small Star of David.
The small fascination turned to wonder: an Italian Jew! (I
always carried that association, though it was entirely
false, but she belonged in *The Garden of the Finzi-Con-
tinis*, if anyone did.) I'd been afraid the world would run
out of Jewish girls before I found one. She always had an
otherworldly aspect, a face like an exceptionally clear
nineteenth-century photograph, a mysterious ancestor in a
family very different from my own.

So: she was a tall, lean girl with an ample bust, with the
face of other dark, gaunt women made sexy or at least interesting by Joan Baez and the early sixties. Her time had
not quite come. (She lived long enough to see herself mentioned as a "model of beauty"; I told you she had a reality
confusion, and that didn't help, believe me.) Her manner
was shy, a little ironic, and no one, so far as I knew, had
befriended her. She seemed to know nothing of contemporary American literature—the only test of true knowledge—and that attracted me. Since she knew everything
else, we were equal.

These were the final years of an innocent era, when studious, untraditionally attractive women could be assumed
to be living alone, waiting for marriage to men much like
them. But now, at midnight in the library, she seemed
dressed for bed, like a housewife who'd gotten up to let in
a repairman, still webbed and puffy in the face, body exud-
ing a clumsy warmth that was positively exciting. Maybe

she'd like a beer, I thought. Who could resist going to Kenney's with the real writers and listening to me carry on about Canadian writing? In my element, not hers.

I turned abruptly, brushing against Rachel's table in one long, forceful, sweeping stride (I was coming at her like Tarzan on a vine), and then I let out a stately yelp. Rachel jumped and I found myself bent double in pain that issued from no special place, a pain that had a specific shape and color, rather than origin or target. It was a sharp, purple pain, it made me think of ice picks and stilettos, the word "puncture"—the nastiest word I know—lodged itself in my brain. I took one step and her table lurched with me and the pain became excruciating—and localized—and for an instant, I saw a face I could love. Rachel Isaacs, the brilliant and aloof Dante scholar, ran to me, almost throwing herself on the table to take my arm.

She'd seen the source of my agony. I'd been thinking: My heart! How unfair, with my book unfinished, and only twenty-two.

I tried to move and found that I couldn't. A vast, lugubrious pin held me in place. My leg was numb. I thought: gunshot. A maniac in the stacks, one of those gun-toting southern boys— "I'm sorry I dumped on your story, Ben Lewis!" Purple arrows exploded from every nerve end. I moved and a shot rang out, just as Rachel enclosed me in her arms.

It was freakish, of course. There was no rifle, no ice pick, just old, dry library wood. The side of the table contained a flaw. One small snag, hardly enough to lift a thread, except in the thigh of an ardent lover. It had caught my trousers as I swept by and something devilish in the angle of the grain and the thrust of my step (the force of my desires, Rosie)—no diamond cutter could have split the grain so neatly—had sliced off a foot-long varnished dagger of birch into my thigh. It had pulled out from the table like a crude gate with my last step, and now, stupidly, I watched it for a second with a child's glee: Boy, wait'll they see the bandage on this baby! I'll have a scar! The first wave of pain subsided, I even giggled as I shivered, until the flow of bright-red blood spread from my shoe and alerted me to the fact that an artery was severed and I could bleed to death in the periodical room in the arms of a girl I'd been wanting to meet. I felt sick, but I couldn't move. Merely by drawing near me, Rachel had stained her khaki slacks dark brown. My leg was cold, numb, weak; I sagged, but was pinned in place by the weight of the world's longest splinter.

Standing, I passed out, then came to, with a ripping of cloth. She had pulled the arm off her raincoat and had tied the sleeve around my thigh and was tightening it with her pen. (She—whose family considered changing shoelaces an act of self-sufficiency!) Dozens of students clustered around, but in total silence. There was a puddle of blood under me now. I felt utterly calm and foolish and my heart was fluttering. Someone moved toward me and broke off the heavy chunk of splinter; the shock registered throughout my body, but now I could sag to the floor.

Rachel was kneeling in my blood, she could slide in it. Her Star of David dangled in my face, I could see down the cleavage of her Hawkeye sweater. A sweet final sight. "You're very kind, Rachel," I said.

There was serenity in bleeding to death. I must remember this, I thought. I thought of Washington's leeches, I thought of the kitchen puddle in my *Atlantic* story, I wondered idly when nail clippers had been invented— when would it be anachronistic to use them in a story? What's the origin of the word "raunchy"?—I must hobble over to the Unabridged and look it up. So many things to look up, so many things to know, like the fights between orthodoxies of poets in Toronto, or the New Perth poetry I'd been reading about in *Meanjin*, or race consciousness in the new Caribbean novel I'd read in *BiM*. I wondered how so many people could gather so quickly, and mouths, moving, remain so silent. Someone else cradled my head on his knee. I was probably paler than Rachel now.

And it occurred to the writer in me that being so unfocused, racing out to embrace an indiscriminate cosmos, this omniscient giddiness, was death. I'd lost a bucket of blood and the brain was emptying itself first, just turning in its chips. A femoral artery—I was proud of reaching out and grabbing a slippery word like that—had been sliced, and in a sudden arbitrary move, I'd snuffed out my thirty novels, my immortality, and I would die in a library younger than Keats! My dozen stories, I quickly assessed— nothing like imminent death to sharpen the critical faculties—weren't good enough for a . . .

Rachel broke her pen tightening the tourniquet; she was given two pencils. I saw my book bag with the binder inside, kicked from the blood to give her more room.

At Student Health that night there was an emergency operation. An amputation saw was used to cut the splinter back to skin level. I was given six pints of blood, and finally a fairly routine splinter, the driving tip with the sledgehammer force behind it, was partially extracted. Pieces of wood were inevitably lodged in the muscle, and a silver-dollar-sized hole would have to be kept open with hot saltwater compresses for a few days, until the fragments worked their way to the surface. "They're wood, after all, they'll float," said the doctor. I've never forgotten that mechanistic vision of the body, my body; it seemed to me one of those epic images that I'd paid for, but could never use till now.

"Good thing your wife was there," he said, winking at Rachel, who offered no resistance. "We can joke about it now, but it's one of those weird things that the medical books are full of. Save a patient, and lose an article, eh?" He showed Rachel how to make the saltwater, and I purposely turned away. You could say she was a hostage to my accident. That's how we met, and got more acquainted on our first date than any couple in modern history. I was on pain pills and a local anesthetic; I couldn't be counted on to look after myself. "Now we know who put the 'casual' in casualty," she said, smiling.

Rachel had a car and drove me back to my converted garage. She held me up as I walked. The place was its cold, usual mess. My chair was an ancient Goodwill armchair wide enough to sleep in (hence the bundled blankets in its seat) with arms wide enough to hold dirty mugs of coffee, bowls, a couple of paperbacks, and a few pages of recent writing. She suppressed a shudder. "I know," she said. "Maid's day off."

She put water on to boil. I had no salt. "I'll be back in half an hour. Stay warm," she said. I hadn't believed it until she showed up with a box of plates, a suitcase, books, and a small silo of salt. She put me to bed and said she'd stay the night. The narcotic effect of painkillers left the sexual issue unsettled. I woke every few minutes; I saw her studying and writing, then dozing, in my chair. It was a sign to me of the depth of kindness, not passion, that I'd drawn out of her. She was an angel. My novel was never found; probably the bloody thing was pitchforked into a dumpster.

Only one oddity kept running through my mind those first few hours together. Maybe it was the medication, maybe I was only half awake. I had raised my head and was studying the woman in my chair. Without looking my way, merely flipping a page of whatever she was reading, she asked, "You are circumcised, aren't you?"

Nothing is ever as automatic as it seems. One might assume an easy transition from Samaritan to lover when the course of a woman's duties takes her to a man's apartment, to the tending of his naked flank, and the sharing of his convalescent bed. We could easily have passed that first night and maybe the second as strange bedfellows and nothing else. She brought dash and orderliness to my life: bottles of dried oregano and basil, Chianti, various pastas and cheese sauces, all done on the double-burner hot plate. She ate white meats in those days; the second night she made a version of coq au vin; well, it dazzled me. I had avoided cooking anything with a potential for causing clean-up difficulties. I rotated grilled cheese, spaghetti, and ham-and-cheese sandwiches on a weekly basis.

She gave no indication of expecting more. Those were not casual times, sexually speaking. When the dentist was in, we had to keep quiet—he would have thrown me out. That long first night she read and wrote in my chair, under one harsh spot from a three-prong pole lamp, sipping tea from my special Lovett mug, initialed by the penile ceramicist herself. She never sleeps, I remember thinking. It had been snowing outside, and I wondered how I would do the dentist's walk. If I don't, I'm out. If he sees a girl, I'm out. Those were the practicalities bouncing around the outer ring of consciousness. Closer to the center were those recent obsessions over nail clippers and the origin of "raunchy." (I still haven't looked it up, and now I'm a thousand miles from the nearest Unabridged.) And at the center was Rachel Isaacs. (Whose last name I had to ask; we nearly made love that first night not knowing each other's names. Whatever else you may discover about the two of us, that would have been the most uncharacteristic.)

The pills wore off around four o'clock. A leg like a toothache. More hot salt compresses were applied. She returned to the chair, looking sleepy. She bunched the blanket over her shoulders and turned off the light. My room was utterly dark, the darkness was more psychological than physical; I could lie awake in the dark, feeling the walls and ceilings only inches away, feeling entombed. But this time in the dark, I remembered the last profile of Rachel in my chair. The girl I'd made the aborted move on, four hours earlier. The girl who had been my only reason for staying with Dante, all those weeks. What the hell was I doing in bed? What would she think of me, if I didn't make a move? She'd laugh at me!

So I arose, wanting her. And the nature of my rising, the awkward, premeditated lust in the dark, sealed the nature of our relationship.

Yes, it was lust. Something very different from any other experience of my life—it was something to be consummated immediately, before we talked, before I knew anything else about her. Something related to desecration. I didn't know where the chair was, and even the thought of bumping something in the dark and opening up the leg wasn't enough to stop me. The apartment was loud with someone's breathing. I was thinking only of the warmth waiting for me under the Hawkeye sweater; it was the vision of Rachel at the library table, not Rachel in class, that moved me toward her now. Every blind half-shuffle I took was aimed for that chair; I realized after five or six that I was utterly turned around in the dark, without the slightest idea of where the bed, the chair, or the bathroom was.

"Richard?" she whispered from somewhere behind me.

I turned to face her. I imagined a dozen faces, a dozen chairs.

"No longer mute? No longer inglorious?"

I was on her chair in a second, aiming to plant myself on the two arms, but I missed. One stiff arm missed the chair entirely, the other clipped her around the neck, and my leg took the full brunt of the fall. The groan was for all of it, the leg, my pride, my shame.

But we were both in the chair now. I was in her lap, roughly speaking. She straightened out her legs to give me more room. I could feel the warmth of her face, I could feel a few tickles of her hair. "Want to come to bed?" I asked.

Sometime in the night, she'd undone her Indian braids. The full, lustrous black hair was down, and brushed out. "Priapus proposes," she said, "but diaphragm disposes. Don't go away."

The pills must still have been working. My mind was skittering along like a drunk's, in that twilight before sleep and sickness: "Go to bed!" I was remembering as one of the cruelest commands in the language; "Come to bed?" as the kindest question. The love we made that night I also remember. Not one of the most proficient moments; more like Siamese twins obeying a crude sexual command. But when we awoke, we knew we would move from the dentist's, and stay together.

There, Rosie, I have fulfilled my promise to you.

I graduated that spring and decided to move to New York. Rachel might have stayed back in Iowa to get her doctorate, but she didn't. I think she loved me; if you have evidence to the contrary, keep it to yourself.

Chapter Seventeen

If you live long enough on the Upper West Side of Manhattan, it will come to pass that—

every transient dream and every permanent nightmare will be fulfilled, and

you will have drinks or dinner with every hero you ever had, and

you will meet with madness on the grand scale, you will see genius at every stage of deterioration, and

you will use your wife abominably, and she will use you, and

you will think twice about your honor, and you will discard, or reach for the deck accordingly, and

you will perform acts of such grace and dignity, and others of such blinding stupidity, that your self-image will be forever knocked askew, and

you will find that all the lessons of art and politics and psychology that you thought were dead or abstract are still alive, and

you will be obliged to define for yourself the meaning of Hell: Is it "other people" and "the inability to love," as you learned in school, or is it a concept as simple as, say, Auschwitz?

The best and the worst of your culture will pass in front of you, and

you will find out on some summer's day when you've drugged yourself to all those lessons and heroes and defective geniuses, and you've begun to accept the bitter knowledge that Manhattan will not sing for you, that suddenly even your marginal life will come to an end, and

you will act in concert with your demons.

New York for Rachel was the fulfillment of her talents and travels and contradictions—Los Angeles, Italy, Iowa, her Jewishness, her poetry, her films, and her flat-out genius. We liked New York's old-fashioned conservatism, the way it preserved, and didn't plow under. New York held on to values. It respected anonymity, it made way for differences.

I like to think New York in the mid-sixties was very much the way I was: half hard hat, half intellectual. Endlessly expressive, but a little confused. Just like me, it was slow to assimilate, it held back. For Rachel, New York was like the best of Italy, but with neighbors. In New York, you could hold out against the twentieth century, or launch yourself into the twenty-first—it didn't matter. You'd always be a contemporary New Yorker first.

Leela used to say, "I am a Hindu if I marry a Hindu or not. If I eat meat or not. If I dress in Western clothes and go to Christian churches. If I neglect every single Hindu holiday, I am still a Hindu."

I don't know what I am.

We were living in worse quarters than anything I'd known in Pittsburgh, with bugs like I'd never seen before.

The house I grew up in was free of pests, except for pigeons where the basement should have been. We had three rooms on Amsterdam, where it was mainly black and Puerto Rican, with a scattering of Jewish widows on rent control, a few bargain-hunting young professionals, some actors and actresses, and the occasional writer. Rachel was taken as Puerto Rican or Italian or Jewish by anyone in a mood to project. When I think of her now, I realize she could have passed as a native of any place from Portugal to Punjab.

The bugs! Rachel was a pacifist, and the roaches were a continual challenge. What stopped her was a practical question: Isn't a dead roach, especially a squashed one, worse than a live one that has the decency to hide most of the day? I used to write in the Columbia Library, while she worked at home. I didn't know what "work" she was doing, though I imagined it had to do with her thesis. Her proper role, as I saw it, was to support me for the two or three years it would take me to make us independent. Then there'd be a rose-clad country home in New England, with a Village apartment to take us through the winters.

It's 1964, in case you're dating this. The odd thing is, I was almost right. She did teach down at NYU, and I got an advance on my novel in less than a year. In 1964, we made about twelve thousand dollars. The next year, with the novel out, we cleared over twenty. I didn't know what a fluke that was. On that kind of money in 1965, two people lived adequately in Manhattan if they shared with the bugs.

Christ, Rosie, what did I care about the bugs? I was heading for immortality! Cedric Salkind gave me a chapter in his *Looking Forward, American Novels of the 60's*—little Richie Durgin, up there with Pynchon and Heller! Of course, his book stayed in print long after mine, an embarrassment he solved by dropping me and adding Vonnegut in the next edition.

("That's the price we pay, Richie," he told me later. "When you're out there on the cutting edge, not all your bets pay off.")

So, I would come back from the library around three in the afternoon. Rachel heard me coming up the stairs and she'd be standing behind the door.

"Open it carefully," she'd say.

I'd squeeze in.

Behind the door were three overturned coffee mugs. Sprouting over the countertops and floors were all the glasses and cups we owned, plus some of the dinner plates. It was as though a very circumspect person had thrown a tantrum. Under the glasses I could see roaches, pushing at their new horizons. Every item of crockery held its inmates.

Rachel stood in the kitchen, hands pressed against her cheeks as I tried to dispose of them. "The final solution," I joked (in the beginning we could joke about most things), and she would help centralize the roach pool, pushing all the cups and saucers and plates into one wide area. After many failed attempts to slip paper under the plates, she agreed to drench a sheet of newspaper with enough Raid to stun them as they shot out of the gate. They did their stiff-legged dance as I flipped them on the sheets, and when the morning's *Times* was plastered with roaches, I'd funnel them into a lidded receptacle and drop them in someone's garbage. This was my homecoming ritual. This I did every day. I never thought it strange; if anything, I thought of it as very New Yorkish, something we'd chuckle about in our sunset years, rocking on a porch somewhere up the Hudson.

But you and I know, don't we, that the Broth of Life was beginning to thicken. Her poem "Roaches," for one thing. She was entering that allegorizing phase of her life, and beginning to see me and everything around her and everything she read in a historical light. She wouldn't have minded nearly as much if I had just sprayed like a maniac and killed everything. What she couldn't take was that touch of consideration, letting them escape into a lingering death.

I didn't deserve the name Adolf.

We could have been happy out here in India, Rosie. We also have bugs—huge, tenacious things—they infest the kitchen and the bathroom and they make noise when they walk and they can even knock a teacup over if you try any bell-jar tricks with them. So no one bothers. They are felt to have an equal right to everything. They are not associated with filth in my servant's mind (they may even have been his relatives living through another existence); he sweeps away their bodies only when they've died and the house lizards have not done their job.

Last month, as I was sitting on my little porch, wondering if the monsoons would ever get here and if they'd be able to wash away the pig blood on the driveway and wall, a young man in tattered khaki clothes stopped his bicycle in my driveway, made a respectful bow to me with folded hands, and proceeded to pry off the heavy iron manhole cover in my driveway.

With the air of a performer, he suddenly dived into the bowels of my drainage, surfacing every few seconds with great handfuls of new and old feces. Armies of dung beetles materialized like huge black walnuts from a butterscotch pudding. Out on the street, his two young assistants, boys of five or six, did a stiff-legged barefoot dance of death on my driveway—those beetles were fast, but little boys are faster.

"Good work, sa'ab?" he beamed. "Keep drains clean? Every week I am coming, okay?"

Well, this too, is allegory, Indian style. A vision of the cycles of the world. My cook came running out almost immediately—dung beetles were boiling up the drainpipe as she peeled potatoes in the sink. I didn't move from my chair as the sweeper and my cook had a go at it. This was the sweeper's little calling card, like those old Hoover salesmen who used to toss a baggy of dirt on your carpet when you opened the door, then offer to vacuum it up. So now our driveway is shit-plastered in ways you wouldn't believe, littered with corpses the size of small mice, and dappled in blood to the height of a man's shoulder.

I need all this to keep my perspective.

Chapter Eighteen

Those were the years we found each other mutually miraculous. From Iowa into the third or fourth year in New York we found ourselves saying, "Really? Amazing!" to most ordinary things in our past. I lost all sense of what was truly odd in my life, and because I was so impressed with the simple things in hers—things that had cost her nothing, things she thought of as natural—I never learned about the big things, the momentous events, like having a baby. I strained mightily to tell her everything about Pittsburgh and Lovett and I could see her eyes glazing over, but there was one small story that she used to ask me to repeat, and then she would tell it to her friends. It embarrassed me, but she could make people laugh.

My parents pronounced some ordinary words very strangely. I had copied them, of course, until teachers told me they were wrong. The first was "widder" for widow, and the second was "shadder" for shadow.

So as not to be embarrassed again, I drew my own conclusion about that tall thing with rungs that my father used for climbing the sides of buildings. If he called it a ladder, it had to be a laddo. I might have been ten or so before a teacher asked me what in the world a "laddo" was, then showed me the word in the dictionary, and I was forced to change.

Rachel loved the story. She loved anything that had to do with language and tricks of perception, and I must admit that even today "laddos" and "ladders" occupy discreet image-files in my brain. I have pictured laddos standing free of walls and disappearing in the clouds. Ladders are heavy, noisy, paint-spattered things that never take you high enough.

Once in New York I caught Rachel frowning over a line in the paper. "I don't know Dutch," she said. "Why does the *Times* use Dutch?"

"The *Times* obviously doesn't use Dutch," I said.

"Well, look then."

The offending phrase was ". . . knocked for a loop."

"So?"

"What is a loopknocker?"

"Come on, Rachel. 'Knocked for a loop' is English."

"Oh, knocked for a loop. All right."

That's how she saw the world. She had freak vision and sometimes it let her down.

From Rachel I demanded more complicated memories. The Kurt and Lotte stuff, Raymond Chandler's knee, Rossellini and the Swede, the few stars she'd met, or whose kids she knew. What are their deformities? Who's gay, who's crazy? Who's sleeping around? She wasn't that interested.

So I learned her European anecdotes. She and Marco hitching through Europe, staying in hostels and visiting the galleries. In Basel, a city of art and commerce, of exhibits in the banks, she and Marco had been in a rug store.

Marco liked rugs; he liked painting rugs. The salesman tried to gauge his taste. "Too crowded," Marco kept saying, then, "Too spare," and the salesman beamed with inspiration.

"Yes, this carpet is crowded. It's like Stravinsky. I know what you're looking for, but we haven't got it, signore. No one has it. You are looking for Vivaldi's *Symphony for Classical Guitar*. Serene, that is what."

She needed things like that, in order to live. So do I, now. She was willing to trade moral sanity for aesthetic perfection.

I was not always that way. Back then, I wanted fierce, Lawrentian love, some sort of grand, innocent passion. I remember a time very early in our Iowa living arrangement, just after moving out of the dentist's garage and into a basement apartment, a few weeks before our marriage. It's probably the event that decided me on marriage, on having met the Collaborator in my life's design. We were lounging one morning on our pull-out bed, naked. She was running her fingers lightly down my cock, as though merely assessing its smoothness. "So beautiful, really," she said.

I did the same for her, thinking it a prelude. "This isn't bad either."

My cock gave a lurch, an incremental leap in hardness, and she smiled distantly. Now she looked at it. "See how it responds." Her hands were always the perfect degree of coolness; I can't remember a time when a touch from Rachel anywhere was not welcome. She cupped my balls, like a seductive torturer about to squeeze without warning. I reciprocated with a moistened finger around and over and in her, which she seemed not to notice. She slowly brought her face down and brushed her lips, her eyelids, her cheeks against it, while my finger went berserk in rotation and agitation. "Oh, it's beautiful, beautiful," I kept saying, wondering if this was my opening. I drew closer, aiming for that moist clot of pink wrinkled skin, and then Rachel squeezed. Not hard, but a gesture that froze me. "What the hell are you doing?"

"It's so lovely. Your cunt is so lovely." I could feel it closer than it had ever been, that fierce Lawrentian love.

"Don't be silly." She sat up, and spread it wide for me. "You call this beautiful? It's not beautiful. It's nothing. Literally. Your cock has all the qualities of beauty, not to mention utility. It's a proper art object. But this—how would you go about making a cast of this?"

Spread out like that, it did look like something from a Broadway novelty store. She was on her feet now, thrusting it in my face. "You want to lick it? You want to lick my cunt?"

In one grand gesture I grabbed her with both arms, and I twisted on the bed and she was torqued on top of me. I went after her head-first. If I'd misread her signals the first time, this second time I didn't care. She had to know there was something besides aesthetics in the world, that I could be driven to possess the aesthetically ugly and I really didn't give a shit what she thought of the functional allomorph between my legs. I won't dwell on the sexual connections between us, Rosie, but that was a day of heroic, fierce, exhausting love, engraved on my memory. It even brought a little color to her cheeks. Bruises, bite marks—call it Pittsburgh love.

When I woke after a short nap, Rachel was sitting up beside me, totally naked, arranging her hair. She was putting earrings on, and her gold chain with the Star of David, and as she touched her lips with the tube of lipstick, I was possessed one more time. I was on my stomach, but I could have balanced straight out on that pedestal of a stiffened prick. She reached first for her necklace, as though I were a chain snatcher and not a rapist, and I slammed into her with such force that her eyes rolled back and her teeth clamped down on her lower lip and her nails dug into my back. It felt as though I had dipped my wick in molten wax, and the sounds that gurgled from our throats were new to us. This was not one of those proficient sexual moments when the parts are functioning with cool self-determination while the brain ponders batting averages, but one of the frenzied instants when mind and body and maybe a third force have all kicked into high gear at the fusion of lust, and love, and even tenderness.

I was afraid to look, when it was finally over; I was afraid I'd hurt her, that she would stagger to her feet, get dressed, pack her bag and leave. I could imagine anything, that I was guilty of any crime. I hurt all over, and I feared that I had broken the most marvelous plaything I'd ever had.

"Well," she said, and slid further down the mattress. "If I smoked, I'd smoke a cigarette now."

"How do you feel?" I asked.

"Missing in action." She combed my hair with her fingers, and now, even looking at those sharp red nails, at the gold chain, I wasn't turned on anymore.

"I come not every day to woo," said I, wishing I'd memorized more of Petruchio's speeches back in Lovett, when I'd used them to great advantage with Janet.

"What you lack in subtlety, you more than make up for in low animal heat."

I was studying her face, minutely. The wrinkles on her lips, the arch of her nose, the cheeks returning to chalk.

God, it took a lot to bring the blood to the surface of this woman! In profile, she was perfection; her face seemed cut from the very air. But straight on, to grasp it, I needed it broken into a thousand little patterns, like sun on water, on birds' wings.

She sighed. "How did all this start?"

"You admired my poor abused organ."

"Yes. I remember."

"And you got pissed off when I admired yours."

"I'll never forgive you."

"Or forget, I hope."

"Art is long, life short."

"Is every animal so talkative after making love?"

She then turned on her side and wrapped her arms around me, slipping her hands to the back of my neck. This was the moment that has seared through me for all time, Rosie, when a woman brands you with the intensity of her love, or of her need. "Darling, I am. I am an animal of words." She smiled, I felt a stirring, but suppressed it. I'd said once she had Ernest Borgnine teeth; thank God for that small imperfection.

I thought we had gained a purchase on immortality that day in Iowa.

New York wasn't such a mystery to us. I had my old friends Newman and Goodman from Iowa, now back East; I had a novel contract and those months of anticipation when every phone call was announcing something new and glorious: a movie interest, a paperback sale, an interview show. I had wondered what a publisher did with the year of lead-time between acceptance and appearance, and now I knew: They strung you out tighter than a violin string; I expected music every time I scratched.

Meanwhile, we had New York to distract us. I knew I'd love New York—it was the culmination of all my avid provincialism. I grew pudgy on sidewalk pretzels. I couldn't believe the glut of distractions, the food, the shopping, the art, the movies, the bookstores. My advance on the novel had not been huge, but it was more than my father had ever seen in a year, and it came in a lump sum. It seemed mountainous, inexhaustible, and whenever I managed to deplete it, new sums were added, thanks to paperback and foreign sales. All without a job. I practiced humility in letters to Stur Foster.

One day in the second year, after the novel had come out and gotten its reviews, I wrote up an outline for my second book. Bigger and better than the first, with a lot more sex. Hugh Talbot was my editor, not quite a legend, but a heavyweight. He'd come from England twenty-five years earlier, and in that New York way had managed to remain perfectly English, while picking up the crust and drive of a New Yorker. So, when he called me in to say, "Frankly, we don't look with favour (I always saw his words spelled that way) on your new project," I was crushed and confused. Which side of him had I failed to rouse? I must have still been smiling, so he went on.

"We were proud to have been your publishers for the first book. I trust you were pleased with our performance. But I've sent this outline around the board, and frankly, we're all a trifle disappointed in it."

"How big a trifle?" I asked.

"A rather huge trifle, I'm afraid."

Proud and brittle, I gathered the pages and stuffed them back in the folder and stormed out. Secretaries who'd gotten to know me over the spring and summer didn't look up. I expected a phone call from Hugh Talbot or from my agent, begging me to reconsider. I told Rachel what I'd done and she, who was writing in the kitchen, didn't look up. "I'm sure it's for the best," she said.

"Hugh Talbot probably is the best," I heard myself saying, aware for the first time of my stupidity.

"That's what I mean," she said.

I threw the folder on the bed and went for a long New York walk. Down Broadway to the bookstores, counting the reserves of my novel. I munched on a pretzel and shuffled on. How do you start all over again?

My first novel had already been out a month; what had I done lately? Rachel hadn't even read the book after I described it as a childhood and adolescent romance. (I realize now I purposely discouraged her, goading her into calling it a symphony for undescended testicle.) She never read any of my things, unless she did it in secret. We never talked about them. And to be perfectly truthful, I was a little relieved. Seeing a lineup for a new Truffaut film, I joined it.

Jules and Jim is my all-time favorite. It lies somewhere near the core of my sentimentality. I'd first seen it with Janet down in Garnett Place. It fused for all time an ideal of sex and art and friendship. After that film, it's a wonder we hadn't all separated in groups of three and gone upstairs to experiment. Anything by Truffaut, no matter how disappointing, was an opening-night event.

I must have been standing near the head of the line. Within minutes a giant tail of movie buffs had curled around the corner. I love movie lines; you see the most interesting faces in them, and overhear the most interesting conversations, especially on the Upper West Side of New York. Any movie in the world could be cast from a movie lineup on the Upper West Side of Manhattan.

So I was lost to everything but passing faces, just sucking them in and trying to remember bits and pieces. Well, there I was standing, momentarily blank, when a woman tugged my sleeve and asked, "If you're alone, do you mind if I go in with you?"

I made space, even before looking her over. It was one of those intermediate fall days—early November, I suppose —when a heavy knit sweater was all you needed against the gray winds. Hers looked hand-knit, and her face was nearly lost in its high collar. I immediately thought: New England.

"I know you," she said, "I mean, I know your picture. You had a book out a few weeks ago. It was in the paper. I haven't read it."

I excused her. My personal involvement with publishing stopped with recognition, not sales.

"I'm terrible, but I don't even remember your name, just your face. The book had a real long title and it was about Pittsburgh. That's pretty good, right?"

"Rates some popcorn," I said.

"My name is Carla Goodings," she said. "I don't usually do this. I mean, pick up strange men in movie lines."

"Is this a pickup?" Am I strange? I should have asked. And there I was again, ready to leave with Carla Goodings, and forgetting the woman at home. I am loyal to proximities and that's about it.

In fairness to myself (that's what this book is all about, isn't it?) I should also say that I am loyal to experience and to adventure and to the promise not so much of sex, but of new stories.

"What next?" she asked after the movie, and I said I should be going back to work. "Me too." She shrugged. I had her name and her address and I knew she was a painter. She lived below Gramercy, where artists had been given converted loft space. She seemed too young, too fragile to be an artist. What did I know? I had no expecta-

tions about painters, except that they should look de-
mented and act abominably.

"I suppose you could come see my loft," she said.

With painters, the smaller and weaker they are, the
bigger and bolder their art (I've discovered). Carla had to
stand on ladders and chairs, and drop her canvases down
with pulleys to the sidewalk. I've always admired the engineering skill of artists, all the mechanical expertise they
pick up. Carla had more tools than my father in her loft,
and she knew how to handle all of them. I've always felt I
belonged in a junkyard, working with scrap and crowbars.
Time has come around to satisfy me.

And I can imagine your saying about now, Rosie, What
a fool. He's been living for two years now with Rachel
Isaacs while she was probably writing three quarters of her
poems and the first of her stories and he hasn't once indicated the least awareness of what was going on under his
nose.

The kitchen table, Durgin! There she was—where the
hell were you?

Chapter Nineteen

. . . and it will come to pass, if you live long enough on the Upper West Side of Manhattan, that your marriage will subtly change poles, the energy will flow in different directions, and no temptation will be foreign to you.

You will serve new functions.

All the clouds that had been gathering will suddenly release hailstones the size of grapefruit.

You will leave your old morality hanging in the closet and put on street-smart shades and a surplus jacket; you'll hustle and cheat, bow and scrape, and you'll wake up some morning a few years down the line on an unsheeted mattress, down with sticky puddles of old wine cut with cigarette butts and a woman beside you whose name slips your memory. . . .

I always felt Rachel's stay with me was provisional. I could imagine a hundred times a day—as she closed a book, as she opened the refrigerator, as she glanced at the mail or looked up from the television—her saying, "Well, that's it. I'm tired of this and I'm tired of you and I find our endless dialogue fatiguing in the extreme. . . ."

I was trained for outbursts very early in our marriage,

back in Iowa. I was trying to be a model husband. All I knew about marriage (aside from the crude approximation of my parents') was from watching the marriages of my Iowa friends. Marriage was obviously a cinch, much easier than the complicated, messy, tragic things we read about in Big Lit. The pitfalls seemed so easy to avoid. A little kindness, an offer to help out with the dishes, to hang up the clothes, to drive her to the supermarket and even push the cart—what could be easier? A few compliments didn't hurt, even if I wasn't good at it. It always sounded tinny when I beamed, "Hey, honey, this is good! What do you call it?"

(I called her "honey" in the beginning.)

Here's something for you, Rosie. Back in Iowa, in our basement apartment, I came home from classes, tossed my jacket on the unmade sofa bed and called out, "Hiya, honey, I'm home!" The typewriter was going in the kitchen. The typing didn't stop. I stepped into the kitchen, loving and expansive, nostrils flaring, a groom's silly grin plastered on my face. "What's for dinner? I'm starved."

She stared at me, took the sheet of paper in both hands and jerked it out of the machine, then pressed it inside a folder. Oh, boy, I thought: I've stepped in it now. I'd been married about a month. She stood, put the typewriter in the case, then carried it back to the closet.

"Honey?" I asked, "something wrong?" She came back to the kitchen, and stared at me. Something in school? I wanted to ask.

I must have been smiling, still trying to show my sympathy.

"I should thank you," she said. "I have been looking for the cruelest words in the English language. Quote, Hiya honey, I'm home, pause, what's for dinner, question mark, close quote will do quite nicely."

"Oh, come on. I was showing my appreciation."

"Were you."

I felt a surge of self-righteousness. That's what husbands do—come home from work and ask about dinner. Hadn't she ever watched television? That's what the men of America do, for Chrissakes—stand in kitchens looking goofy. And if wives acted bitchy, it meant you weren't spending enough time with them dishing out compliments, or maybe you weren't satisfying them in bed. They were skittish, no doubt about it, but eventually trainable. I made a note to myself: Check out the sex angle. Lay it on heavy tonight.

Maybe flowers.

"What did I say?"

"Everything. What you said was, quote, Here boy, my shoes need shining. Or was it, Smile for us, honey, and let's see your teeth."

"What the hell are you talking about?" This was the time for a little self-righteous anger. Nip this shit in the bud. This was disrespect, but I exercised self-control. Nothing undignified. "Let's go out, then."

"No, I want to cook."

She was being perverse. "Good. So what's for dinner?"

"What did you bring?"

"I've been teaching, remember?"

"What suggestion do you have?"

"Christ, Rachel, that's your job. I don't know."

"It's up to me. Good. I'll have spinach salad and a hard-boiled egg. I don't think I will ever eat meat or cook meat again. And if you ever want to eat here again, I think you'd better buy a good cookbook and start reading it."

"Honey—"

"I am not your honey. I was going to tell you that anyway."

Oh, I stormed out and went to the bar and probably had three or four quick beers and a schooner of popcorn. I hate spinach salad, the way it insinuates itself on the edge of your teeth, the fine grit that never washes out. Life would be considerably diminished without my nightly short ribs of beef, my hamburger, or my morning bacon and eggs.

It would be particularly dim without Rachel to cook it. This basement apartment was the first one I'd ever rented with a proper stove and refrigerator. No more window ledges for the milk, no more hot plates. And now no more wife?

By the time Goodman showed up at the bar, a little surprised to see the groom out alone, I realized I didn't have much of a case. I'd wanted a bright, creative, crusty Jewish wife—the very thing he'd warned me against. I'd wanted complexities in my life—he'd fled them. To complain that Rachel didn't have supper waiting for me and had suggested that I study a cookbook—well, it sounded like whining on the replay. Goodman's wife, innocent Wisconsin farm girl that she had once been, had left him early in their marriage. This was in his undergraduate days in Madison. "How'll I get laid?" he'd yowled at her as she got in the taxi. She'd turned around and pantomimed how he'd do it, using both hands and lots of knee action, to the taxi driver's smirk. My situation wasn't so drastic. And their marriage had been the happiest I'd seen.

I didn't get a cookbook, but I came back to the apartment with some bread and sliced cheese. Back to grilled cheese. The next night I came home earlier and asked what she thought I could cook. She started me on spaghetti and tomato sauce, showing me how to sauté onions and mushrooms. In a week, I'd moved up to the simpler pastas, then broiled chicken. She never went back to meats, and gradually she cut out eggs. We learned to alternate our cooking nights, which labeled me "henpecked" and "shlemiel" even before we left Iowa. One need not cease growing or learning, even in marriage (this was a revelation to me, Rosie). The cooking arrangement, who shopped, who cleaned was never a problem after that.

(She'd admire me now; I've taken on Indian cuisine, mostly vegetarian, with a passion. I go down to the village market every day, bargaining for the vegetables, grinding my own spices, leaving only the long hours of simmering to the cook. At night I sit on the floor with Dev and we eat with our fingers, tearing off chapatties or making balls of the rice to polish the plates.

(What kind of man is this? I often wonder, the Pittsburgh and Iowa selves peering in, looking down at the squat balding American and the dark-haired little boy making slurping sounds as they eat with their fingers, licking off the gravy as it runs down to their elbows.)

Not everything was worked out in Iowa, and there were continual surprises, things I didn't learn and couldn't absorb. One night, when I was rewriting patches of my second novel, Rachel asked if I would mind "looking over" a few things she'd written. I was flattered. What did I know of Dante? I smiled.

"No," she said, "some stories."

(It can be said, finally. "The rest is history.")

Let me backtrack just a little further; there's a context to this. She had never admitted to me, aside from showing me the poems she'd written in Italy, that she had any deeper interest in poetry or fiction. Her interest in the Workshop ("crude talents in a big hurry," she called us), which she never even visited, was purely sociological. She considered my writing, and the writing of my friends, "synthetic," not organic. She considered our frantic competitiveness "nouveau riche," and she referred to the journals I kept reading down at the library as "how-to" magazines. Dentists and plumbers, she thought of us, keeping up with advanced technology wherever it surfaced. She was right; we were awful. She was right to call us bureaucrats, and our teachers undersecretaries. It was the only way we had of catching up with the aristocrats of our generation, those from literary backgrounds and better schools and (it can now be admitted) with greater talents.

Rachel never read her contemporaries. She never read paperback books or journals or newspapers. ("You might try the feel of a hardcover book someday," she once said. "If it was written before 1960, I don't have to," I answered. "Hieroglyphs ain't my speed.") So far as I knew, she didn't read in the twentieth century. She had a scholar's taste for original sources and for original thinkers: her preferred reading was letters and notebooks, diaries and journals. Her light reading was biographies.

What it all meant was that she and I were opposites. I was the snob, she the democrat. I required certification, I read the *Times Book Review*, I kept a mental chart of writers who were up or down. Like any nouveau riche, I was terrified of being seen in the wrong literary neighborhood, in the wrong company. If I went slumming, I wanted credit for it. Rachel was more exacting, less restrictive. She could enjoy cookbooks and gardening tips, she could read military history, Catholic devotionals, travel books; she could cultivate friendships with shopkeepers, clerks, engineers, and some of the old Jewish widows in our neighborhood—she wasn't a snob, like me. She merely demanded that people or books be interesting, honest, and delightful, and when they failed, she would quietly withdraw.

She was an aristocrat. Take that as a partial context.

The other was more immediate: the visit of her father, and the unpleasantness that ensued. We were sitting in the kitchen of our Amsterdam apartment in January 1967. There was half a large bottle of Chianti still on the table. We had no plates, a result of my rampage of the night before. In about a week, I would start teaching an evening class in composition and English language at Rutgers in Newark. Temporarily, I thought.

I'll get to the rampage in a minute.

It had been an even worse time for Rachel. She'd had a fight with her father (over me, I'd thought) the night before and she'd just canceled her usual trip to California for his birthday. He'd been a total stranger to me until the day before, when he'd shown up in New York and called from a pay phone just down the block.

No son-in-law in America had craved acceptance as much as I had. I was hungry for a proper father. Five years after my own father's death, I was finally grieving for the things I'd bottled up during his life. When guilt replaces a love that never existed, you're prone to complex sentimentalities. I'd been going around with that sentimentality in my gut; it animated parts of my first novel.

We put him off for half an hour in order to get some food, and cleaned out a winter's clutter like demons. How to explain the roaches, the dirt, the barred windows, the cramped, minimal existence? My lack of a job? Our charming, heroic bohemianism? You can start by calling it failure.

And then he was on our doorstep. Rachel let him in and

I stayed back, letting them hug. When she said, "Daddy, I'd like you to meet Richie," he only looked at the point of my shoulder and scowled. My outstretched hand (I'd been debating a bearlike hug) withered in the space between us. We were both about five-six; he was then sixty-six, stout and bald, with curly white hair forming a rim. He was tanned, and there were broad moles and freckles on his California scalp, though his eyebrows were still black and bushy. No resemblance to Rachel. I wondered if Californians traveling East in the winter kept an out-of-date, shabby topcoat hanging in a closet, or if maybe there was a rental service at the L.A. airport, specializing in gloves, scarves, boots, and coats. I'd expected a thick accent, but there was none; nothing different from any New Yorker of his age. His words were all a little hardened, each word too distinct.

"Ben! I'm so glad! Rachel's told me so much! It's been such a long time!"

"Long? It's never been." Every time I spoke, he turned to Rachel, as though to ask, "Is this guy serious?" and as though requiring the services of an interpreter. For a moment, it seemed that he didn't know, or had forgotten, that Rachel had married, that I was family. Whatever it was, I exercised an unwelcome claim on his attention, and none at all on his affection.

I was still grinning like a buffoon.

He sat in the Goodwill chair I'd brought from Iowa. "I'll bring tea, Daddy," Rachel said, and I was left alone with him. I checked the walls for roaches: none for the moment. The place was for once orderly, but bare and dark and grim. He chose not to look at me. He scoured the walls, and I winced with every crack, every cobweb.

"What brings you East, Ben?"

"Business, what else?"

"Television?"

"Didn't I just say business, Mr. Durgin?" The tea was slow.

So I was not to call him Ben. And obviously, I was stupid. When Rachel entered with the tea tray, she sensed the tension. This was a new side of Rachel—the hostess—bright, perky, almost giggly. The strain must have been killing her.

"Mr. Eisachs has come East on business, Rachel," I said. "If you'll excuse me."

In the kitchen, I poured a shot of Scotch. The prejudices of my people stated (among other things) that Jews never drank and disapproved vehemently of anyone who did. This did not immediately recommend my reentry, shot glass and bottle in hand, but it remained an option.

Father and daughter sipped tea. I heard words like "Mommy" and "blood sugar" and others like "studio" and "script."

"Darling, come join us," she trilled. I gulped the Scotch and took a sofa corner as far from both of them as I could.

"Daddy's here to discuss an option. Not here, exactly—he's off to London to discuss it."

I nodded. He seemed to be chewing a response, jaws working, nothing coming out. "Interesting," I finally said. One of Rachel's words.

He waved away my interest. "I'm hungry," he said. "What's close?"

At last, something I could relate to. "Great!" said I, "there's a terrific little Hungarian place—"

"My daughter and I find goulash an abomination. I don't trust gypsies, and I frankly doubt your ability, Mr. Durgin, to direct me to anything remotely palatable."

The words "cold cherry soup" died on my tongue. I cannot describe the sophistication I'd felt, making an acquaintance with cold cherry soup. That was New York, Europe, Art, Domestic Exile. Rachel had even learned to make it for me.

He turned to her. "Where shall we go?"

"I think I know a place."

She stood, and from body language, interposing herself between Ben and me, reaching in the closet for a raincoat while blocking me from getting it for her, I knew, *knew*, I was not invited. Ben-Zvi was already at the door, adjusting his shabby overcoat and scarf, his back to me. When Rachel looked at me, it was to shake her head gently, with a sympathic frown, to reach out for my hand as I sharply withdrew it.

"Ben?" I called. I could see his shoulders bunching. He didn't turn, or answer. "I take it I'm not invited?" I waited.

"Ben?"

Finally he turned. "Am I stopping you? It's up to my daughter."

"No, it's not. Don't blame her, buddy." I put her behind me and cut the distance between us. An old hatred was flowing. I could feel it lighten my arms, clench my jaws, beat in my brain. I was a gorilla of outrage. In another step I'd have his lapels bunched in my fists; I'd have his bald scalp wrinkling against the wall.

"Richie!" Rachel cried out.

Ben peered around me. "He's crazy," he said. "You married a crazy. He keeps you locked up here and poor and he's crazy too." He took a step toward me, so did Rachel from behind, and she pulled my arm just as Ben bumped me hard.

"Get him out of here, Rache, I swear to God I'll throw him out if he doesn't leave—"

I turned to her, my fists shaking.

"We're going, we're going." She whirled her father around and pulled him to the door. "You!" she said, "I'm ashamed of both of you." But she said it to her father.

The only thing in this world I cannot tolerate, Rosie, is deliberate rejection. Being ignored totally, being devalued. Criticism, yes. Even cruelty. But not contempt.

They left, but I wasn't finished. I started with the tea tray, the cups and the pot, and spiked them on the floor; then I grabbed the dinner plates and heaved them against the walls, smashed the glasses against the refrigerator, and made the worst shambles of our crockery that I could—the Cossacks had come. I stopped short only with the type-writers and the books and pages of Rachel's writing. (What if I hadn't? What if, in my unconscionable rage and my hurt feelings, I'd taken all those thousands of pages I thought were drafts of her thesis, and destroyed them?) But I pulled out everything else—clothes from the closets and drawers, sheets from the beds, towels. And then I performed the definitive surgery, the one thing I couldn't retract: I murdered my old Lovett avocado tree, wrenching it from the metal pot, uprooting it and whirling the clotted roots high overhead till fetid clumps of soil were spattered over everything.

The living-room floor, the kitchen floor, everything was nothing but garbage and broken plates. Let her, goddammit, clean up this shit! No more tolerance for her delicate feelings about roaches, no more squeamishness over final solutions. Ben-Zvi was only acting out what Rachel had told him—obviously. She was leaving with him, obviously. I'd heard what the supreme authority in her life thought of me, so why not be hung for the steppenwolf I was? I'd denied too much of my best self these past ten years: no drunkenness, no fights, no women, no ill-bred reactions to disappointment or rejection.

Not anymore!

They would know! They would see it and know my
pain! And I would take my pain downtown to someone
with dirty nails and poor diction and nothing but instinct
and talent and workshop training. Down to Carla Goodings.

Chapter Twenty

The Carla Goodings Connection, for what it's worth.

There comes a time on the Upper West Side of Manhattan when infidelity enters your life, usually to stay. For a man like me, bigamous to the core, I'd been morbidly monogamous for ten Wanda, Janet, and Rachel years. And see where it got me, I thought, that night. Insulted, and stepped on like a worm.

I have not always behaved like an excessively proud man, but I sniffingly insist on being taken seriously. (I should be using the past tense.) And when I brooded on it, I saw that Rachel had never quite paid me proper homage. She'd never read my novel and stories except to scorn them. She'd never thought well of my friends, and she'd ridiculed my ideas. She'd found clever ways of sabotaging my pride. In the ultimate betrayal, she'd even dared to find my mother "amusing."

I was obviously looking for excuses, and I had them. Carla had paid me the proper respect that first (and only) afternoon, picking my face out of a movie lineup, signaling her interest.

Linseed, color, dirty clothes, clutter: I loved it. I love

painters, I'm in awe of them. They're strong and unreflective; even their agonies are heroic. Five minutes in Carla's studio, and I was playing professor to her mumbled "Yeah, maybe you're right, y'know"; ten minutes and I was holding a wine bottle and a crumbly joint, bracing a ladder while she painted, telling her about laddos with a practiced skill.

"You writers," she said, "you can make fun out of anything."

"Can you come down and play?" I asked, speaking of fun. The laddos of my childhood had all been missing a topless artist like Carla Goodings. I fantasized about climbing up. Brute Ascending a Laddo.

The canvas was enormous. One of those Frick meta-paintings. She was executing her own Bellini canvas, a faithful but blurred reproduction. The focus was on the fireplace, the wallpaper, the old black museum guard in his gray, ill-fitting uniform. Bits of other paintings—a Van Gogh—peeked from corners, but were cut off by the edges of Carla's canvas. This, to me, was great art. It had social and political depth. It put art in a human context. If I could forget the purpose of my visit, I might even have trembled before it. If Carla had ever read poetry (or anything else), she might have titled it "Musée des Beaux Arts." She'd caught the play of muscles in the guard's jaw: the man was obviously talking to himself.

I suddenly remembered the word. "He's blue-gumming! The old guy's a blue-gummer!"

"A what?" She was down with me now, sharing the joint and swigs of wine, and I had my arm around her bare flesh. "That half-singing under the breath—that's called blue-gummin'."

My God, it all comes back! Nothing is ever lost. Ten years earlier at Forbes Field I had asked an old woman what a chow dog was and she'd told me and she'd been laughing at me ever since. "Every team gotta have a chow dog! Chow dogs is for blue-gummin' the empires!"

I identified with the bored, outgunned guard. I saw the purpose of making him, not the paintings, the center of attention. I wanted to possess the woman capable of such vision and such energy. I knew what the guard was telling me: Forget the paint and go for the lady.

There was an old horsehair Victorian sofa in her loft, and a mattress with an untucked sheet, and we dove for the mattress, tearing off our clothes on the dash, and not quite making it. I was on her, still over the dusty floor, and we had to scramble those last few feet for the mattress, rolling for it, hollering the way painters and welders and blue-collar types were supposed to, in making love. Well, it was satisfying and famishing too, and when Carla studied me afterward it was with both hands, her lips, and a Polaroid.

Carla kept a file of cockshots. It was a thick file, with names and dates and places written on the back. It made me blush—girls weren't supposed to fight back like that. "My wife thinks cocks are beautiful," I said, wondering to whom, exactly, I was being disloyal.

"They're good and bad. Some are boring. Some are even pretty. They're more interesting than breasts, that's for sure. Someday I'm going to do for cocks what Botticelli did for tits."

The world knows about Carla Goodings' cockshots now. The world smiles; it's fun. But I was uncomfortable back then. I was on the brink of a New World, one just over the edge from Janet and from Rachel, and I wasn't ready for it.

She had that clear, forthright New England sturdiness, as

though she should be out picking apples instead of measuring my cock and plotting its dimensions on a sheet of graph paper. Just a ruddy-cheeked, large-boned, buttery blonde from unbroken Puritan stock, with a tough, wiry body. No surprises; body and face seemed continuous, unlike Rachel. Rachel, I realized, was all delight. Rachel was a prize.

What had I done to her? Not this little game with Carla —what had I done to the cement with Rachel, what would she do when she saw the mess I'd made, when she had to deal with the challenge I'd thrown down: him or me? What right did I have to do that? And if for some incredible reason she'd choose me—what had I done to deserve it?

She had to be back by now. And maybe was gone for good.

Carla was dressing, slapping on a blue work shirt and her jeans over that hard, ready flesh. I missed softness, whiteness, voluptuousness. I flipped through dozens of cocks; I wasn't off the top mark by much (there were grades on the back), and after a few shuffles, I couldn't recognize myself at all. She was back on the ladder. I went to the refrigerator and found a bowl of egg salad and lathered it on some bread.

So much for my infidelity.

This is not a dignified memory, Rosie.

I walked back. It was only eleven o'clock when I left Carla's loft, and I had about ninety blocks to go—time enough, I figured, for Rachel and Ben to get back to the apartment, call the cops, and pack a bag. I had no doubt that over sauerkraut and schnitzel or whatever he considered proper food, he had already proposed the obvious: Forget this guy—he's a loser. I don't like his looks. Come back to California, don't waste yourself on slime. Not only slime, he'd be saying. Crazy. Hot, crazy, probably drunk with a goyish temper. Does he beat you?

There were many desolate blocks to walk. On any other night, I would have been mugged; not that night. They could hear me ticking a block away—I was dangerous to anyone's health. Or maybe I looked too wired, too much the undercover cop.

Ninety blocks is sufficient time to contemplate one's deficiencies. What became abundantly clear, after about a block and a half, was the innocence of Rachel in all this. After five blocks, the great similarity of her father and her husband. Maybe I should pack a bag; I should clear out.

Given my sentimental love of *Jules and Jim*, I was deep-down prepared to like Rachel's lovers, just as I expected her to like mine. We would have some sort of Lawrentian *Blutbrüderschaft*—if I was generous enough in the spirit. So that would be my approach, if she cornered me. Only, I preferred to think of myself as the fetish-object, roughly handled by sensual women.

Around about Twentieth Street and Lexington, I was assailed by a different presence. It came to me as a story, fully formed and worked on as I walked.

On the long walk home from his mistress's bed, Frank Keeler was besieged by ghosts. He was still on lower Lexington when his father—a man Keeler had last seen in a plain pine coffin five years earlier—hissed at him from between the garbage cans in front of a Szechuan restaurant.

"Hey, kid, got a minute?"

Keeler had all too many. "Dad, I thought you were dead," he said.

"Laid off. Mind if we talk?"

"*If we keep moving.*"

The old bowlegged shuffle was familiar. It was his father, all right, and Keeler reached for his cheek. Five years ago, there'd been ice under his skin.

"*You get used to it,*" said his father. He pressed Keeler closer to the walls than he liked to walk, in Manhattan.

"*I've been watching; don't think I haven't. I even read your book.*"

"*I always wondered if the dead were watching.*"

"*Look—about tonight. What were you proving?*"

This was a tender spot. He and his wife had fought, and Keeler had done some spiteful things to the plates and glasses.

"*You shouldn't have pulled up the avocado, Frank. I figured you'd protect the avocado no matter what. I felt safe there.*"

"*What could I do? You're no stranger to spite.*"

"*You have a better head than me. Be patient. I was built this way for a reason.*"

The voice was fading, a distant station.

"*I thought you and Mom were my special burdens. You were what kept me from other people.*"

His father seemed to snicker. Keeler had never thought of his father outside of Pittsburgh, but in New York, he fit in tolerably, probably as well as Keeler did.

"*Rachel's a good girl.*" He hesitated a step, and Keeler stopped. His father was bathed in radiance. "*Consider closely the women in our lives. What Rachel has made possible in yours, what your mother made impossible in mine. Think what my life could have been. Think what your life might have been.*" His father skipped across the garbage cans and stood on the trunk of a parked taxicab.

*Then the lights went off and a familiar raspy voice ac-
cused him in the dark.*

"*You're a fool,*" *it said.* "*She's too good for you.*"

So one's relationship with the dead continues to mature.
It's a useful thing to know, in a collapsing universe. When
my father died I was twenty, and I still related to him as a
teenager; he was to me (at best) the spiteful carpenter to
be pitied and avoided. And now, at twenty-six, I saw him
as I should have all along—as the clearest version of myself
I would ever have. Bitter, spiteful, groping—and resigned. I
remembered on that walk uptown his only "saying" (as
opposed to my mother's torrent of clichés): "Nothing succeeds like success." To him, it explained everything—why
the Pirates kept losing, why rich people got richer (we
didn't have to expand it to "Nothing fails like failure"). It
was a principle rooted in genetics as well as politics and the
monetary system; to fight it was a bull's pathetic courage
in the corrida—make yourself a trophy.

I thought of Dylan Thomas' poem on the refusal to
mourn the death of a child by fire-bombing; how, at
Lovett, that poem had struck me as a personal code of
honor—I had encountered it in my magical junior year in
Stur Foster's writing class, after my father's death and just
in time to start my own story. And as I walked, lines of
the poem kept returning. But, worse, memories of my father kept intruding. Those endless losing Sunday double-
headers at Forbes Field, the hope we kept investing, the
disappointments. "Gonna look after me in my old age."
And I could hear the voice and see the smile and the tap-
ping of his temple all over again. The sexless marriage he'd
known—as though sexuality in marriage were a rare thing,
more a function of education and imagination than any-

thing visceral—and for a moment I tried to conceive of a life as he had lived it: without leisure, dreams, or imagination, without love, but richly supplied with anxiety, pain, poverty, bitterness, and crushing boredom. The only thing he had that he loved was a three-pack-a-day cigarette habit.

And I tried to imagine his landscape.

Then, Rachel's. Rachel's in Italy, in Iowa, in California. An abundance of everything but basic belonging, and her deployment of talent and brains and incredible effort to get the lone thing my father gave me—a place to come from.

The dark blocks of lower Park and Lexington were comforting. I dreaded the coming on of midtown, hitting the West Side at Columbus Circle, walking up Central Park West to the Museum of Natural History, then cutting over to Amsterdam and home. It was one o'clock when I clumped upstairs and fitted the key in the lock.

If Rachel had been waiting with a gun, I would have understood. I tried to enter quietly, but the door scraped against a broken plate. A living-room light snapped on: Rachel in my chair.

I expected it then, Rosie, just as I expected it every minute of my married life: She would look me cold in the eye, not bothering to raise her voice, and announce, I'm leaving you.

"Maid's day off?" I asked. She'd cleared a path through the rubble, concentrating the debris. I didn't know which way to head—to her, past her, back out the door. Her face gave no hints.

She was wearing her old Hawkeye sweater. Her hair was down, in braids. And she stood and came slowly to me with her arms out. She had been crying; her flesh was hot and dry. I think back to this now as the grandest gesture of our life together; she was saving my life a second time.

She didn't ask (she assumed correctly) where I'd gone; she didn't ask why I'd gone on a rampage. I felt terrible. The story she told me in bed was approximately this: Ben-Zvi had come to take her back to California and she'd told him to butt out of our affairs. Some furies are implacable—I know that now—he had simply decided when he heard of our marriage that I was no match and he'd become a front-line obstructionist. That was when I learned the words *Shabbes goy*—the Sabbath gentile who turned on the lights for pious Jews. That's what I was to my atheistic father-in-law.

Then he'd mentioned his big plan, the one he'd come to get her approval for. His autobiography wasn't dead! Only this time, he was scripting it for television, not the movies. And, get this (best of all! he'd said), it wasn't for England at all. It was for German television. He'd already translated it. The Germans had all the old footage, and prints of the movies he'd seen in the twenties and worked on. He would go to Munich for the summer and work with the hot young names in German television (they've since become the hot young names in German cinema). Old friends were interested in acting. It would be one of the biggest things ever attempted on German television—obliquely about Nazism and the Holocaust, of course—but concentrating on a life in the arts, on the German century.

"I told him that bitterness is the mother of nostalgia," she said. The idea of returning to Germany sickened her. Hilda, of course, had refused.

My own feelings were more equivocal. For Ben-Zvi, personally, I wished nothing but misery. But for a writer with a dream, I could muster sympathy. Remember, until later that same night (early that same morning and continuing through the day), I didn't know that much about Rachel's attitudes to Germany or the Holocaust. I didn't know the poems and stories she'd been writing. She'd even owned a Volkswagen, back in Iowa—in my generation, that was a signal you looked for.

(This was the last day of innocence in our marriage. She knew I'd seen a woman. She also knew she'd married a madman, or maybe just a brat. And in a matter of hours, I would learn that I had married a genius and been entrusted with her keeping.)

Deep down, then, I could support Ben-Zvi's condemnations of America as easily as I could support Rachel's horror of Germany. Why would any European stay in America if he could honorably get out? Europeans dived deeper and came out dryer than Americans; they smoked more and never got lung cancer; bricklayers knew Mozart and waiters sang Verdi . . . and schoolgirls spoke six languages. I knew enough, however, not to say, Why shouldn't he?

"I told him if he went to Germany, I had no father."

I was dying to confess my own sins, though they were growing paler by the minute.

"Look—about tonight, earlier, I mean—"

"I told him what I thought of his behavior."

"Nothing compared to me."

"That's true."

"Christ, did I feel righteous! I sailed along under a righteous head of steam."

"Where did you sail off to?"

"A walk."

"I see."

She saw, of course, though she didn't mention it for months. (One day in the spring when we received the notice of an opening, "Carla Goodings at the Frick," Rachel handed it to me and said, "Your friend, I believe.")

The truth of the matter is that on a single night, she lost a father and gained a husband, and I lost a wife and gained an institution.

In the dark hours of early morning, I awoke to a gentle rocking on the bed, and the soft moan that I interpreted first as crying, then as a kind of singing.

I pretended not to see. It was Rachel, of course, but a Rachel I'd never seen before. She was praying in the old Jewish way, davening, striking her head softly and repetitively. It was the prayer for the dead, and out of a deep superstition, I never asked her about it, or whom it was for. But I heard it so many times that night, repeated with such urgency and secrecy, that it burned into my brain.

Chapter Twenty-one

A couple of years ago, we sent a spacecraft into the solar system. Maybe we'll live long enough to absorb all the data. I sit here in timeless India, fascinated by all of it. The *Times of India* relays the pictures; Indian astronomers offer instructive commentary. A few years ago, the *Times* even relayed the pictures of Pittsburgh's Carleton House Hotel being blasted into rubble. I winced. I'm at that point in my life when the dead speak more insistently to me than the living.

If you remember your space data, Rosie, you may recall that Jupiter has a moon, Io, that is called the most active body in the solar system. Its surface is in constant volcanic eruption. Constant. The reason is the proximity of Jupiter, whose gravity keeps Io's core in volatile soupiness, sort of sloshing around under a frail skin.

We didn't know about Io in 1967. If so, I would have diagnosed myself as Iotic, the disease as Iosis: the result of orbiting too close to a larger gravity. That's approximately what happened the night after her father's visit, when Rachel showed me her work of the past three years. I put up a feeble attempt at escaping it, with my novel, but basically

I was caught. She published a small book in the spring of
1967. Then she gave that May reading at the Ninety-
second Street Y, the reading that made her a star overnight,
and she gave that West Coast reading that you attended in
the fall. And the *Selected Poems* came out, and the stories
started appearing, and she was dead in January 1968.

The point is, we were both iotic; we both circled larger
bodies, our cores in perpetual eruption. There's another
moon out there somewhere (I'm far from research facili-
ties, or else I'd dig up its name) with its own little satellite
—let's call that little satellite (lumpy, pocked, wobbly in its
orbit, doggedly constant) Durgin. Rachel is Io, the beautiful daughter, and the planet she circles—still circles, will always circle—is so enormous we will never plot it.

Or if you want a simpler concept, think of this. Trapeze
artists will sometimes refuse to perform. A given night, a
certain combination of air pressure, temperature, things
they can sense with their skin and their inner ears. "Too
much gravity," they'll say. Too much, invisibly, weighing
her down.

Rachel had too much of it all: talent, expressiveness, language, disembodied pain. If I were ever to commit suicide,
I know it would be from enormous personal suffering,
some inconsolable private grief. Her life, as I understand it
(correct me if I'm wrong) was relatively painless. It's as
though she picked up signals on a radio band we couldn't
hear. Things acted through her.

We stayed in the next day, sipping tea and sweeping
china. Her father, leaving that night for Europe, didn't
even call. Rachel had always been to me a Temple of
Reason—dry, hard, unforgiving; irony was her armor.
Now I saw this . . . desecration, Rachel as ritual-obser-

vant, Rachel as daughter, wife, and hostess, and I saw for the first time how dependent she had been on her father, and now was on me. I'd assumed she was the strong one in the marriage; I might go out and achieve a measure of fame, but she had the authority, the brains.

I also had thought of myself as the madman, the deranged partial-genius, the guy with unpredictable habits and justifiable hungers. Rachel was my rock, my stability. I depended ever so slightly on her scorn, her irony. I had no irony. I was innocent of history; I'm all greed and lust and hunger; I trust myself and hate my enemies. I'm not confused, ever. And the work reflects that, or did, until confusion entered my life. And I had no way of handling it.

Until you mentioned it in your letter, Rosie, I had no idea that Rachel depended on me for stability, respected my ego and my ambition. All the things I called immature in myself (and noted for eventual correction) she clung to; she needed that callow Pittsburgh self, she identified with my mother in ways that I found baffling.

What a partnership we might have been!

We were sitting at the kitchen table that evening after my dinner of pasta, polishing off a bottle of Chianti, when she asked me, "Do you mind if I read you a poem?"

"Whose is it?"

Unperturbed, she extracted it from her folder. "It's called 'The Filmmaker's Daughter,' " she said. "It goes like this."

You dropped me where the compass
had no meaning.
East, where mountains grew,

and snowflakes fat as sea gulls
settled in the passes.
East, where deserts tore the moisture
from my coastal eyes
and the Sierras wore rims of snow
like, you said, ermine stoles
at a premiere: this dream,
Father, has no meaning.

To hunch against the unrinsed breakers
and doze away a lifetime's sorrow
under the savage palms
of Santa Monica has made of me
the inconsolable, the prisoner of your
accidental escape. I have no
Holocausts, Father, only what you didn't leave me
and the Germans didn't take.
Though sometimes I forget
You are German too.
History sings for you
with occult melodies.

Why do I demand
more savage distractions?
I can say it now, Father:
you have botched a second chance and the rasp
of palms, the thump of hooves
down the silted drive, the pools of idleness:
they are chains.
They are ghosts demanding food,
they are nanny's curses,
they are the broken crockery—Father!
There are clots of blood on my walls.

I can say it now outside your hearing:
The compass that steered us here,

the thirty years of Rose parades and
parties on the Palisades, the sour indecision
that left us hostage to your exile
and the cruel consolation of a vulgar
hospitality: they are without meaning.

Not ever thinking the unflushed virus
you carry, the virus you passed
to others, the virus isolated
but not extirpated, not ever thinking
of deformities visited
on the children of shadows,
fed by ghosts along the shore,
given salt to teach us
too much community
might strike us dumb again.
Given toys to teach us
an arrogant humility.

In those days, Rachel read just as she spoke; she'd never given a public reading. She turned the pages over to me (just as I'm turning them over to you); she never included this poem in her readings, and it doesn't appear in *Depth Perception* because it related, she felt, only to herself. "It's my kaddish," she said. But she was a performer in her way —when she gave that reading at the Ninety-second Street Y, she had people weeping, she had others on their feet— audiences wanted to devour her where she stood. Maybe you remember that at Berkeley, Rosie; maybe that's the secret you're trying to recover.

Me, too.

I was crushed. She'd written the poem after saying her prayer, while I slept, with the smashed crockery still on the floor. It might have been the start of her saying good-bye; first to her father (whom she never saw again, as she had promised), and then to her mother (in her "Rhein-gold" poem), and finally there was even a poem to me, which I still have.

I suppose some critic, if not you, has come up with the inescapable fact that her last forty poems, and not just the one to me, are suicide notes, or prayers for the dead.

She read all day. Funny poems, like the ones she'd written about my mother without ever showing them to me, like "How Many Books?" or "Saint Carmen of Steato-pygia," referring to one of the jammers on the Oakland roller-derby team. And poems she'd written in Italy before "Neighbors" (which ended her Italian phase), love poems to Marco, poems on paintings, nature poems, even devo-tionals. You have those poems somewhere in the papers; the world has them. I won't comment on them, since I only know the context of three poems—the one I just quoted and "Neighbors," and the one to me that last morning, which I'm not ready to give up.

Later that night, after reading her collected works, and having dinner at the Hungarian restaurant—cold cherry soup and goulash—she took out another notebook and started reading stories to me. Normally I prefer to read fiction myself (I'm grateful to poets whenever they want to spare me the effort), but not with Rachel and her sto-ries. She gave them magic, and added warmth to their irony.

The problem with her kind of writing is simply this: What to do when reality is too monstrous for irony—the "banality of evil" problem—or when irony is too stern a measure for a simple human truth? You end up looking callous in the face of tragedy, or intolerant of simple weakness. That's what we discussed after she read me the story, or is it the fable, of "Julia."

I remember when she started reading "Julia," I stopped her after the first sentence, when she indicated it ended with an exclamation point:

All Julia wanted after the long dirty train ride was a shower and a warm, soft bed!

"Hold on!" I interrupted. "You can't use exclamation points in serious stories." I felt a little protective about fiction in our marriage—it had become my threatened little promontory of expertise.

"Okay," she said. " 'warm, soft bed, period.' " Then she looked up from the page and added, "Maybe you should wait till you know where the train is going."

It took me a second or two to catch on. "Oh, God."

"I'm sorry. I really wish I could write stories about myself. Or California, or even Americans in Europe. But when it comes out, it's always about little girls in . . . the other Europe." It wasn't a long story, so she riffled to the end.

"Here's the last line. Maybe it shouldn't be said so directly, but . . . *Since no one who made that trip or visited that camp is alive to tell the story, I have told it again for all of them.*"

She described her recurrent dream to me, one that's reflected in her poems and stories, if you look hard enough. She is standing on the riverbank. We were out walking on a beautiful spring day in the unspoiled countryside. There is a river next to us, forest beside us, birds twittering in the trees, and a warm spring sun beating down. We sang, we ate, we drank some wine, and when she gets up again, I have disappeared. She hears distant shouting, "Raaachelll—" and far on the other side of the river she sees me, waving my arms. And the sun is falling behind a mountain ridge, the spring air turns colder, and the river churns with ice and trees and houses and live-stock and bodies—always parts of bodies.

How did I get over here? she wonders. She can see a secure modern city on the other side. Planes in the sky, highways, suburbs.

I don't want to corrupt these memories with bits of literary criticism, but that's what we did: we were, after all, literary people, however impure my motivation. The finest parts of my character were embedded in writing, the most generous moments of our lives had been given to books. My own arrogant humility, if you please, is found in those thousands of hours reading quarterlies and then collections and in hewing to that promise I made at Iowa to read a book a day until I'd sucked into myself everything obvious and even a few obscurities.

In the last year of Rachel's life, we lived in a literary bubble. There was the question of her spreading fame, of course, the demand for readings and the obscene attention (and the almost silent appearance of "Smoke" in all this), but there was, more to the point, the tranquil intensity of those months when I sat at home to answer the telephone while she wrote, and I tried writing a few stories till a new novel idea pushed itself forward. It didn't. I toyed with writing a comic novel, something delirious about the incongruities of our backgrounds—I didn't know we were six months from ending it all, and that the incongruities would be left for me to solve, this way, to you.

During the last few months, after she returned from that reading tour in California and refused to see her father, I felt like a drowning man, himself holding a loved one by her fingertips above the water. And I could feel her grip lightening, day by day. I knew I couldn't hold on to her, and letting go myself was no answer.

Then, one morning, I felt her grip for the last time. All the aching was over. She seemed happy. She cooked a big breakfast. She decided to bake some bread—that's a symbol, isn't it, of continuity? She went into the bedroom and wrote the love lyric "Sauterne," and killed herself while the dough was rising.

"Call it," she wrote, "the twittering of the moon."

She was being generous. It wasn't the moon, it was me. My visits to Carla had nothing to do with it. (And apart from writing her own series of museum-guard poems, Rachel had nothing to do with Carla.) And it wasn't her lover, Jack Toomey (the political historian at Columbia), because we weren't competing for her love; we seemed to be at our individual best together.

Jack Toomey is the man in her diaries. Since he's not literary, he's someone you should talk to. He knew her in different ways. He was her guide to Morningside Heights, to coffee with Hannah Arendt and her circle. Jack's a decent man, but something of an astronaut—too perfect in quantifiable ways, if you know what I mean. (The first time she met him, in the Columbia Library, where they were searching for the same old journal, she found him too clean-cut, too Waspy, too "Mormonical.")

After she died, Jack wrote his famous study of the Constitution. Some even said he'd put the Constitution on the couch. He literally saw it as an embodiment of the national character. If the society was sick—this was the early seventies, after all—the Constitution was its autobiography. He psychoanalyzed it, and its implications for the national character, the limits of its freedom, the depth of its vision, its hopes and contradictions, its aristocratic pluralism, its vast and intricate design, its sweeping claims and lyrical despair—as pathology.

The relationship between Rachel and the Constitution might be worth exploring.

I remember a favorite old Iowa bull session: brilliance versus genius. Most of the writers that dazzle us, make us think twice about entering the same competition, are brilliant. The glare off their work is like a polished mirror's. It is so easy to ignore the duller finish of genius, the many sides and layers that make it up.

Brilliant she surely was, in every measurable way. Was she also a genius? (I don't think the two are in any way connected; you can't get promoted like a chessmaster). Geniuses bind us to their world, they see the world whole, and they are aggressive in creating it. If you had asked me when I started this if Rachel was a genius, I surely would have answered yes. It was an article of faith with me that I had stumbled into marriage with a genius, and therefore I was exempt from any blame for its collapse. Geniuses just do things that the bright, and even the brilliant, cannot control.

But she wasn't a genius, Rosie. She was too defensive, her world too fragmented (had she survived, she might have achieved that peculiar half-genius, half-brilliance of a Kafka), I think (to sound reactionary), there was not enough health in her world to sustain it.

This is where my pain enters. If she wasn't a genius, if she lived on my side of the room, if we were knowable to one another, and especially if she relied on me and even loved me (as you say), then I am the villain of the piece. And my life here is an attempt at salvation.

Rachel once told me a bitter joke. It sounded cynical
enough to have been one of her father's Hollywood jokes.
A psychiatrist's wife commits suicide. When a non-shrink
confronts him, "Isn't it an indictment of your profession?"
he answers, "Not really. We'd been divorced six months."

What a bastard, I thought. And I laughed and laughed.

And something else, Rosie. These pages I've been sending you—they aren't a novel, and they're not quite an autobiography either. They are the recordings of energy-
bursts from a distant star, the little bit we've been able to
pick up here, at the edge of a scruffy universe, with defective equipment.

Chapter Twenty-two

It seems like years ago that I mentioned I'm nothing more, here, than a glorified carpenter. Emphasis then on carpenter; now, on glory.

I'm the biggest employer in Faridpur, even bigger than the Asian connection of New York Mets logos. Forty carpenters work for me, our income is high, and nearly all of it in the form of foreign exchange. What I do, basically, is go to New Delhi every few months, visit friends in the various embassies and ask if they've seen anything in wood they'd like copied. Big things—stereo cabinets, wall systems, bed frames, formal dining tables. Teak, rosewood, mahogany—it doesn't matter. Costs and weight and transport don't matter to my clients, since they're diplomats.

When Leela and I came here, her father was a village *mistri*, the kind of carpenter who fashions small writing desks or bookshelves from discarded scrapwood. He had the ability of all craftsmen in this culture—cooks, tailors, mechanics—to look at a picture, commit it to memory, and reproduce it perfectly. Leela's American earnings over the years, remitted faithfully, had resulted in a creditable version of a southern California mansion.

We came over for just a summer, immediately after getting married in Lovettville. Dev was conceived here,
though born back in the States the following winter (I'd
taken my bride back to New York, where she found immediate library work and I went back to my network of
part-time jobs.) When Dev was just beginning to walk,
Leela started developing back pains. At first the doctors
told us it was not uncommon—she was thirty-nine, after
all, and the birth had been stressful. Then she started losing weight. By the time we got the proper diagnosis, it was
of course too late.

So we came back a second time, for her death. She refused chemotherapy, radiation (only enough to permit her
a few weeks' remission) and surgery; she began instructing
me on her relative indifference to the death of her body, as
she referred to it. It was good that she did so, for it became
my duty to lay her body on the funeral pyre and to thrust
the burning branches in her mouth, where oil had been
poured.

When that was done, *papaji*, Dev, and I went back for
tea and I realized that this was a place that made sense to
me. I was a son again and I was a father, and grieving was
not acceptable behavior.

"I am the son of a *mistri*," I told *papaji*. "Allow Dev and
me to stay with you."

He wept, for the first time, with gratitude. And we
began this slow climb up the ladder. My demons are
tamed, Rosie, though I realize that India cannot be my last
stop. If I am healed, I have to return someday.

Two of my wives have died. The middle—she took the
name of Digger as a cover for her kleptomania and other
deficiencies—was one of those weird turnings a man might

take, in grief and self-pity and nihilism. It lasted four months, a kind of 120 Days of Sloth and Swinishness. Trauma precludes much memory—she was like a lightning bolt across my life—and in those four months I was served with old processes; I was taken into custody; our apartment was searched for drugs and stolen property; I was pushed around by some of her milder confederates; I was the respectable (till then) front, used and (thank God) abandoned. These are all the banshee wails of my life's midnight, an indication to me that populations exist, inside me and just outside the gates, ready to march if I let them, on anything I ever valued.

Even now, I'm sometimes gripped with the horror, here in the celibate sands of Rajasthan, that my second marriage is still in force, that somewhere along the line I forgot to sign a paper, and my third marriage is thus annulled and I will be obliged to return to Digger and support her various habits for the rest of my life.

I once noticed numbers tattooed on her wrist. *My God*, I first thought, Digger, of all people, was a Holocaust survivor! She saw me looking. "That's my social security number," she laughed. "Jake had a needle, so he burned it in. I like it—it's convenient."

It's a nightmare I face every time I go to Delhi and pass the rows of American and European beggars outside the American Express offices in Connaught Circus—that one emaciated female with a streaked, dirty face, blue-white skin, and hunger-hollowed eyes will grab my arm and pull me to the gutter again.

Enough of her. My ghosts, otherwise, are gentle ghosts; they grow with me, and I still address them. One of my oldest fantasies was that, by closing my eyes and invoking a name, I could project that person into my field of vision. When I was teaching in Bridgeport or Newark, and riding the bus back to Manhattan, I used to cry out to Rachel; she would answer, and I would show her exactly where I was. "Fort Lee, Rache, coming in on time. Bus will drop me at West End and Seventy-second." It was always a surprise when she didn't get the message.

I still do it. I walk the village alleys here, or sit out with my carpenters going over the hasty sketches and measurements, and sometimes my eyelids fall and I can feel Rachel or Leela wanting a stroll. So I'll get up from Ram or Govind, tell them to work it out as best they can, and we go for a walk, I and my ghosts, along the parapets of Tamerlane's wall, or out along the millet fields where the women are always stooped, or deeper into the village, where all the boy tycoons of Faridpur commerce gather for tea and a foul little cigarette, sipping cloudy tea from communal cups.

I have become more of a mystic than I ever thought possible. It's the effect of this land only partially. That stag in Cooke's Forest is part of it too, and the moilings in a drop of sperm. I was always a mystic, though I've tried to murder the impulse.

Let me circle back, Rosie, backfilling as I go, till we come again to that day in January that you want to know so much about. The day that my life balanced on; twenty-nine years of comparative ego buoyancy before it, and these twelve years of dense star-stuff since.

A little over five years ago, I was subletting a two-room apartment on Columbus Avenue, facing what seemed to be absolute extinction. I was an adept at packing up on a moment's notice—a typewriter, three boxes of books and papers, plus a suitcase crammed more with plates and favorite mugs than clothes—and I'd be out of one address

and into another inside of half an hour. I was good at spot-
ting sublet notices in the local laundromats, just as I was
good at approaching various institutions for part-time
work whenever I heard of a death, divorce, or breakdown
in the lower depths of a local English department. For five
years in Manhattan I had been stringing together part-time
jobs on contingency bases, educating myself in half a
dozen fields of literature, getting by with just a Lovett
B.A.

My name appeared on no mailbox. I was grateful for
any disguise.

I expected no mail, and was afraid, after Rachel's death,
of the things people left behind when they saw my name. I
kept my eyes open for dancers and actors, those blessed
animals that never read. I was responsible for watering
avocados and feeding cats, and taking messages from
agents and producers—the world I'd left behind.

It was at just about that time, when I was sleeping off
the effects of my thirty-seventh birthday, spent alone, that
the phone started ringing. It was early—anything would
have been early—and the voice on the other end asked for
"the novelist, Richard Durgin."

It was a southern voice; the combination of South, novelist, and my name sobered me up.

"Dwayne Harvey Lewis," he said. "I'm the new chairman out here at your old alma mater, Mr. Durgin. Sorry I
never had the privilege of teaching you, but, well, maybe
we're fated to meet after all."

I'd stretched uncomfortably to grab the phone, and as I
untwirled the cord and turned over, I could hear Dwayne
Harvey Lewis asking in that Big John Connally accent,
"Mr. Durgin? Are you there?"

"Right," I said.

"First of all, Mr. Durgin, I have to ask one big question. Are you free?"

With my favors? I wondered. In approximately two days, my temporary job would end, and there had been nothing, anywhere. In my years of degradation, I had not explored the unemployment lines. "Very free, Dwayne Harvey."

"And my second question is what's your social security number?"

And so I learned that Stur Foster had suffered a stroke, they needed a writer to teach for the next three months, for which there was only one logical choice—Stur's most famous student.

Could I cut my New York commitments and come out to Kentucky for the spring?

"I can't call the offer princely, Mr. Durgin—it would be more in the nature of a sacrifice for you, I'm afraid."

The sum was more than I'd seen in a full year's teaching. It might even cause me tax problems for the first time since the first novel.

I told him I would consider it an honor, since it was, after all, for Stur that I'd be doing it.

"Can we reserve a place for you in Ramsey Hall, then?"

"What?"

Ramsey had been converted, before Dwayne Harvey Lewis' arrival, from a girls' dorm to a faculty residence. All the dorms now were coed, and all of them were uphill.

With little prompting, I pictured a cozy master's residence, a sideboard stocked at college expense, a quilt turned back, a bone-china casserole steaming on an antique farm table. On the bus out to Lovett, I dreamed of leather armchairs, walls stripped to their honest Baptist brick and crammed to the ceiling with books. (Whatever else I had discarded of my old honor and dignity, I remained devoted to reading, if not exactly to writing. Thanks to the anxiety of preparing lectures in freshman survey courses, I'd even mastered most of Shakespeare, Chaucer, and the Restoration; I was still an uneducated fool, but not an illiterate one.)

Something cheerful and welcoming and, above all, mine. And if I dared to think of it at all, there would be a Lovett girl to come home to. I was going to be a shark now myself; even football players backed off from a professor in heat.

Ramsey Hall wasn't just barren; it had been looted. A Roman villa, after the vandals. Twenty years before, there'd been chandeliers, ballroom mirrors, burgundy carpets that propelled you across the floor with a kind of coiled grace to a spiral staircase that made every girl a princess as she descended to meet her date. There'd been deep sofas and high-backed armchairs where supple young couples could forage for sex less detectably than in a car. I remembered a carved oak reception desk from where the wives of retired Baptist missionaries would call the maidens down.

I'm such a goddamn fool, I expected all that to have remained, that touch of graciousness, never realizing that it had passed from everyone's life and not just from mine.

A People's Army must have done the conversion. In place of the desk and mail slots stood a splintery old library table waiting to stab anyone who brushed up against it, littered with old letters, opened envelopes, magazine wrappers, and even a few copies of the New York *Times*. Amazing—the warmest part of the week in my senior year had been the Wednesday drive into Lexington with Janet and sometimes a professor, for the past Sunday's *Times*. An advance, then. Someone was subscribing to *Scientific American*. Someone else to *Rolling Stone*.

A young married couple were receiving gallery notices from Louisville. There was a Leela receiving an aerogram from India. My little Lovett was growing up: there were Jewish names, an Indian name, and a notable lack of the Bonnies and Chrissies of my Kentucky youth. There was even a bulky envelope for me, containing the keys and a television request form. (I avoid television sets the way I avoid splintery library tables.)

And so I made my way across the scrofulous carpet to a serviceable staircase at the side of the foyer, up to my room in the dorm that had set my head and heart afire some fifteen years earlier.

I had feared being oppressed by continuity, that I would know too much, be too popular, that old passions would grip me, old enmities surround me. That first evening I walked to the chapel along the brick path; I sat in the back listening to choral practice, I walked to the front, pacing off the sixty feet from the lip of the mezzanine to the stage. In my fraternal youth, we'd had a pledge who wrapped match heads in tinfoil and lined them up on the mezzanine rail. As he heated the foil the matches would ignite, sending hot pellets of tinfoil on the stage. Speakers, singers, musicians, the dean of the chapel would slap at their necks, thinking they'd been bee-stung out of season.

Most of the academic buildings I knew had disappeared. The Union that I'd wasted a year in was gone, and in its place stood something proper to a Big Ten school, with bowling alleys, a delicatessen, and two small theaters. My fraternity had disappeared, of course, as had all rumors of its existence; it was now the alumni headquarters. I ate a hamburger that first night, seeing none of the professors I had known, calling no one, and walked back to my room, thinking it all, as Rachel would call it, "Jersey Turnpike."

There was a note for me, pushed under the door.

It was from the head librarian, Ms. Mehta. A very proper little note saying how pleased she was that I would be on campus, and that I might enjoy visiting the Richard Durgin Exhibit in the main foyer of the library. She apologized for having to do the best with what she could get on short notice. She signed her room number, on the floor above me.

It couldn't hurt, and it wasn't that late. Anything was better than that room.

There's an image, hard to shake, of the Indian woman in the American university. Plump and sari-clad, efficient and hard to understand, married to a computer scientist or a doctor. Living poor and stashing it away. No visible fun in her life, children in school doing very well, cleaning up on scholarships. She jingles with gold bangles as she walks.

That was not Leela. She was about my age, slim, dressed in slacks and a sweater, with short hair and contact lenses. I'm not implying attraction, only surprise.

"I know you from your pictures," she said. "Please come in. A drink?"

"Only tea, please, or coffee."

Love-sick as always, I nevertheless exempted Ms. Mehta immediately. My fantasies were as immature as ever—I was back at Lovett! I was choice! (I know now what I wished I had known then.) The Indian librarian was a nice lady, in her thirties, probably married to some guy back home, more westernized (and attractive in a westernized way) than the few Indian women I'd seen in New York, but that was it.

She was also attractive in a totally different way. She was the world's leading authority on Richard Durgin.

She was the Rosie Chang of Durginness.

"I first went to the registrar's office," she told me over tea, "and looked up all your records. Many of the professors are still here, of course. Then I went to each of them and asked if they had any of your old papers. Some still did. Then I went to the library and took out copies of your books and, I believe, all the stories in the various little magazines."

She looked so serious. She pulled up her sweater sleeves as she talked.

Oh, Rosie, she was so dark and downy; she was the Mona Thwait of the converted Ramsey Hall.

"Then I asked Mrs. Foster for permission to use some of your letters to her husband."

"I have more manuscripts with me," I said. "I've kept my corrected galleys." (I even had copies of favorable reviews, though I wasn't about to admit it.)

"I think I have managed to find most of the important reviews," she said.

"Amazing! I never read them, of course."

I must have cared for her, somehow, lying so furiously.

"The letters to Stur Foster are very beautiful, I think. They reveal you as a man of integrity."

She didn't really mean it, I thought at the time; she's foreign, after all. I remembered sending those letters, how hard I'd worked on them to sound modest and unaccomplished, owing everything to Stur and the encouragement of Lovett. I did owe him everything, but I wasn't big enough to say it that way, then. Now it was too late.

"And did you get a chance to read my books, too?"

And then she smiled, Rosie, and if you believe in universal gestures, you know what the smile meant. Yes, she had. And she liked them. Loved them, in fact. She didn't say any of that, but she communicated an essential fact to me, that first night back at Lovett: she was a woman of this time and place, as well as a culture foreign to me (yes, why do I keep doing it?). She only said, "Yes, I have read them all. In fact, I had the novels even before I knew you were coming. I'm a reader, Mr. Durgin."

"Dick, or Richie, please."

"Will I have the pleasure of escorting you through the exhibit tomorrow, Dick?"

In ways that New York never was, Lovett and Iowa were, to me, the world. It was strange, hearing a perspective on Lovett that was both alien and intimate. Leela knew the staff, she relished gossip, but I detected no special mention either of a displaced husband or a current attachment. Her rooms were only slightly less impersonal than mine—a batik instead of my "Old Kentucky Home" calendar, some plants, a round brass-topped table. Her tidy breakfast table was set for one.

(A bachelor has special vision.)

As for your interest in all this, Rosie, I waited for mention of Rachel and none was forthcoming. Leela was a librarian, not a modern literature scholar, she burrowed but didn't connect. Deep down, I suspected that Lovett would be no different than any place else—that if they had me on campus, someone would want to interview me about What Really Happened.

Resistance dies hard; I should have gone down to my room thinking: I have met the path of my salvation. I should have thought the ways of redemption are sweet and mysterious. I should have asked her— Are you alone, Miss Mehta? Instead, I thought only, Now there's a strange little lady. She knows me better than I know myself.

Chapter Twenty-three

There's a comedy here, if you look for it.

The subject of a thirty-seven-year-old (as I was then) easing himself back into the dating pool is undeniably comic in a Neil Simon sort of way—looking first for unattached young professors (by definition there are none), then for the higher-level secretaries and departmental assistants, and finally surrendering (as you knew I would) to the widest possible pool of contacts—mid-seventies undergraduate women.

The comedy of thinking yourself supremely sophisticated, just weeks out of New York, and half a dozen years out of a legendary marriage (and a couple of years out of your most secret degradation), and discovering—Humbert Humbert that I always was—that time has been racing forward while you were learning to write long sentences with a minimum of punctuation and the children born in the middle of the fifties (your decade, as it turns out) have been doing healthier things with their young bodies.

If you were Richard Durgin at Lovett in the spring of 1977, you read your students' stories closely between the lines, you developed the antennae of an alley cat. Sex was in, even at Lovett. When I'd been a student, my women classmates rarely wrote in a female point of view; they didn't know how a woman sounded. Now we knew (just as we'd always suspected back in our freshman year), they went back to their dorms after a date and announced, "Fuck, am I horny!"

Rising to the lure, I suggested that my horny senior, Miss Fitch, accompany me to Lexington one evening for a movie.

She pointed out a motel halfway there that would do quite nicely. She was nineteen, from a Cincinnati suburb, where her father managed portfolios. We churned on the double bed for the requisite minutes, stared at the television for a movie, swam in the indoor pool, and returned to the room for another bash.

"I like my lovers to show their vulnerability," she said. She especially enjoyed a sigh, tears, a whimper, apologies for acts—mainly—of omission.

"You're nineteen. What do you know of vulnerability? Where did you read it?"

"Vulnerability is the new sexiness." She pouted, combing out her golden hair.

That was mid-April. Kentucky summer, the month or two of border-state perfection. Stur Foster passed on, just before Derby Day, without a sign of recognizing me on my visits. Ungraciously, I immediately thought of replacing him, but the chairman never called me in.

"A lot of us write," I overheard him once in the halls. "And Stur was never really on staff, you know, officially. There's not a hell of a lot to replace."

So that era ended, the time when even guys like me could discover a talent they never knew existed, those twenty years of elite democracy practiced by an amateur teacher and writer. Sitting here today, Rosie, I think they were probably right; better not to replace the irreplaceable. That's not the way I argued five years ago.

I had only one course to teach—Stur Foster's old Advanced Creative Writing (which now carried full credit) —and I was dreaming, Rosie, of a life worth living all over again. Time for writing, except that I couldn't write. But was I ever eloquent! I taught like an apostate denying his defection; even with my own talent slipping away from me, the secrets of the craft slashed through my hands, each narrative strand leaving a nick and a scar as it burned past me.

So I was eloquent, as the gift departed, and I was preparing myself for a life of serious teaching—but nothing was offered.

So it will come to pass, if you ever return to the campus where you'd been tested and where you first tasted fame and glory, that no one really cares who you were, or that Lovett Social Club emerges, in memory, as another version of the American Constitution (Jack Toomey, take note), and that the professors you respected have become the crusty Old Guard, identified with their years of opposition to the sixties reforms. And you have no friends among the younger staff, who are the sixties reformers, turned mellow and hedonistic by the seventies. You are fifties, that decade you never consciously watched passing. You share an office, on the one day a week you meet students, with a man your age who identifies himself as a "Beatist." "You mean Baptist?" you ask at first, but no—he's done a thesis on Kerouac and Ginsburg and Snyder and Alan Watts and he's compiling chapbooks from incoherent ramblings of the survivors. The fifties are his magic time, too, but a hustling

fifties of New York, Denver, and San Francisco, and he
has no interest at all in the surface life of the fifties. He's
convinced himself that we all lived in coffeehouses listening to jazz and mad comic monologuists, that we boosted
cars and fled to Mexico, that sex and dope and booze were
as free as the verse and the novels and the action painting. . . .

And almost, he convinces. The fifties were my power, I
think; they gave me crust and backbone, they gave me a
coherent social vision and a place to come from, and they
were free to admit to any of us growing up through them
that yes, they were superficial, and yes, there were things
in our immediate past and in our present and immediate
future that did not bear much thinking about.

The fifties were my vaccination.

It was as though the fifties were a giant engine, boosting
us into the future, confident and unquestioning and blind
to all reckoning and warning lights. And ever since, we've
been backfilling, correcting the flaws, tinkering with the
assumptions, reopening the old files. We know more than
we ever thought possible, and the engine is dying and we
will never know again that innocent confidence of Richard
Durgin and Wanda Lusiak, holding hands in Pittsburgh,
imagining the personal heli-attachments, the piling up of
wealth and hygiene that was promised to us.

Those were some of the things that Lovett brought
back. Because at Lovett in the middle seventies, the students still believed, and had every right still to believe,
never having seen poverty or having suffered reverses.
Minor corrections—the retirement of T. Lysander Crommelin and the admission of perceptible minorities, the liberalizing of residence laws, the blind eye to drinking, the
breakdown of dress codes, the cracking of the fraternity
system (and the necessary destruction of the Social Club,

which had subsidized inequity more than it had pushed for reform)—all these minor corrections added up to imperceptible reform, and left Lovett at relatively the same place in a liberalized society as it had been in 1957. The routine assumptions of my Lovett students would have been radical pronouncements, the common sexual practices would have gotten us expelled, their impieties were our blasphemies—but still, they were innocent, conservative, socially blind and historically impaired young people of wealth, breeding, and unchanneled intelligence.

They depressed me profoundly. Still, had I been called, I would have dedicated my life to them. They no longer called forth my old class hatred. And none of them, thank God, had even heard of Rachel Isaacs, even though the hagiography was well advanced in other parts of the literary world.

Leela took me through the exhibit that first morning; she'd displayed old term papers (just the "A's" of my English-major years), the *Atlantic* story, poems I'd published in the various campus magazines (and had forgotten about), and the sheaf of letters to Stur Foster.

Who is that guy? I might have liked him. With the two books, the reviews, the chapters devoted to him, the stories, the pictures—he was quite the young comer, at thirty.

"Were you really a carpenter's son?" she asked me as we stood in front of the *Atlantic* story.

"Almost precisely as described."

She was smiling a little too benignly at that. "Why?"

"Because I am a carpenter's daughter," she said.

(I should have asked to see her hands. I should have asked her to hold out her hands.) I said instead something stupid, like, I didn't know they had carpenters in India.

And she answered sharply, "What do you think—that we all live in mud huts?"

We toured awhile in silence.

"Did you hear strange voices this morning?" I finally asked.

"When?"

"It was still dark outside. I thought I heard a man shouting out words."

"When I sleep, Richard, I sleep."

"First I thought it was some kind of new addition—you know, a town crier or something. Then I got angry: who the hell starts shouting things at five in the morning? But when I got to the window, he was gone."

"There are many strange things on this campus. You don't have to involve yourself, so you should feel happy," she said.

I wanted to mention a few of my own strange involvements. She probably wasn't ready for Gideon Ramsey's boar hawg. The statues, thank God, were gone.

The voice outside the window continued for several days. The mornings were warm and bright and full of bird sounds anyway, so I was accustomed to waking up before six o'clock; five o'clock was not an imposition.

It seemed impossible that no one else heard it. On the third morning, I could make out the words—unpleasant ones they were, too— "Whoooore," and "Adulteress" —but I couldn't see the shouter. He had to leave by five o'clock, when the dawn began, because Ramsey Hall's jogging contingent took to the hills at about that time. They, of course, heard nothing.

This was not a prank. There was misplaced passion but no humor, no direction involved. Who, in this day and age, even used the word "adulteress?" (What faculty member, more to the point, isn't a whore or its male equivalent?)

One night in the second week, two distinct voices took up the chant.

Perhaps student activism at Lovett had taken a striking new turn. Maybe we should go up to the student dorms and shout out a few epithets of our own. Or maybe, of course, since no one else seemed to care, I should set myself up as a one-man investigator.

Too bad the old high-backed lounge furniture had been removed. But at three o'clock I went downstairs, slouched under the staircase, and waited. Ramsey Hall was a far more active place than I'd even considered; on the upper levels, doors were being opened and closed, and hushed voices were suppressing giggles all night long.

At a quarter to four, I went outside and crouched in the wisteria at the end of the veranda. That veranda we used to snuggle, or grapple on, now bare and even dusty.

The bellowing commenced without my noticing the bellower's arrival, as though he too, had let himself down from the dorm by a rope ladder. I jumped at the first raspy, manly throat clearing, coming from nearly on top of me.

"You whore. You wake up. Adulteress, I am calling you—"

And I was on him in a second, old third-string Homestead wrestler going first for the knees, lifting him, and dropping him on his back. He was strangely light, and I didn't fall on him immediately as I'd intended; instead, I made eye contact with his terror.

He was perhaps seventeen, with round dark eyes and a slight mustache. Obviously not Lovett; the boy was Indian. He had turned on one shoulder and was trying to regain his footing; I took an ankle and flipped him over.

"What the hell are you trying to do?" I cried, and now I was sitting on the small of his back, wrenching his foot back. "What's this all about, before I break your foot?"

He screamed. I pulled harder.

"Who are you?"

More screams. Lights went on above us.

Between gasps, I made out the words, "The son of the whore."

Up from Clay Street, I could spot a man running—campus security, I thought—except that he was Indian, too, and older, and carrying (I recognize it now) a cricket bat.

And there on the porch in her purple robe stood Leela Mehta, advancing down the stairs.

I was feeling a little like Custer. The boy seemed no immediate threat, so I released him. He was slow getting to his feet. "Up!" his father (I assumed) shouted.

"Both of you, leave here at once!" That was Leela, her voice suddenly accented, and commanding.

"Is this the man? Is this the man you have insulted my good name with?"

"Look, buddy," said I, advancing on him. He was my height—which is not to say much. "You heard the lady." And to myself I thought, Who the hell am I to be saying this. She was on the first step, just behind me. They would have to go through me to get her.

"You know these clowns?" I asked.

Of course, she had to. I'd already figured it out.

"You come, right now," said the husband. He added a string of new commands in his own language, to which Leela responded, "I will die first."

"Go back inside and call the police," I told her.

"I am calling the police," said the husband. "You have

raped my wife and assaulted my son. You will be going to jail for the rest of your life."

"Go back, Leela; he's crazy."

And she did; I could hear the rustle of her robe on the dusty veranda, and the choking back of her tears.

"Okay, now then. You want to fight? One or both—I'm ready. And the cops can pick up the loser."

I was in a high old mood—hadn't had a fight in fifteen years or more. But they wouldn't give me the satisfaction. The father pointed out his son's limp, his "broken leg." He would have the pleasure of seeing me in court, he said. The pleasure of seeing an adulterer and child abuser behind bars.

Step by step, I started advancing on him, and when we were six feet apart, he started pulling back. "I don't know that lady at all," I said, "but I know the two of you plenty well. If I hear one more morning like the last two weeks, I'll have the pleasure of seeing you in jail, got it? Now get off this campus and get out of that lady's life." I took two quick steps, then stamped the ground, and they were in full flight.

When I turned, Leela was standing at the door, sobbing against the door frame. It was a little after four in the morning when the parked car pulled out from the curb, and we went inside.

Chapter Twenty-four

The heart is a crazy broker, Rosie—who knows where it'll place its investments next? I was thinking only: Get this lady some tea, and she was sobbing on my shoulder (and God, was her face hot!); my only concern was getting her up the stairs before the faculty marathoners came skipping down.

And by the time we reached my floor, I was carrying her across my threshold and tucking her in my bed.

"I am not an adulteress," she kept repeating. "He is saying that because I left him to take a job."

"There, there," I said.

"His pride is hurt. He has poisoned my son against me. He can only think in those old ways—rape, adultery. I am ashamed for myself. What must you think of me?"

"His pride's not the only thing that'll be hurting, Leela."

"He has written my parents saying I am a loose woman. They are demanding a huge settlement from my parents. . . ."

Tribal things, I thought. We were sipping tea. For all I knew, parents could sue in India. "I hope your father's a sensible man," I said. "Tell them to fuck off."

It just slipped out, not the thing you say to your Indian-lady librarian, but she seemed to smile before saying, "My father is too polite to tell them to fuck off. He wouldn't listen to anything bad."

"Good for him."

"He'll threaten them with hammers and nails."

"Carpenters don't take shit, that's for sure."

"Only their daughters," she said, then added, just before my chorus, "and sons."

She bowed her head, looking down at the bedspread, I thought; I stared at her blue-black hair, looking for gray, or even white roots. None. Then I noticed she wasn't staring at the bedspread. She was staring at her open robe, and at one strap of the nighty that had slipped off. When she looked up again, she was smiling, and I helped with the other strap.

The ghost of Mona Thwait came to life that morning—it was only five o'clock, and I was culminating some kind of lifetime passion with Ramsey Hall and Leela's black, Rachellike hair, and the adrenaline from the near fight, and awe for this lady's reserve and beauty (now weirdly pitched) and her evident respect for my writing, and avenging myself on a lifetime of library tables and looking up at departmental meetings in which I had no permanent stake but still was required to attend (and is any woman sexier than a thirty-year-old assistant professor reading a report on curriculum change at four o'clock in the afternoon, when everyone is evidently going through the motions and words are detached from meaning and you sit there, watching pale, overworked lips reading words that can only drive you deeper into sexual fantasy)? Anyway, you know what I mean—this was it! This was the moment when everything familiar and exotic, dowdy and extravagant, tempting, forbidden, and savage was driven to the surface and I dived, and dived, until I had made her an adulteress lurid enough for any culture.

"Thank you," she said at eight o'clock. "I'm feeling much better now."

Well, that was my Leela. And as she tried to get out of bed we found ourselves still bound to an amazing discovery: that she didn't have to work that day and that I didn't care if Lovett offered me anything; we only cared to stay in bed until starvation drove us out, and that wasn't until late afternoon.

Three years later, on a funeral pyre in India, clarified butter was poured in her mouth, and I thrust burning branches in her face till the butter caught. Kibitzers stood around taking bets on my probable failure, clapping and shouting encouragement, while our baby son sat on his grandfather's arm and some of the carpenters and their wives sent up howls of grief.

I did a professional job. Leela had instructed me, as had my father-in-law. At the time I thought how wise was this ancient culture, cauterizing the grief so rigorously. No Forest Lawn sentimentality. But I realize that's a Western interpretation: all rituals over here are to prepare you for entry into the new stage of life.

After you have done a thing like that new passion is unthinkable. Remarriage is an act of sacrilege. Her face still floats before me, and she sits with Dev and me on the floor as we eat. She sits with me today as I write this. She has made of me a kind of brahmachari, a priest. She has ended my lusts.

Back when I started writing this, I said to myself, Rosie Chang is going to know more about Rachel Isaacs than I ever could, but not one word of truth will emerge from it without the stories I can tell.

I exaggerated my importance, and my knowledge.

There's only one more thing I know, and since we've come to the grim moments of my life, let me tell the tale of Rachel's passing.

It is winter in Manhattan. I have not been writing, but Rachel's work is suddenly everywhere (poetic fame is a mayfly's curse) and my mood, as I recall it, cannot be good. Jack Toomey, of course, is not subject to moods, and is not in direct competition. Mormonical as Disneyland, my friend Jack.

She has written her life's work—all those twenty thousand pages you have will be coming into print for decades, won't they? I know three or four poems, two stories, and am hustled out of the apartment (never by Rachel, just by the contemptuous stares of her interviewers) while the fame machine gears up.

With the marketing of Rachel, she is growing increasingly passive. Jack Toomey and I discuss it; we make plans, using the last of our savings, to take a vacation as soon as her book of stories is published. Somewhere warm and illiterate, without satellite relays.

One night, following expulsion by a television crew, I came in after a long angry walk. I'd been working out an argument: either we cut these parasites off, or else I leave. It's not that I'm jealous or begrudge your fame—your work deserves every bit of it—it's just that you've become a different person; they're making you into a zombie. You're exhausted and they're using your poetry to psychoanalyze you.

When I entered, the apartment was hauntingly clean. She was sitting in front of the television staring at a stupid comedy show. Very much unlike her.

I started with my reasonable ultimatum. (I'm terrible at these things. The moment I get angry I realize I love this woman. What would I be without her, who is really to blame?) She nods, but she's not listening.

"Rachel, are you listening?"

"What is this thing?" she asked.

"A stupid comedy show. Very popular."

"Every week they do this?"

"It's a comedy about life in a Nazi concentration camp."

"Which side are we supposed to like?"

"The good-guy Nazi guard and the wise-guy American are always getting the better of the loveable but bumbling S.S. officer."

And even as I said it, I knew I was squeezing the wound till it opened. I was out to puncture her.

"It's called *Hogan's Heroes*. I doubt that it rhymes with anything."

"Bergen's Belsens," she mumbled. Then she snapped her fingers in a frenzied little ditty, like a fifties rock song, "Who put the cream, in the crematorium?"

"Great gobs of whipping cream," I said.

"I guess I always knew," she said.

What can I say, Rosie? I was hurt and I was bitter, and deep down I probably resented her sudden fame, purchased, I thought, in ignorance of America. If she didn't know *Hogan's Heroes*, she didn't know me, either; if she couldn't swallow back that kind of gall, she couldn't cope with the years to come.

So take that, Rachel.

No one had vaccinated her against America.

"I think I'll go to bed," she said.

I think all the police reports mention that Rachel's body was discovered by me the following afternoon. That's not the truth. The facts are simply these: She was asleep when I went to bed, and she was up very early on the last day of her life. When I got up, I saw her in the kitchen punching down bread dough, and I smiled to myself as I showered. A good sign. Homely, wifely virtues and all that.

That afternoon there was a football game I wanted to see, as did Jack. He came over around one o'clock, to an apartment fragrant with baking bread. Rachel passed him in the hall, barely acknowledging him. We were both accustomed to it, but still he asked, "What's with Rache?"

"She felt a poem coming on," I said.

Actually, she'd been writing a poem all morning between punch-downs of the dough. All I knew was that its name was "Sauterne," about cooking wines. She wanted me to know that, in order to understand the poem.

We were engrossed in the game. She called out instructions from the bedroom about putting in or taking out the loaves.

Around half-time she came out of the bedroom and said she was going for her bath.

We were watching the game, eating fresh rolls, calling out how good they were, and plotting the vacation that afternoon as Rachel lay in the hot bath. When the game was finally over, it was Jack who started looking for her. "Rache? Rache?" I could hear him in the bedroom and in the back study. "She go out, Richie?" And I couldn't honestly remember.

He went into the hall, then down the stairs. I took another roll, then noticed the bathroom door was closed, though the light inside was off. She was sitting in the cool, dark waters, her eyes still white in the reflected light, her face and neck and shoulders whiter still.

"Rachel, for God's sake; you had us worried." And I snapped on the lights to a world of blood.

It seems that some people—like me—are destroyed when the world fails to conform to their vision. And others are destroyed when it does, down to the smallest detail.

I've replayed our last night and morning a thousand times, and that's all I can come up with—she was waiting for one last treachery. A final proof. I think of most suicide as impulsive, an almost flippant response to some unforeseen and entirely unworthy indignity. Almost as though we take our life only when its value has been so degraded, so whittled away and laughed at, that we despise it ourselves.

Even now I remember old conversations with Rachel, moments that I should have taken more seriously, back when I was struggling with existentialism and literature and falling upon all those undergraduate profundities (late, as usual) with my usual blood-lust.

"Hell is the inability to love!" I howled.

"Nonsense," she said.

"All right, then, hell is other people."

"Bullshit," she said. "Hell is Auschwitz."

Or a later exchange. I had put one of my characters into an existential nightmare. "Help!" he cried, "nothing's connected." Rachel, with the clarity of a paranoid, was faintly amused. "Everything's connected, darling—don't you know?"

Her father had betrayed her, and she had not forgiven him; Jack and I had probably disappointed her, but not in ways she couldn't forgive. (I've made her sound too brittle; she was a forgiving, compassionate woman, before the critics turned her into a "Passionara" for our times.) The country was betraying her with Vietnam, though she never mentioned it. She was always "political" in her art, but rarely topical.

And so to answer the first question you asked me, Rosie Chang—why did Rachel kill herself?—I'd say she killed herself over a silly, evil television program. The program provided the final evidence she was looking for, or the thing she most feared finding: proof that the European millions had died in vain, and that her country and her times were incapable of absorbing the lesson.

And I had delighted in rubbing it in.

I had always feared that I would be the one to let her down, that, by a stupid or unthinkable gesture, I would reveal myself to her, somehow, as a Nazi. She made me realize there was a lot of the Nazi in me, no matter how I worked on it. I resented her lack of Americanism, her California background, her Europeanization, her sophistication, her schooling, her breeding, her haughtiness; her dismissal of my pop-song and television and movie and sports and Pittsburgh and bitter-lumpen upbringing . . . I resented her (what else to call it?) rootless cosmopolitanism.

She'd never heard of Patti Page. A million sordid facts of my world she'd never been exposed to. Like a Fiji Islander, she died of the common cold.

Take this as the most damaging confession I can make. I may have been innocent of the actual crime, but I was the agent of her death. All those early critics who accused me of crimes I didn't commit—they were right, for all the wrong reasons. Not for the crimes I committed, but the help I omitted. If, as you say, she admired me for some things, even for my ego and my self-confidence, even that is gone now.

Maybe you know more. Maybe (I even pray) I'm wrong. Maybe somewhere in those twenty thousand pages are the keys to my own salvation. Her face haunts me still, and in her world—and mine—there are no torches I can bring to burn it away.

FOUR

Bagni San Stefano
Sept. 25, 1982

Dear Richie:

So now I know. Your last pages reached me here, in a small *pensione* about half a kilometer from Rachel's old Italian convent school. I walked up the path yesterday and sat in the long, sloping yard behind the stone buildings where she'd lived and studied for three years. I even sat on the stone wall—the land here is all rock and angles, old and beautiful—in the very place that Rachel described so perfectly thirty years ago, and I watched the train cutting its way up the slope to this village and the ones higher up; through tunnels and switchbacks, each reappearance bringing it closer. She had called it "the reincarnation" of the train, and had imagined each recurrence as a re-creation, a new historical epoch. Very Augustinian, the nuns had written, with approval.

It is peaceful, here. I could think myself an Italian, or at least a non-Chinese American, with very little effort.

I don't know how to respond to Rachel's death. It's so ghastly, so appalling, so squalid—yet what else could have caused it except something so wretchedly American? Something she couldn't defend against. It was the final collision of innocence and catastrophe, if I want to stretch my thesis to its insane limit. I understand the difficulty you faced, and I respect your withholding it till the end. It is the evidence of your understanding, I think; a mark of at least partial redemption, if that's what you're seeking.

(It must be the ecclesiastical setting here. Who am I to be giving absolution?)

The good news—I hope it's good news—is that I have the time and the money to visit you in India. I have things I want to leave with you—offerings from Rachel beyond the grave, and from me, struggling to mediate. I am grateful for the draft of "The Filmmaker's Daughter," and I can give you dozens of such poems that she never sent out or published—some of them about you.

It's true—I have mountains of facts about Rachel that you will never possess, but whatever truth the book contains will be built on the story you told.

If you can give me two weeks to answer more questions, who knows—I may be able to spare you thirty years of guilt and recrimination. Thirty years to get on with the rest of your life, wherever and however you choose to live it.

May I confess, after all these months of playing the sage Berkeley professor that I also get a tingle, thinking that we're about to meet? Well, there it is; a very professional, involved, unobjective and totally unironical confession from your "Cheena-lady."

See you next month, DV.

Yours,

Rosie

Epilogue

It is one of those countries where a foreigner calls a small boy in the boy's language. "Narinder Singh!" he shouts, and the boy stands under the balcony. "Sa'ab?" he asks. In their language the man asks if his father is driving the taxi today and the boy hesitates to answer. "I'll get someone else, then," he says, and the boy suddenly remembers, yes, his father is at the taxi stand, on the other side of the trash heap.

The man is holding an air letter from Europe.

"Delhi, sa'ab?" asks the boy. "Sa'ab taking taxi to bus, bus to Delhi?"

"Tell your father to bring the taxi around to the front. I'll be waiting."

He stands on the porch, watching the long-legged child, his own son's closest friend, bound across the makeshift cricket pitch and out over the steaming trash heaps of the village, scattering the pigs with their pink, spotted litters, the dogs, and buzzards. He scrambles over the old wall and disappears.

The man has done it often enough; this time it is too fatiguing: Going to the taxi stand under the grove of gul-mohar trees, where all the taxi drivers sleep, these days, under their vehicles. Finally deciding which set of feet to rouse, which of the Sikhs to engage in battle. To establish a fair price it is necessary to rouse a nest of quarrelsome Sikhs, waiting for one at least to break the tariff.

The others will crawl back under their cars. The selected driver will stretch and pour himself some tea. He will unwire the trunk and take out an old gas can. Gruffly he'll order the boy over and then extract a small wad of rupee notes, instructing him to buy two liters at the nearest petrol pump, and hurry right back. It will take twenty minutes. The gas will be poured in, the can restored to the trunk, and the lid wired back down.

"Sa'ab taking bus to Delhi?" he will ask, it being the man's practice to take the bus to Delhi every three months. He is, however, out of rotation. It's only been a month.

Narinder Singh will inform him that yesterday China-lady sent a letter. And Dev has told him, the privileged friend, that China-lady is coming for a visit.

There has not been as much excitement in Faridpur since the American arrived, married to the *mistri's* daughter.

Either you develop a tolerance for all this, or you go mad, Richard Durgin thinks. Usually he can handle it.

He knows he has half an hour at least. He sits on the porch, looking out on Tamerlane's wall, watching his son practice his cricket bowling, watching the pigs and peacocks and vultures. It comes to him that because he never learned to pray for his father, he has learned the shradh and kaddish for his wives.

Swaying lightly to these ancient chants, he takes a poem from his billfold, reads it again, and repeats the lines: "How unlike me to do this thing, this warmth of pure surrender . . ." and touches it lightly with a match.

Outside, the taxi pulls to the door.